KIDNAPPED

ON

SAFARI

KIDNAPPED
ON
SAFARI

A THRILLER

PETER RIVA

Skyhorse Publishing, Inc.

Skyhorse Publishing books may be purchased in bulk at special discounts for sales promotion, corporate gifts, fund-raising, or educational purposes. Special editions can also be created to specifications. For details, contact the Special Sales Department, Skyhorse Publishing, 307 West 36th Street, 11th Floor, New York, NY 10018 or info@skyhorsepublishing.com.

Skyhorse® and Skyhorse Publishing® are registered trademarks of Skyhorse Publishing, Inc.®, a Delaware corporation.

Visit our website at www.skyhorsepublishing.com.

10 9 8 7 6 5 4 3 2 1

Library of Congress Cataloging-in-Publication Data

Names: Riva, Peter, 1950- author.
Title: Kidnapped on safari : a thriller / Peter Riva.
Description: New York, NY : Skyhorse Publishing, 2020.
Identifiers: LCCN 2019037926 | ISBN 9781510749009 (hardcover) | ISBN 9781510749016 (ebook)
Subjects: LCSH: Television producers and directors--Fiction. | Safaris--Africa, East--Fiction. | Kidnapping--Africa, East--Fiction. | Terrorism--Africa, East--Fiction. | LCGFT: Thrillers (Fiction)
Classification: LCC PS3618.I833 K53 2020 | DDC 813/.6--dc23
LC record available at https://lccn.loc.gov/2019037926

Cover design by Erin Seaward-Hiatt
Cover photo and illustration credit: © ugurhan/Getty Images (sunset); © Friedemeier/Getty Images (elephant); © in-future/Getty Images (white texture); © focusphotoart/Getty Images (red texture)

Printed in the United States of America

With special thanks to:

Joanne DeMichele—a trusted voice;
Kim Lim at Skyhorse for excellent editing;
Sandy and JoAnn for enduring read-aloud sessions;
and my mother, Maria, for setting a high bar that I could not
possibly hope to attain.

Dedicated to:

Those readers who want the real East Africa with a
rip-roaring adventure thrown in.

TABLE OF CONTENTS

KIDNAPPED
ON
SAFARI

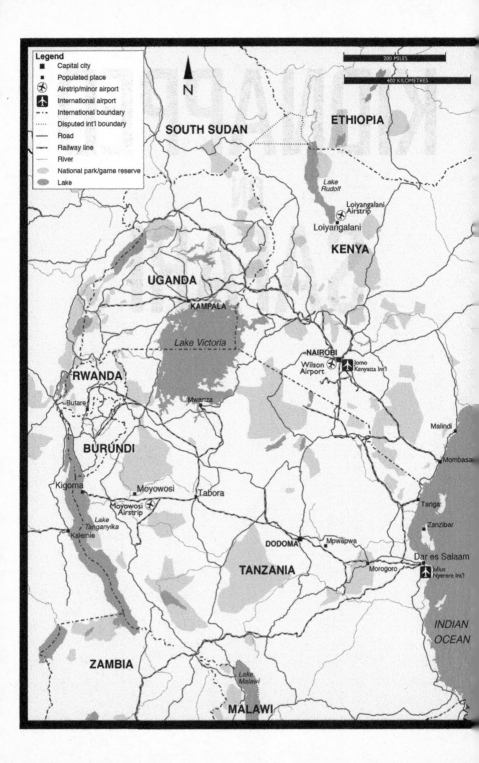

CHAPTER 1

Lake Rudolf, Northwestern Kenya

Driving north along the dusty dirt track on the eastern shore of Lake Rudolf with his trusted guide and devoted friend Mbuno, an elder statesman of the Liangulu tribe who was at the wheel, Pero Baltazar was at peace with the world. He was doing what he loved best—filming the last vestiges of the authentic wild. And he was doing it with his wife, Susanna; his best friend, Heep Heeper; and Heep's wife, Mary. He looked back around the Land Rover, focused his eyes on his wife, and grinned. Her eyes crinkled and her smile reflected her shared sense of calm, safety, happiness, and, above all, the feeling of having escaped the realities of an otherwise very harsh world. Here, in nature, they could let their guard down and simply revel in the filming project they were embarking on.

A great part of television producer Pero Baltazar's regard for the dry region in northern Kenya was the El Molo tribe that eked out a living, mostly by spearfishing in the shallows. Among the reeds were to be found some of the largest freshwater fish in the world—giant, shallow-water Nile perch that regularly reach up to one hundred pounds. *Mighty, peaceful fish; who knows how old?* Pero thought.

Moments before, Mbuno had spotted a young El Molo man approaching the lakeshore carrying a four-foot wooden fishing spear with a barbed tip and a long handwoven lanyard. A man, likely the boy's father, walked by his side, encouraging him.

Stopping the Land Rover in a cloud of dust, off to the side of the road, Mbuno simply said, "He is fishing; it would be very good to film, I think." No one ever questioned Mbuno. Besides having been through dangerous adventures together with Pero, Mbuno's knowledge of the wild was unsurpassed. A suggestion from Mbuno was as good as a command for Pero. Everyone piled out and readied camera and sound equipment. Bill "Heep" Heeper, the show's director and videographer, was joined by his wife, Mary Threte, the show's on-camera talent. Mary was known to millions as "The Crocodile Lady" for her bravery with and around water reptiles. In a previous documentary that Pero's team had shot, Mary actually swam with a behemoth of a sea-going crocodile in the open Indian Ocean. It won the team their third Emmy. Pero knew this new show's popularity was entirely dependent on the capable, beautiful, and brainy Mary and her on-camera appeal.

As Heep and Mary readied themselves, two assistants checked batteries and the Sony Betacam. One of them, Tom Kane, was originally a BBC sound engineer for the brilliant wildlife documentary trailblazer David Attenborough, with several years of field experience. Tom was fit, suntanned, and able. The other assistant, Nancy Breiton, a video equipment specialist on loan from Sony, checked that the camera's unique color chip was seated properly. Used to off-road adventures in developing nations, she was worried the bumpy drive might have dislodged it. When she gave Tom the thumbs up, he held up the clean white back of the day's shooting script, and Heep hoisted the camera and performed white balancing. They were ready to shoot.

Watching his crew efficiently ready themselves with haste, Pero thought, *This is a real family affair now*. Pero's wife, Susanna, née Reidermaier, the inventor of the Silke Wire, an almost invisible personal microphone, bent over Mary's collar and made sure her thin microphone system was on and ready. She checked her digital recorder and transmitter connected to the Betacam, a unit no bigger than a cell phone, and mouthed *ready* to Pero. Everything was indeed ready.

Meanwhile, Mbuno had approached the young El Molo man and his father and started haggling. Pero saw the surprise on the father's face when Mbuno asked if they could film the hunt. A price was negotiated, with Mbuno heeding Pero's rules. Pero believed it was never fair for his crew to be paid by studios for filming wildlife action that was sometimes undertaken by natives who often got nothing in return. If Pero and his team were filming, the rule was that everyone who participated was paid.

Mbuno was proud of his friend Pero; had been for years.

Mary checked her figure-hugging gray wetsuit with red seams, unzipped the top by about six inches, and glanced at Susanna to make sure the mike was still okay. Susanna gave her a thumbs-up. Mary waded into knee-deep water, following about five yards behind the boy who was advancing steadily into waist-deep reeds. The father stood next to Mary, looking anxiously at his son and the fingers of green vegetation moving ever so slightly beyond.

The boy stepped carefully and inched through the shallows into the reed bed, careful not to possibly wake a slumbering giant. Then he stood motionless for nearly ten minutes, spear aloft, waiting. Pero glanced at Heep, who was crouching down at the water's edge, video running. Pero wondered if they would have to switch to fresh tape but also knew that Nancy had a stopwatch out and was keeping track.

Suddenly, when the spear strike came, the explosion of energy shocked everyone in the crew except the steady Heep. Muscles in fish and man were exerted in a life-or-death struggle through the shallows. The fish took off, its massive power pulling the spear, lanyard, and young man, with only the waving spear indicating the fish's presence inches below. The boy's legs kicked as he tried to stay above the water to breathe. Even among the wall of reeds, the power of the fish dragged the boy tens of yards toward deeper water. The father cried out a warning that the boy could not hear. Yet the young man's training had been sound, for feeling the fish was gaining ground, the boy turned his body sideways, creating a drag on the spear's lanyard, slowing the monster. When the pace slowed enough, the boy began to dig his heels in the soft mud, head above water, while calling out to his father for help, "*Baba, nahitaji msaada!*" (Father, I need help!)

The boy's father had been expecting this. Immediately witnessing the might of the fish, he had already started forward in haste. By the time the son called out for help, the father was halfway to the boy, running against the force of the water, using his arms and hands like paddles. As he reached his son, he called out instructions, "*Wewe kuvuta, mimi itabidi kushikilia wewe . . .*" (You pull, I will hold you . . .) Placing his arms around the boy's stomach, he leaned his weight back, both struggling against the force of the fish.

In the shallows, Mary, and on shore, Pero and the camera team, were enthralled by the timeless pageantry. The spearfishing scene was not one they had planned to shoot for the show, yet the three old friends, Pero, Heep, and Mbuno, knew this was an African scene reaching back millennia. Not an artifact as much as life-sustaining, present-day fact. The El Molo way of survival in the desert lake region demanded traditional expertise. And the whole crew knew they were privileged to film and bear witness.

Mary, too, was enthralled, but keeping a wary eye out for the water-ripple trace of any crocodile, she thought, *Surely, the death throes of the fish will attract a croc*...

When the fish finally slowed and rolled onto its side, the father reached underwater and pulled a blade from his belt, passed it shoulder-high to his son who carefully inserted it into the fish's brain, causing instant, humane death. "*Wewe ni wangu!*" he cried out in victory. (You are mine.) He and his father beamed with pride. They jointly towed the fish, later to be weighed at over ninety pounds, toward Mary.

Mary jumped into action and helped tow the fish to the shore using what little Swahili she had, "*Haraka! Mimi naona maji kusonga*..." (Hurry! I see water moving...)

The father looked over his shoulder and scoffed, "*Ni tu mume.*" (It is only the husband.)

Slightly out of breath with the load and a sense of hurry, Mary called out to Mbuno, "What is *mume*?" Mbuno translated and Mary exclaimed, "Oh, the fish's mate, in such shallow water? Why doesn't it run?"

On reaching the shore, Mbuno helped drag the fish up the bank and explained, "They go in shallows to lay eggs. Then the man comes and makes them good eggs. He was waiting; he thought she was in the nest on the sand with eggs." He knelt down and examined the underside of the female, squeezing the flesh. "She has laid, there are no eggs here. It is a good thing."

The boy's father, however, had misunderstood what Mbuno was saying about the eggs, thinking Mbuno was saying the fish was no good. The old man began to protest that a price had been agreed upon. Mbuno cut him off but understood the confusion. The father had thought the money being offered was for the fish, if caught. Once the fish was back on shore and the crew did not seem to want it, the father thought the deal was broken. It took Mbuno several minutes to explain that the money was for filming, not for the fish. However, the pride of the father and son, still both smiling, made them insist that the crew take half of the fish as a gesture of extra thanks.

Pero had the fish loaded into the back of the Land Rover. They drove back to the Oasis Lodge where they were staying, cut the fish in half, borrowed some ice for the El Molo father and son's half-fish, and then, along the way to the rest of their day's filming, dropped them off, with cash. Pero thought about the morning's filming. *This was a good call—bravo, Mbuno.*

That night at dinner at the Oasis Lodge, eating their part of the superb Nile perch, the owner of the hotel, the trim, fit, sun-wrinkled Wolfgang Deschler, ambled over. He was still slightly annoyed at Pero's largesse, as he called it. "You paid him for the hunt, and then you gave him half the fish? The El Molo are *piraten* if they think you are made of money . . . I'll have to pay them double now for the fish I pay them to catch for the hotel."

Pero was having none of it. He had already angered "Wolfie," as he had nicknamed him years ago. On arrival this trip, Pero had insisted that Mbuno, their guide and friend, would have a normal guest's room instead of the concrete bunker normally reserved for drivers and safari help. That argument was short and Wolfie gave in, reluctantly. Wolfie always regretted changes in operating norms in his hotel. Now the argument was over fish. Pero pressed on, "Look, Wolfie, if I had hired them to fish for food, I would have paid them anyway, right?" Wolfie nodded and Pero smiled. "So, think of it this way, you are charging us full price for dinner, even though the fish is free, right? So you and the El Molo are equally, what shall I say, profiteers?" With that, Wolfgang had huffed, then laughed and turned away, getting back to running the only viable hotel on Lake Rudolf's eastern shore.

CHAPTER 2

Early Morning at the Oasis

Pero Baltazar loved the sun's first light in the northern provinces of Kenya, especially early morning at the Oasis Lodge at Loiyangalani as he sat on his room's verandah while his wife, Susanna, slept in. Watching the doum palms gently sway in the breeze, Pero sipped a hot cup of tea, chai, brought to him earlier by the hotel waiter. Eventually, as the sun broke the horizon, Pero thought he heard Susanna stirring, then the bathroom water running. Without turning around to check, he motioned to the waiter, Amal, who was hovering always within eyesight, and asked for tea for his wife. "*Tafadhali kuleta mimi kikombe cha chai kwa mke wangu. Na maziwa. Asante sana.*" (Please bring me a cup of tea for my wife. With milk. Thank you.)

If a man could love to live with almost nothing, so it was for Pero up here—the coming dry heat, the wind shifts he knew would be timed precisely to noon, and especially the barrenness of the place stretched out before him. And there, in the middle of the vast, flat, desert landscape, slept a shimmering, hurt-your-eyes blue expanse of lake, running like a ribbon south to north, disappearing far into the horizon and eventually feeding the Nile. Pero thought the eastern shore of Lake Rudolf—which he still refused to call by the recent, government-sanctioned, politically corrected name of Lake Turkana—was paradise.

As always, Pero refreshed his memory of this most primordial place on earth. Lake Rudolf had witnessed the earliest advent of man and numerous species of animals, the most famous and largest of which was the Nile crocodile. Pero ran his mental filming checklist—hippos aplenty; camels gone feral; cheetah; packs of wild dogs; snakes, including the dangerous spitting cobra; distant oases with palm trees; and, always, birds that migrated from as far away as Siberia joining resident scavengers, Egyptian storks, and a whole manner of vultures.

Remembering all this, Pero smiled and thought, *I wonder what Wolfie's payback for the fish payment will be this morning?* He knew there would be one. Wolfgang ran a tight ship here in the remote northern territory. Regional tribal issues could be difficult, especially if the western side of the lake tribespeople, the Turkana, kicked up a fuss for the tourist dollars that only Wolfgang brought in. The planned new hotels on the western shores of Lake Rudolf also made Wolfgang nervous.

That calm morning, sipping his chai, Pero did not need to wait long to find out what Wolfgang's retribution would be. Heep and Mary, hand in hand, walked up to Pero's verandah. Mary was giggling, but Heep was fuming. In his singsong Dutch accent, he said, "You won't believe it, Pero, Wolfie's drained the damn pool again!" Pero laughed. "No, it's not funny, Pero. Every time we've come here for the past twenty years, we arrive, sleep, get up in the morning, and the pool is drained."

"Can't you use the other one?" Pero asked, smiling broadly, already guessing the answer.

Mary's cheeks were turning red from suppressed giggling, "Now, now, darling . . ."

Heep looked at her sternly and then at Pero. "Also drained. He actually looked at me and said there was a condom found in the pool, as if it was mine, oh, ours. He said the pools needed to be sterilized! Wolfie's a germaphobe, there's so much chlorine in the empty pool now he could sterilize a whole hospital!"

Pero could not help it. He started to laugh. Mary looked pleadingly at her husband as she, too, broke out in open laughter. Heep frowned. "What's so damn funny?" But his face showed his anger was not real, and his resolve not to laugh was breaking. He gave in.

Pero, Heep, and Mary laughingly said it together, "Wolfie, the pool drainer!"

Susanna came out and asked, "What's so funny?" Pero explained what had happened and continued, "Look, it's really a joke around the world. Even John le Carré stayed here researching his book *The Constant Gardener*, and Wolfie drained the pool then, too!"

Bemused, Mary asked, "You two go through this every time? Why?"

Heep explained, "It's okay. Up here, it is like the Wild West. Wolfie has to maintain control or he would be long gone, run out of town, or killed. No one but Wolfie could run the Oasis here; it's his fiefdom, it's his domain—the El Molo know it. They know that without him standing up for them in Parliament in Nairobi, the Turkana tribe on the western shore would have been given the eastern shore as well. It's politics, and it's tribal pecking order . . . pure East Africa."

Pero added, "One more thing . . . Wolfie has the only non-salty, non-brackish water for a hundred miles. Sort of gives him the winning hand. I'll apologize for the fish, and the pool will be full tonight after filming, okay?"

With a passing "silly boys!" said with a laugh over her shoulder, Susanna went to have a cold shower before heading over to breakfast. Heep, smiling, nodded to Pero and trotted off with his bride.

CHAPTER 3

Mamba Kisiwa na Simu ya Dharura— Crocodile Island and an Emergency Call

The day's shooting went well, starting with a morning call at eight. Pero had hired a fishing boat with Honda outboards, and they embarked from the hotel dock and headed two hours up the lake to Crocodile Island. The water was calm in the early morning, crystal clear, birds dipping beaks on the wing to drink. As they approached Crocodile Island, looking down off to the side, Mary spotted a small herd of hippos. Heep filmed them, lowering the waterproof camera as the blue-black, corpulent giants danced along the shallow bottom near the shore of the island.

The morning's planned shoot was filming the crocodile sand nests, the enormous females waiting just offshore, slowly treading water with powerful tails. Mary donned her wet suit, powered up her video camera, and went snorkeling in four to ten feet of water. Heep and the crew remained in shallow water and used the main underwater camera, filming her filming the crocs. The crew soon found themselves standing in five feet of water, as close to fifteen-foot crocs as anyone sane would ever want to be.

While Susanna had adjusted her Silke Wire microphone on Mary's wet suit collar, she expressed fear for her friend in waters teeming with wildlife.

Mary placated fears, addressing the whole crew: "Don't worry about the mother. As long as you do not get between her and the mound on shore, she will not be interested in you. The ones to watch out for are the juveniles from last year, about four-footers. They will be looking for an easy meal, preferably their cousins about to hatch. That is why she is here, to protect her young. It is the pirates that will be dangerous. But they are afraid of the waiting mother, so you can stay closer to her, and they should stay away."

Mbuno was listening, nodding, but his eyes were focused, looking offshore, keeping a wary watch. Mbuno did not care for *mamba*. (Crocodiles.)

All up and down the beach, Pero could see mounds; some already burst open, others quiet. The ones nearest the water were twinned by visible slowly stirring currents just offshore, revealing a waiting mother.

At the mound that Mbuno and Mary had previously selected together, with their ears pressed to the sand, the emerging baby crocs were filmed suddenly bursting out of the sand nest, slithering, squirming toward the shore ten yards down the beach. Egyptian storks had spotted the hatching and swooped down, taking easy meals. Yet the remaining babies continued to squirm to the water and safety. Once in, they unhesitatingly swam straight toward their mother's mouth, already gaping, an opening of about six inches. The beefy mother hung there motionless, protecting her babies in her gaping jaws. Mary was close by, filming with a small camera. Heep was twenty feet away filming Mary near the croc, catching on video the hatch-lings scooting past Mary on either side, finding their mother and safety. Mary's microphone picked up the sounds of rippling water and the soothing noises she was making from behind her snorkel. She seemed to be humming a tune. It sounded like a child's nursery rhyme. Pero knew the voice-over script would add words like *protective* and *motherly instinct* when they would edit the film. Mary's incredible oneness with the scene was palpable. *Perfect video*, thought Pero.

As they were considering a new mound to film, Pero glanced at his watch and warned the crew he wanted to be on shore or on board the boat before noon, which was fast approaching. Mbuno agreed. Heep wanted to stay in the water longer to get more shots, but Mary trusted Pero and Mbuno and convinced Heep to pack up and get out of the water. It was just in time.

The steady twenty-mile-per-hour wind had been blowing from the west across Crocodile Island, which protected their shoot and equipment. As Pero felt the wind slacken, he called out, "Five minutes, no more! Hurry!" The crew sprang to work, packed up, and jogged to the boat. Once in, Pero could feel the wind picking up, but coming squarely from the east. From the east it would bring the desert dust, strong lake waves, and sear-ing heat. Within seconds of noon, exactly, the temperature rose to over 110 degrees; the lake waves, previously calm, peaked at three feet; and the air was thick with dust.

The course back down Lake Rudolf was otherwise unevent-ful, except for Susanna complaining of seasickness as the boat pitched and rolled. She had been stowing gear, bending down instead of facing the freshening alkaline Rudolf spray. Pero hugged his wife of only nine months and encouraged her to stand for air. "*Nein, nein*," she exclaimed, "My sound equip-ment must be properly . . ." With that she leaned over the side and fed the fish her breakfast. For the rest of the journey, Pero wetted a handkerchief and wiped her brow. She looked better by the time they got back to the jetty.

As the assistants, Tom and Nancy, unloaded the boat and started packing the Land Rover for the mile-long drive back to the lodge, Pero, Mbuno, Heep, Susanna, and Mary sat on the dock, in the lee of the boat, out of the wind. When you are filming in the bush, it pays to take time to review where you have been and what you have left to do. Pero felt this was such a time. The sun was hot, the lake was cool, the breeze was at their backs.

Pero was surprised at how much they had already filmed in just two days, "I think we got plenty of croc footage today. Mary, you were great as always. Along with yesterday's gift of the fishing scene and the croc pack we filmed near Sibiloi Park—"

Heep interjected, "We counted them last night, over one hundred and sixty on that sand bar."

Mary added, "The hippos were really weird in Sibiloi Park marshland. I've never seen hippos on land like that during the day." The crew all knew that hippos killed more people in Africa than any other species, and on land they were especially dangerous. Farther north, up the lake near the beginning of the river that fed the Nile, there were croc and hippo attacks every year. Hippo attacks outnumbered croc attacks by a wide margin.

Pero was thoughtful. "Yeah, well, the footage of the hippos chasing you and Mbuno was pretty surreal, but I don't think we can really use it except for promos."

Heep chimed in, teasing his wife, "Of course, as your shirt was wet at the time, it may be somewhat useful."

Mbuno did not get the joke. "But we had been in the water . . ."

Mary had understood and dug her husband in the ribs with her elbow. Everyone, even Mbuno, laughed.

In a more serious vein, Heep got back to business. "Remember, I was filming that herd underwater today—that'll be good footage, and with a few cuts to shots of them going in or out of the lake yesterday, we can tie it together."

Pero nodded. "Okay, but maybe we'll try some extra hippo shots tomorrow morning. But what I wanted to say is that our great croc luck today just about covers what we absolutely had to get. What is left is an evening with the El Molo in their encampment, maybe a firelight dance with them and Mary . . ." Pero paused, a thought emerging. "And, yeah, maybe we could get to that northern village near the hippo pools and interview the locals there . . . Wolfie said that ten children have been taken over the last few years. That could be important footage. So, let's say hippo interviews in the morning, and maybe the village in the afternoon if Mbuno can arrange it?"

Mbuno said he would try and negotiate with the local chief warden's office and the Nairobi "assistant" they had had to hire. In Kenya, everyone knew there were politics and government involved in anything foreigners wanted to do. Their Nairobi-appointed coordinator from the Ministry was an affable fellow, currently enjoying the hotel hospitality and free food and his hundred-dollar-a-day cash fees from the crew. They liked David because he did not oversee every moment of their day or plans, unlike some previous nosy "minders" they had experienced.

Pero summed it all up. "So, I'd say we stay here another two days comfortably, and then we can move on. Agreed?" Everyone nodded.

Mary and Susanna wanted to know if a decision had been made on where exactly they'd be going next. Pero explained he was waiting on permits to decide a schedule, but most likely it would first be into Tanzania, back to the oceanside croc farm they had filmed with Mary once before, as those visas had already been granted and the ones they had applied for to Uganda and Burundi were yet to come through. Mary whispered to Susanna that she loved the beaches there, saying, "Last time I met the biggest female croc I've ever seen . . . we're pals."

As it was past two in the afternoon, Pero told everyone to take the rest of the day off. No doubt the pool would be full, and he would see everyone at dinner, at six.

And so as the day wound down, everyone relaxed. Susanna felt better, no longer seasick. In the hottest part of the afternoon, everyone jumped into the pools, which were indeed full and refreshing. When dinner came, even Wolfie was in a good mood and joined them for Tusker beers around the campfire in the chill desert night air. Nancy, the new crewmember, had a harmonica and played a foot-stomping Old West tune she said she had learned as a kid in Utah, when riding the range. Her tune was joined by everyone beating on the nearest log or rock to punctuate the horse-trot rhythm before people melted away into the darkness toward their rooms. Soon the Oasis was dark and silent, even the generator turned down.

The emergency call came in at breakfast. They could hear Wolfie's shortwave radio belting out his call sign, repeatedly declaring, "Come in 5Z4WD, most urgent call for Pero Baltazar." Pero got up and made his way to Wolfie's office, asking Amal, their waiter, to get Wolfie. "*Kwenda kupata bwana Wolfgang haraka, tafadhali*, Amal." (Go get boss Wolfgang quickly, please, Amal.)

Pero knew better than to touch Wolfgang's sole means of communication with the outside world. Besides, Wolfgang had once allowed him to use the radio transmitter set, commonly called an RT set, to reach out to Pero's old contacts at the CIA and State Department in Washington. Pero had been a runner for them, collecting papers and making note of fellow passengers at airports when asked, fortunately infrequently—nothing dangerous, nothing remotely exciting. Then two events had caused Pero to get deeper into the world of anti-terrorism than he ever wanted. Unable to cope alone those two times, he had involved his friends, including Heep, Mary, Susanna, and, of course, Mbuno, who were once again on location with him, this time along the shore of Lake Rudolf. Pero desperately hoped this emergency call had nothing to do with his old Washington contacts.

He had quit after the Berlin package incident, after he had nearly died, mainly because he had married for the second time in his life as soon as he had left the hospital and recovered. Susanna was a brilliant sound engineer, as devoted to Pero as he was to her. The name of Pero's first wife, Addiena, who had died in the Lockerbie disaster, was tattooed on the underside of his right forearm. He used to sleep with it across his heart so he would not forget her after she perished. Her tragic death was the reason he had offered his minor services to the CIA in the first place, wanting to do something to thwart terrorism. It was heartwarming for Pero that his new wife, Susanna, now insisted she drift off to sleep lying to his right, making him put out his arm for her to use Addiena's name as a pillow. "She loved you and you, her. It is how I can remember her, thank her, for teaching you how to love, you *dummer Mann*."

Susanna's native German expression of "dumb man" had been a scolding term for him originally deployed during the

Berlin dangers, which was when she had revealed she cared for Pero deeply. Since then, it had become a term of endearment between them, their bond cemented by past events.

Adrenaline pumping because of the radio call, Pero weaved his way past tightly packed breakfast tables, careful not to allow his large, six-foot frame to disturb fellow guests. He heard Amal calling out to Wolfgang. By the time Pero got to the radio office, he could hear Wolfgang replying, "I am coming, I am coming." The RT set was almost a living thing to Wolfgang, and Pero was used to hearing the man talk to it as a father would his child. Pero, waiting at the door, opened it for Wolfgang, who entered, sat, and flicked the on switch all in one practiced movement. He keyed the mike, gave his call sign 5Z4WD in answer, and said, "What is the message?"

The voice faded suddenly, coming in faintly, and Wolfgang gently turned the tuning dial. "Okay, Nairobi, I read you now, the sun's up here so this may break up." A woman's voice came on the radio, asked if Baltazar was available, and Wolfie told her he was present and standing by.

"Message from Flamingo Tours, for Pero Baltazar, urgent, Mwana Wambuno, on safari, Moyowosi Game Reserve, missing for over ten hours. Safari clients being flown back to Nairobi. No trace of Ube. Over." Ube was the nickname of Mbuno's nephew, Mwana Wambuno. Pero immediately knew Mbuno would take the news of his favorite nephew hard.

Pero asked, "Wolfie, may I speak directly to her?" Wolfgang nodded and indicated the mike button. "Pero here, who's that? Sheila Ndelle? Over." Sheila, the backbone of Flamingo Tours, was also the sister of the UN security police chief and totally reliable.

"*Ndiyo*, over." Yes, came the reply.

"Hi Sheila, give me all the details you have, and also, where's Tone? Over." Anthony Bowman was the owner of Flamingo

Tours, known to everyone over the decades as simply Tone. An ex–white hunter, Tone ran the best safari outfitters anywhere—expedition tents, private toilets, dinner with white table linens, client's wishes always fulfilled.

"Hi Pero, Mr. Anthony is down at the Tanzanian Embassy trying to find out more information, if there is any known terrorist or poaching problems in the area. There wasn't any when we sent the clients there. All we know is that Ube took three clients out on a walking safari yesterday morning, camera clients"—by which she meant not hunters—"and they took leopard images in the tall grass, a kill of a bushbuck, treeing the carcass, you know the drill." Pero did. Leopard was one of Africa's big five—lion, leopard, rhino, elephant, and cape buffalo. Originally a hunting list, these animals still presented a challenge for the lens hunter. "On the plane's HF radio, briefly, the clients have reported that suddenly as they were heading back to camp, Ube told our two bearers to make the clients crawl back to the Land Rover and fly back to Nairobi without stopping or talking to anyone. They said Ube told them to do this quietly if they valued their lives. They did as they were told. They have no idea what Ube did or where he went." Sheila paused. "But, Pero, they said they heard a shot. Over."

Pero's producer instincts kicked in. "You say the clients are en route for Wilson Airport? Over." Wilson Airport was on the western side of Nairobi and the jumping off small airport for most safaris and the Flying Doctor air services. Wolfgang glanced at Pero, clearly wondering why Pero should be interested in the clients since he knew Ube's disappearance would be of paramount importance to Mbuno and, therefore, presumably to Pero.

Sheila's tone also had an edge. "Yes, yes, they are inbound but had to wait for Tanzanian air traffic control for permission to depart. We had a plane waiting, in case, for medical reasons on the client's instructions. They will be back in about two hours. But it is Ube we are worried about, and we need to tell Mbuno. Over."

Pero nodded. "Agreed, I'll take care of that. But Sheila, listen to me, please, I need you to go immediately to the airport, see Sheryl at Mara Airways, arrange for a Cessna 414 for us here immediately, plane and pilots—note, I said pilots—on loan, indefinite period. Over." Sheila gave her confirmation. "Good, then call the Langata police station and ask for Sergeant Gibson Nabana. He's the one I shot during that terrorist attack two years ago, remember? Over." Sheila laughed and said she remembered it well. It had made the front page of the *Daily Standard* paper. At the time Pero had needed to gain control of a difficult confusion of authority at Wilson Airport and had only slightly wounded the sergeant. They subsequently became good allies and, since then, drinking buddies. "Okay, Sheila, tell Gibson to stop your clients and confiscate every piece of camera equipment they have. Tell him that I will be in Nairobi as soon as possible. Look, we need to review every shot to see if those camera-happy clients caught anything that can help us figure out what has happened to Ube. Once Mbuno and I see what is there, or not, we will reboard the Mara Cessna and proceed to . . . where was the landing strip? Remember that Sheryl at Mara Airways will need to have that information while you are at Wilson Airport, okay? Over."

Sheila understood the flight would have to leave Kenya and land in Tanzania, an everyday occurrence as long as the paperwork was filled in properly with Customs and Excise on both sides of the border. "The Moyowosi Airport we used for the clients was actually at Mgwesi at the southwestern end of the Lake Nyagamoma, and then there is a three-hour slow drive into the game reserve. Should I lay on transport? Our drivers are still there, packing up the tents. I have not given them instruction to drive back to base. Over."

"Yes, Sheila, hold your people in place, reestablish the camp, but move it at least a mile or more away. We'll use it, and we'll pay the fare. And one more thing, your clients will get back to Wilson before we do, so you have to make sure to tell them, before they land, that if Ube had reason to get your clients out secretly, whatever his reasons were, it is serious and if they value their lives they will not, I repeat, *not* talk with anyone. And keep them at the airport. Over." Sheila said she understood and signed off.

Wolfgang looked over at Pero and simply said, "I guess you'll be leaving then. The pool is full; I was thinking about draining it, but you might as well use it before you go while you wait for transport." It was as friendly a gesture Pero had ever heard the owner of the Oasis make.

CHAPTER 4

Jija katika Hatari—Flee into Danger

Pero immediately left the office after securing Wolfie's promise to keep everything secret and asked Amal to bring Mbuno to join him on the verandah outside his room.

It took Mbuno seconds to hear what Pero knew and to assess a course of action. "You have asked for a plane?" Pero nodded. "Visas for Tanzania are ready." It was a statement. Mbuno was completing a mental checklist as Pero knew he would. If Pero was the producer, it was always Mbuno who seemed to know the right course of action. Mbuno asked, "Who do we need . . . to come with us? We are a team, well perhaps not the two assistants and certainly not the minder. But I think Heep and Mary and Susanna will insist they help you somehow." Pero wanted to make the point that he already knew they all would have to act in support of Mbuno, Mbuno's plans, and Mbuno's expertise.

Mbuno had been involved in "The Troubles," the time of the Kikuyu-based Mau Mau Uprising, as part of the anti-terrorist forces. It made him an enemy of certain people in the mainly Kikuyu government, even though he had been awarded Kenya's highest civilian medal for his role in stopping the al-Shabaab terrorists who had tried to commit an atrocity that would have been totally unforgivable—roasting over one hundred thousand people in the Kibera slum alive. While Pero had been roped in by the CIA to solve the clues leading up to thwarting the terrorists' plans, it was always Mbuno's expertise that had kept them alive. That and Mbuno's ability to compare men to animals and accurately assess their animal behavior.

Pero went on to explain what he had put in place, to see if it met Mbuno's needs. "Okay, I have a Mara Cessna 414 along with two pilots—so we can have twenty-four-hour standby transportation. Sheila at Flamingo is leaving the two Land Rovers and drivers in place, but they will immediately move the camp at least a mile away. Then they'll wait for us at the Moyowosi airstrip . . . do you know it?" Mbuno nodded. "Hopefully, I have Gibson Nabana holding the men being flown back to Wilson Airport so they do not spread rumors or tell anyone if they may have seen anything in the bush. Ube clearly saw something, but the three clients may or may not have; we'll know when we talk with them." Again, Mbuno nodded. "Heep will review any film, video, or whatever they have quickly and tell us if he sees anything, a clue, anything. That's all I have."

Mbuno was silent for a moment. "It is my fault. I have raised Ube with a strong knowledge of right and wrong . . . right and wrong with man, right and wrong with men. If he saw something wrong, he would have stayed behind to stop the bad thing. He would make sure his clients get away."

"I know, Mbuno, I know. But what worries me is that Sheila said he told the two bearers to take the three clients back to the Land Rovers—crawling on their bellies. That means the danger was real and very close. And then there is the gunshot . . ."

"*Ndiyo*, it is not good he was so worried. The gunfire does not worry me so very much. Ube is very fast, they would have needed more than one shot. He may have seen the danger, stayed on the ground in case he needed to . . . how do you say it? *Kufanya lengo tofauti* . . . ah, to make a different target . . ."

"To decoy?"

"Yes, to decoy the bad men away from his clients. But also, he may not be in danger since the clients got away." He paused, "But what is most worrying is that he may still be there, on foot, in a place of danger. It is a hunting reserve, not a protected national park." Mbuno stood. "We must go." It was a statement between them, a statement of brotherhood, of camaraderie, a reaffirmation of common purpose. Pero felt proud of Mbuno's need for Pero to go along.

During the incidents in Berlin, Mbuno had declared Pero and him to be brothers, a great honor for Pero. Now Pero was determined to live up to Mbuno's faith in him.

Pero knew that Heep, Mary, and Susanna, along with the two assistants, would have everything packed and loaded into the Land Rover within an hour. Sheila radioed Wolfie that the Cessna was on its way—estimated time of arrival was eleven, two hours later. That gave the team plenty of time to talk things out.

Pero took the two assistants outside, stood under a doum palm tree in the center of the Oasis compound, and addressed them as the professionals he knew them to be. "Change in plans." Briefly, he told them what had happened.

Pero was impressed that Tom and Nancy did not ask why Ube was missing, just how they could help. "Look, I don't know exactly what's happened, just that a close friend is in danger and we may have to extract him from a hunting game reserve in Tanzania. What I need from you two is help, not

in that endeavor, but in keeping the shoot moving forward."
They both nodded. "We're taking off for Wilson Airport in
two hours. I do not know who is staying in Nairobi with you;
that is up to a discussion we will have after consulting with
people meeting us at the airport. But I want you to go to the
Intercontinental Hotel. I'll call them when we arrive at Wilson
and book us all in. Stay put, full salary, of course, review the
footage we have shot, make safe copies, you know the drill,
and wait for word. If Heep, Mary, and Susanna do not stay on
at the Interconti, we will keep you informed as best we can
from Tanzania. Okay?"

Nancy spoke for them both. "Sure thing, Pero, easy. Will
Heep leave the Betacam for me to service?"

Pero thought he would and again expressed his hope that
Heep, Susanna, and Mary would stay behind as well. "As soon
as I know what the issue is in Tanzania, we'll have a better idea
who's where and why, but I suspect it'll be just me and Mbuno
going to Tanzania." Tom gave a chuckle, and Pero frowned.
"Why, what are you thinking?"

Tom held up his hands, "My guess is they will all want to
go wherever it is you're headed. We heard the stories of your
exploits in Nairobi and Berlin ... you're a team."

Pero could only nod. It was already worrying him that his
friends might put themselves in danger. Again.

The dirt airstrip at Loiyangalani had the usual herd of
goats grazing on the field when the Cessna made a low pass,
scaring them out of the way. It banked a sharp left, circled,
and made a perfect landing, billowing clouds of sand and dust.
The Land Rover was waiting, with Tom and Nancy in charge
of loading. The two pilots gave a hand, and soon the locally
hired Land Rover was headed back to the Oasis Lodge to pick
up passengers.

Wolfie warmly said goodbye to everyone except Pero, whom he took aside and whispered conspiratorially, "I have a portable RT set; want to take it with you? I would if it were me."

Pero knew Wolfie relied on that means of open communication. He was the first person in Africa to talk with the Mir space station and the shuttle. He had maybe four hundred call-sign postcards from around the world on his wall. But Pero could not see the need to carry an extra radio, and his face showed his doubt.

Wolfie persisted, "I will monitor here, and you can ask Sheila to do the same ... you never know when you might need the cavalry, again." The *again* made Pero raise his eyebrows, so Wolfie added, "Yeah, well, that little party in Nairobi was *Gott verdammt wunderbar*." (Goddamned wonderful.) "Those *beschissen*"—(God-awful)—"al-Shabaab needed killing. We were listening."

The *we* Wolfie was referring to no doubt meant half the world—call signs of friends on Wolfie's wall told the story of connections without national boundaries.

Pero gave in. Wolfie patted him on the back and handed him a small canvas stiff-sided case. Pero peered inside at the olive-green metal box, dials, and headset. Wolfie added, "All you need is any car battery. We'll be listening. I set the frequency, and it's also taped to the bottom." Pero thanked him and was the last to get into the Land Rover. Mary waved to Wolfie as they drove off.

Wolfie waved back with both hands. Pero, ever the responsible producer, thought, *He never asked for the other two days' rooming costs. I'll have to make sure he's covered.*

CHAPTER 5

Wilson Airport, Nairobi

The two-hour flight back from Loiyangalani was, as usual, bumpy in the mid-morning heat rise. As their Cessna touched down, there was the familiar skidding sound of tires on the hot tarmac, accentuated by Susanna quietly retching into the airsickness bag provided. Pero rubbed her back and silently wondered if his wife was getting some sort of local dysentery.

The plane taxied past the refueling tanks and on toward the Mara Airways' concrete apron, following the faded painted white lines on the taxiway. Halfway to the Mara Airways disembarking area, the pilots shut off the left engine and called back to Pero, "We'll drop the stairway as soon as we get to our station. Sheryl says she has a policeman waiting for you in her office." Pero knew the office, with one faded red plastic leatherette couch, one old Coke machine, a couple of chairs at a desk with three phones, a window facing the Mara loading apron so Sheryl could keep an eye on all operations, and, unusually, one of the few working Mitsubishi AC units at Wilson. Sheryl had proved herself more than capable of running Mara Airways for over a decade, and Mara's investors, mostly South African millionaires, simply left her to it and gave her anything she asked for. She was, for all intents and purposes, the boss.

As soon as the stairway dropped onto the tarmac, Pero asked Heep to look after Susanna and the crew, motioned to Mbuno to follow, and they descended into the heat, picking up the pace as they trotted toward Sheryl's cool office. Through Sheryl's window, Mbuno could see the office was full.

"Gibson! I owe you a Tusker for all this," Pero exclaimed as he entered the room.

Sergeant Gibson Nabana responded, laughing, "One beer, boss? You will have to buy me a whole crate!" Extending his hand, he took hold of Pero's forearm as Pero did the same to him. They shook forearms. Then Gibson spotted Mbuno and did a little head bow. "*Mzee* Mbuno, it is again a great honor." He used English and Pero understood Gibson wanted to make sure Pero and the whole room knew he was showing proper respect. After all, during the al-Shabaab incident, Mbuno had captured several terrorists, turning them over to Gibson to get the sole credit.

It was also clear Gibson was genuinely humbled. By using an elder's most respectful title of *Mzee*, he was acknowledging the older man's authority. Mbuno nodded in response but stayed otherwise silent. He was studying the three tourists, filthy and mud-dried, seated on the leatherette couch. It was clear they were nervous and out of their element. Mbuno turned to Pero and simply said, "Please."

"Right." Pero asked Sheryl if he could borrow a chair. Sheryl pointed to one, and he picked it up and sat before the three men. "May I have your names please, in order, along with residence and nationality." Pero was banking on Gibson's uniformed presence to make the tourists talkative in the face of authority.

"I am Harry Winter, Junior, of New York. US citizen." Harry was sixty if he was a day.

The second man said, "Bob Hines, New York. US citizen." Then he added, "Former Marine Corpsman, basically a medic, along for possible medical assistance." He nodded toward Harry Winter. Bob was in his mid-thirties, fit, and sharp-eyed.

The third man, middle-aged and pale-skinned, was fidgeting, turning a wedding band over and over on his finger. He looked up, avoided direct eye contact, and said, "Richard Bachman, Princeton, New Jersey. US citizen."

Pero decided to go for the weakest link. "Richard, why are you so nervous? Speak up now and fast, or this may drag out for weeks."

Richard's head snapped up. "Weeks? We did nothing . . ."

Pero decided to apply a little pressure. He leaned forward and gently said, "Richard, while everything was going along fine, you would have completed your safari and gone home. No one would have been the wiser. But," he paused, "by the time all your bags, all your prescription pills, all your private possessions, and your computer files and phone records have been searched, do you really think there won't be multiple charges? So, let's hear it, now and fast or there will be a search followed by a booking here with Sergeant Nabana taking you to a holding cell while they conduct a more thorough search— and that includes a cavity search."

Richard Bachman from New Jersey folded like a pack of cards. He started by explaining that Harry Winter was his boss. Mr. Winter owned and operated the largest waste company on the Eastern Seaboard. Winter had insisted Richard Bachman come along on the trip because he was an expert with film still cameras, as it was his hobby. They were down in Tanzania, he really didn't know exactly where, and had been on safari with a young scout, he couldn't remember the servant's name—Pero frowned that Ube was being referred to as a servant—and they had photographed each of the big five except for leopard, so Mr. Winter offered a big bonus if they could get one good shot. They went out early and spent most of the time in the muck, with slippery mud, leeches, and grass that would slice your hand. It was raining, and then the scout had told them to be quiet. "He pointed at this lone tree, and there it was, a leopard. I set the aperture and handed the camera to Mr. Winter who took a string of shots. The whirring of the winding motor made the leopard look straight at us. It jumped down from the tree, and the scout told us to work our way backward. That's when it happened."

The ex-Marine started to interrupt, but Pero told him to be quiet for the moment. "Go on, Richard."

"Well, we had crawled and frog-walked back about a hundred yards, back the way we had come. I figured he was herding us toward the small road we had crossed, another fifty yards backward."

The Marine interrupted, "A hundred." Pero nodded at the Marine and then gestured at Bachman to continue.

"There was no way I could have known we were in danger. The two—what are they called—yeah, *askari* with us only had one rifle. And I was getting leg cramps. So I stood."

The Marine commented, "Idiot."

"So what? I'm an idiot? I couldn't have known."

Pero wanted the real answer. "Known what?"

"That there were men all around us. They spotted me and started jabbering, loudly. Our guide knocked me down, and we started crawling away in a different direction. It was terrifying; we were in danger, I guess. Anyway, after about an hour of crawling into ditches, swamps, and more muck, the guide spoke quickly with the two askari and then told us to follow one of them, and the other would take up the rear. Then he stole my hat and gave me his. I lost his. The guide stayed behind. We could hear the voices all around but there was this deep ditch, and he made us get in and swim crawl away. That's all I know. About three hours later we found the Land Rover and left, like he told us."

The Marine took over. "He told us to bug out, do what we're told, and we'd get out safely. He stayed behind as a diversion, I guess. We heard a shot a little while later. We don't know where he is or what happened. We got the Land Rover to the airport at top speed; we never went back to camp. The plane's pilot was having a late dinner, so we grabbed him, waited for very first light, and flew here. I called the Mara people here, once airborne."

Harry Winter decided to exercise some muscle. "Look, we did nothing wrong. I demand to speak with the Ambassador. I'm an important—"

Pero finished the sentence for him. "Nothing. Out here, you are nothing. You abandoned your guide in the field. You fled to save your own hide."

"You can't speak to me that way—I am an American!"

"So am I, buddy, so am I, and I can just imagine how this is going to look in the *New York Times* tomorrow." With that, Pero stood up and motioned Mbuno, Sergeant Gibson, and the ex-Marine to the other side of the room by the Coke machine. "Coke, Bob?" The Marine said thanks, and Pero pushed the buttons.

Pero knew the machine did not take money anymore, but the refrigeration worked fine. He took one out of the bottom slot for the Marine, one for Gibson, and one for himself. Mbuno would, he knew, rather die than drink the sugary liquid. *Now, if it was made with honey, wild horses couldn't keep Mbuno away*, he thought wryly.

Pero needed a few more facts. As he saw it, there was really no charge against the three of them. But he figured the ex-Marine might have more field experience to make a real evaluation. Pero took out his wallet from his safari trousers' front pocket, pulled out a laminated card, and showed it to the Marine. "So, Bob, would you give me the sitrep, please?"

The Marine looked at the CIA identification card, checked the expiration date, and nodded. "Figured something else is happening here. Sitrep, eh?" Bob understood the significance of Pero using the military term for a situation report. "Okay, but do you want these two fellows"—he pointed at Gibson and Mbuno—"to hear this too?"

Pero stared him in the eyes and asked if he remembered scuttlebutt in the Corps about a little terrorist incident in Nairobi a couple of years back. Bob did; he had still been in uniform back then. Pero nodded and simply said, "You're looking at three of the people who foiled that attack. All three and a few more, including an American lady and her Dutch husband out there." Pero pointed out the window at his crew, who were standing in the shade. "And, well, maybe also a couple of Marine F-18s I called on for help."

Bob was visibly shocked. You could almost see the thought process: *a little African guy, not much more than one-hundred-and-sixty pounds, an overweight African policeman, and, what, a middle-aged CIA spook?* He looked out the window at the three women and two men, none of whom had any military bearing whatsoever. Then he thought about the CIA card with the words "Render every assistance" printed on it and decided to comply. His report took under ten minutes. It was thorough.

He told them he estimated ten to twelve different voices, but no vehicles—nothing wheeled could be used in that terrain. Whoever they were, they had quickly made a ring around their position. "I figured they were going for a snatch, a kidnapping." He heard accented command voices, perhaps of German origin, maybe Dutch; hard to say as they were speaking Swahili, which Bob did not understand. He did catch the words *wagen* and *baum*, which he guessed meant truck and tree. "Little Christmas tree is *O, Tannenbaum*, no?"

None of this made any sense to Pero. What the hell would a tree have to do with Ube being in immediate danger?

Mbuno asked more pointed questions. "How did you get past them?"

Bob turned to Mbuno and reported, "In the deep ditch, we crawled for maybe a mile or more, right past the men in the encirclement."

Mbuno knew field craft better than anyone. He addressed the Marine, "*Bwana*, maybe those two"—Mbuno pointed to the men still seated on the leatherette couch—"crawled belly down, but you would watch. Most ready. You would crawl or swim, face up. You saw." It was a statement of fact. Pero had not considered it.

Bob had not thought anyone could know. "Okay, yes, I saw, but in that marsh, I could not see more than boots, a bit of leg. The first boot I saw was old leather, cracked, repaired laces. The trousers were camo, torn and repaired. The man was on his heels."

Pero had to ask, "What does that mean? That he was poor?"

"No, his weight was back, on his heels, not ready to run, amateur for a soldier." It was clear the ex-Marine was assessing combat conditions in case he needed to fight. "The other guy, a little later on, maybe twenty yards, was on the other side of the ditch. We could see where he had crossed, breaking the bank. I figured he was staying away from the edge in case it collapsed, and that's why he couldn't see through all the marsh grass as we worked our way past."

Mbuno said, "Exact picture, please."

Bob turned to face Mbuno. "Stocky legs, muscled. New camo trousers, maybe a uniform, couldn't tell. Machete on the left side—tells me the right side might have had a holster unless he's left-handed. Upside-down AK-47 muzzle tapping back of left thigh, so maybe the guy is six feet tall. Boots: synthetic fabric, olive green, new, laced straight across, German style." Bob paused. "And this guy was fit; even in that mud, he was pitched forward, ready to move."

Mbuno nodded to Pero, and Pero said, "Okay, Bob, that's helpful . . ."

Bob said, "It's the guide, Ube, right?" Mbuno nodded. "When he took the idiot's hat, I knew he would be the decoy. The damn thing was bright orange, a Stateside hunting hat to show your fellow hunters you're not a damn deer."

Pero agreed. "Good thinking. Ube was probably trying to decoy them. Mbuno thought so, too, earlier."

Bob raised his eyebrows, looking at Mbuno. "One more thing, mister . . . those two askari or bearers, whatever you call them?" Mbuno nodded. "They kept their heads. I'd like them in a firefight. I felt bad leaving them with the Land Rover at the airfield. I figured they would go back to the campsite. That might be dangerous."

"How far was the campsite from where the incident happened?" Pero asked.

"They wouldn't have known where we were camped; that's my hope. Ten or fifteen miles by Land Rover, plus the four miles on foot. Is it far enough away? But you have to know, we weren't traveling traceless; we were only taking goddamn pictures."

Pero knew what he meant. A professional could easily trace their route back to camp, step by step, if they wanted to.

Mbuno understood it, too. "It is why Ube stayed. These bad men would not know how many came. If they chased only him, they might not know there were others."

The ex-Marine nodded. "Brave man, as I said. Need a hand rescuing him?"

"What makes you think we're gonna try?" Pero asked.

Even Sergeant Gibson, watching Mbuno's face, chuckled. Bob answered for both of them, "Man, you ain't asking what's next, nor waiting—you're planning. Count me in."

CHAPTER 6

Katika Hatari—Into Danger

B ob was right, of course—a rescue was precisely what they were planning. Bob went back to sit on the couch. As they left the Coke machine alcove, Pero turned to Mbuno and asked, "Have you been to Moyowosi before?"

Mbuno looked concerned. He took Pero aside and explained that Moyowosi was a hunting reserve—a game reserve, not a protected park. And since his tribe, the Liangulu, were forbidden to hunt, he had not been there, nor had he wanted to, for over twenty years as Liangulu were not welcome. Pero understood. Mbuno's ethnicity would be transparent to anyone in eastern Tanzania.

"It may be all right," Mbuno said, explaining slowly. "Authorities are now running the hunting camps, not the local tribes who hate my people. Very rich hunters pay eighty thousand US to hunt elephant there. It is big business." Mbuno pronounced *big* as "beeg," as most Africans do. "And the Kigosi Game Reserve is also next to Moyowosi, and the police run that reserve."

But Pero wanted to know if Mbuno was confident about going to Moyowosi with Pero without any firsthand knowledge. Mbuno didn't answer. Instead, he called the ex-Marine over to walk out with them. "Mr. Bob, do you think you will know the place again? Can you lead us there?" Bob replied strongly that he was sure; once they got to the Land Rover parking spot on the road from the airstrip, he would know the direction.

Pero then asked, "What did you do in the Marines, Bob?"

"I was a field medic, you know, first aid in battle conditions." That especially seemed to satisfy Mbuno, who mumbled something about first aid being a good thing.

The Mara office door clicked shut. Pausing just outside the doorway, Pero turned to Sergeant Gibson. "Okay, Sergeant, we're going to load up the Cessna we've hired and go back down to the Moyowosi airfield at Mgwesi and go into Moyowosi Game Reserve, link up with the Flamingo Tours' two askari, probably stay with them in the tents there, and, with a little luck, find Ube."

Sergeant Gibson knew Ube was Mbuno's nephew. As the whole of the Langata region was the Sergeant's beat, he took in tourist and guide activity at Wilson Airport regularly. If you worked Wilson Airport, you got to know all the best safari guides, and Ube was considered one of the very best, trained by Mbuno since a young age and trusted as a sole safari overseer by Anthony "Tone" Bowman, the ex–white hunter and owner of Flamingo Tours. It didn't take Gibson long, therefore, to convince Pero and Mbuno that he, too, wanted to help. He concluded with, "Ube is a very good man. I am ready."

Pero explained that the cameras and film the three men had were most essential and that he was going to ask some of his crew to oversee it being developed at Nairobi Labs, the professional development lab in Kenya, and then carefully inspect it to find out if the two photographers happened, by accident, to photograph any of the attackers. Or kidnappers. Or whatever they were.

"So, what can I do, Mr. Pero?" Gibson wanted to know.

"Sergeant, the cameras and film must remain in your possession. If there is any evidence there and if it is needed for a court case, it must be overseen at all times by a strong and honest police officer to be considered as proof in court. Can I ask you, *tafadhali*"—(please)— "to help us with this?" Gibson said he would be very pleased, puffing out his chest. Pero wasn't just flattering Gibson; Gibson had proven to be both strong and honest at the time of the terrorist attack at Wilson Airport.

Pero knew it was time to address the two other people on the couch, but before he could reenter the office, Bob held his arm and asked to be allowed to have a go. Pero watched as Bob entered the office, marched over, sat on Pero's vacant chair, and leaned forward. "Mr. Winter, my job was to protect you, provide emergency medical assistance on safari, and see you safely back to Nairobi or home. I consider that task complete." Harry Winter, Jr., nodded in agreement. "As for you, Richard, relax; these fellows have work to do, and you're too small a fish to bother with. But here's the problem you two are faced with. If anyone ever, and I mean ever, hears of your exploits here and the tale of the chase through that swamp, then you will put a man in danger. And I suspect that Mr. Pero here will make sure the *New York Times* exposes the fact that you ran away for your own personal safety despite the danger posed to the guide you left behind. That can ruin a reputation in a hurry. Me? I honestly don't care. Mr. Winter, I know you care. And if you, Richard, are smart and want to keep your job, you will care, too." Both men were open-mouthed. It was clear that the medic-bodyguard was in command. "So, are we agreed? You go back to the Hilton, enjoy a day or two in town, and then fly home."

Harry Winter wanted to know about the safety and return of their safari film. Pero called over from where he was, "Courtesy of the US government"—well, Pero knew that was a little white lie, but he continued—"all your film will be professionally developed and reviewed and then sent to you as soon as possible. The Sergeant here will personally oversee its safety, and experts are on hand to properly screen anything you took, just in case you accidentally captured something vital or of interest. Agreed?" Their response was unquestioning and keen. Bob stood, looking down at them in a commanding way. Pero continued, "Good. And if you need to give testimony later to prove you took an image of interest, I assume you will cooperate?" Again, they assured Pero they would be cooperative. "Good, good. Then the Sergeant will take down your address here in Nairobi, telephone numbers and personal addresses back in the US, and so on. Just to make sure they can get your cameras and film back safely."

Leaving Gibson in charge of the two tourists, Pero and Mbuno motioned for Bob to walk outside with them to join the waiting crew. Heep, Mary, and Susanna, along with assistants Nancy and Tom, were standing in the shade of the building next to their pile of equipment. Pero made introductions, related the story as Richard and Bob had told them, and asked Bob where the camera gear and film was. Bob pointed to a small pile of equipment on the other side of a chain link fence a hundred yards away, baking in the equatorial sun but still inside customs. Pero went back in and asked Gibson for help. Not ten minutes later, the tourists' equipment was cleared through customs, and the camera bags were handed over to the Sergeant who took them inside the air-conditioned office. The personal items from the tourists' safari remained on the concrete, ready to load into a taxi that would take the men to the Hilton.

Heep asked what the plan was. Pero wasn't sure.

Mary looked at Susanna, who nodded and said, "You had better stop right now, *mein dummer Mann*. You are not going anywhere until we make sure it is safe."

Heep, about to speak, was shushed by Mary, who glared at her husband and spoke to those assembled. "Not again, no you don't, you two." The ex-Marine looked confused. Mary looked at him and explained, "These two have been up to some very dangerous"—she paused for effect—"activities. Yes, let's call them that. Okay, the first time around Pero saved my life and my uncle's life . . ."

Pero interrupted, "No Mary, we all did it together."

Mary was having none of it. "Yeah, fine. We helped, but it was your work with the CIA that got us into trouble and got us out and stopped those al-Shabaab terrorists. Right?" She said it so forcibly that Heep, Pero, and Mbuno all nodded in unison.

Nancy and Tom looked dumbfounded but completely engrossed.

Mary continued, "And that was enough excitement and people dying for a lifetime; but no, that wasn't enough for you two. Heep then gets kidnapped and almost killed, you stop some uranium smuggling and get radioactive poisoning . . ."

Pero, needing to keep some of this secret, held up his hands in surrender. "Please, Mary, okay, okay . . ."

She was angry. "No, not okay, Pero. Susanna and I are agreed. No more little plans and scheming . . ."

Pero looked beseechingly at Susanna while pointing at Mbuno and the ex-Marine. "Darling, we just need to rescue Ube. There's no plan . . ."

Susanna was ready. Clearly, she and Mary had a plan. "Yes, you do, I know you. You are already planning; it's what producers do. But listen, please. Let's get this clear. We're a team. You will stay in constant contact, we will have a plane here waiting to come and join you, with force," she emphasized. "Yes, you heard right, with force to get Ube back and then return to our tranquil life of filming wildlife in dangerous places. Correct?"

Heep was smiling by this time. "Sorry, Pero, they went into the back of the plane and hatched plans."

Pero didn't really mind. Mary and Susanna were acting out of love and concern. What worried him was how to divide the team to be most effective. Susanna was right, he was the producer—*aha, that's my angle*, he thought. "So, can we all agree that I need to produce this rescue?"

Susanna took her husband's arm and pinched it, hard. "*Dummkopf*, you think I didn't guess you would try that? No, we will all agree on a plan and you, *mein dummer Mann*, will stick to it. If anything, in the bush Mbuno must be in command."

Pero had no choice. "I give in! You win. Look, here's where we are now as I see it. The three of us, Bob, Mbuno, and I, fly down there and pick up the askari. Mbuno tracks Ube, we assess and radio phone you at the Interconti with what we find, and then make a final plan. Of course, maybe Ube has already returned to the campsite, and all we're doing is flying down and back. Okay?" Everyone thought that would work. "Meanwhile, Heep, Mary, and my darling not-so-*dummer* wife . . ." Susanna dug her nails into his arm again. "Ouch, okay, all three of you will hole up at the Interconti along with Tom and Nancy. You, Heep, and Mary will babysit and then review the developed film Sergeant Gibson will be taking to Nairobi Labs. I have Wolfie's radio if this cell phone can't find a signal." He pulled out a phone from his breast pocket. "I'll call the service repeater and get them to telephone the Interconti or leave a message."

Heep chimed in and assured everyone that the Interconti had an HFRT he would borrow for their room. Susanna told him she already had the frequency of Wolfie's radio set. But Heep wanted to know if Pero had one of the special satellite radios from the CIA on this trip.

Pero groaned and pointed to Tom and Nancy, shaking his head. He had been hoping for secrecy, but knowing it was futile, he explained to everyone he wasn't doing anything for them anymore. "So, no, I have not got one."

Bob wanted to know if he was still CIA or not. "Hey man, you showed me a current ID, pal."

Pero felt Susanna's nails dig in again. "Hey, ouch. Look, I am, I guess, still part of that team technically. But even Director Lewis told me to stay out of trouble, and, no, I am not currently on any assignment and frankly don't want to be again. Enough was enough. I endangered all my friends." He waved at the people standing there. "I don't plan on chancing my luck again." Impatient to end the discussion, Pero explained he wanted to get going but wasn't sure what they would need as equipment.

Mbuno took charge. "Pero, we need what we already have, but we must move very quickly, I think." Mbuno looked down at his feet, clad in the new hiking sneakers Pero had purchased for the whole crew. "These will do. We will need a medical kit."

Bob walked over to the reduced pile of stuff from the Tanzania safari and plucked out a green canvas bag with a shoulder strap. "It's a little wet, but everything inside will be sealed dry. And if we find the tents, I have a full medical kit there, including a defibrillator."

Susanna addressed Pero with a sly smile, "Ah, *mein dummer Mann*, you want to go off on an adventure, *nein*?" Then she narrowed her eyes. "But you will need to transmit what you find, right? Or get in contact if you need real help, is that not right? So, we can hook up my Silke Wire to that transmitter Wolfie gave you, and as long as you are within one hundred meters of it, it'll transmit." Susanna, a serious brain trust on her own, had already worked out communications. She explained in a manner that was so encouraging she never made Pero feel like he was deserting her. "I have made note of the frequency and will have that radio working at the hotel before you even land. Now, I must connect the Silke Wire microphone receiver to the Oasis radio." She lifted Wolfie's green canvas bag and her Otterbox waterproof case with all her microphone equipment and sat down in the shade to connect the units together.

Heep and Pero knew the Silke Wire transmitter was so thin and undetectable that Pero or Mbuno could wear it under their safari shirt collars. The Silke Wire transmitter base had standard audio jack outputs, which Susanna clicked into the microphone input of the RT set. She looked up to make sure they were watching what she was doing so they could repeat it later if necessary. She explained, "Here, look, if you leave the base unit on with cables attached to the Land Rover battery, it will transmit anytime you speak into the microphone wire. That will key the transmitter base and the radio will detect incoming signal and then will transmit. We will be listening. With luck, the frequency modulation will not wander too much. It is not perfect, but should work."

Bob was clearly impressed as he held and examined the Silke Wire microphone in his fingers delicately. The transmitter tube was smaller than a cigarette, about half as long, with a thin, dangling, four-inch wire. On the stub end of the tube was a push button. "This thing? Where's the microphone?"

Pero smiled. "Bob, we'll explain on the plane, later. That is the whole microphone, just the wire. And it's the antenna, too."

Susanna gave her warning: "Yes, but you have to be close to the radio, maybe one hundred feet, no more." Bob, Pero, and Mbuno nodded.

It was agreed that Heep, Mary, and Susanna, along with Nancy and Tom, would hole up at the Interconti to review the tourists' film as soon as possible, and they could also await news or a call for help. Then came the moment for everyone to depart, but before they could look for the nearest cabs, two minibuses arrived. Sheila from Flamingo Tours got out of one and Tone Bowman emerged from the other. It was Tone who spoke. "You still here? We need to get Ube back."

"Agreed, Tone," Pero responded, shaking Tone's hand. Pero was worried how long Nairobi Labs would take to process the film and wondered if Tone might have an idea. Pero pointed out that Sergeant Gibson had already gained possession of the cameras and film.

Tone was glad to have something constructive to do. "Righty-ho. I'll go to Nairobi Labs directly with Sergeant Gibson and get the owner, Hasaan, working immediately." Pero pointed at Mara's office and explained that Gibson needed to keep legal custody for testimony later. "Good, Hasaan can work under police orders then. I'll call the Sergeant's new chief at Langata Station. He's my neighbor. I guess the developed film could be with your people at the Interconti by tonight. That do?" Everyone agreed it would have to do.

Susanna shook Tone's hand, introduced herself as Pero's wife, and explained she would act as the communications center in their room at the Interconti.

Pero felt relieved that Susanna was being professional and not overly emotional. "Well, that settles it. Hey, thanks everyone, but please, one more favor—wait till you hear from us; don't come charging down to Moyowosi until you are sure, okay?" His team gave their agreement, and people started to divide supplies and luggage, loading it all into the minivans.

Mbuno took Tone off to the side, where they had a heated argument. Mbuno prevailed. Tone then addressed everyone. "Okay then, we'll take you to the Interconti. I have already called your man there, Pero. All booked in; they even threw the BA night flight crew out early to make room." People began to load up. Mbuno and Bob started to take the gear they needed to the waiting Cessna, which was being refueled and undergoing pilot preflight inspection.

On their own, Tone and Pero needed to clear the air. Pero started first. "Ube's family to me, Tone. He's like Mbuno's son, really. I can't let my brother down."

"Yes, but he's my friend, too. Both of them are—most trusted. If I stay here and take control . . ."

"No, Mbuno needs control, Tone. Not me, Mbuno. He is the only one I would trust in a situation in the bush like this. It's his kid. He's the expert, he's got to have one hundred percent control."

"Yes, yes, I figured as much. It's just frustrating. Did you know Mbuno was my field agent during the Troubles? He is, or was, the most capable man I know. But still . . . we're the same age. He just told me, dammit, that I would slow him down. Well, my ego took a bruising, I'll tell you, mainly because he is right, of course. So, have no fear, I'll monitor the phones here."

"Ah, but Susanna will have the RT frequencies, and we'll be using that."

"Agreed, and I have an old set at home, so we'll power them all up and maintain watch until you no longer need us. The camp team down there consists of two brothers, Teddy and Keriako Matunga. They are reliable."

"Bob said so. Good to know." But something was bothering Pero about what the three witnesses had intimated. Pero knew Tone had safari intelligence streaming in from all of East Africa. He needed to maintain his edge as the premier tour operator. So Pero asked Tone, "What did you find out from the Tanzanian embassy?"

"Nothing, nothing in the region—no terrorists, no kidnapping gangs in Tanzania yet; only the ones in Burundi, and that's four hundred miles and three tribal lands away. Nothing they can think of. They are as dumbfounded as we are. They are about to call in several hunting safari groups for safety. This has spooked the whole region."

Pero got to his real question. "What would a German or German group be doing secretly operating in the Moyowosi region? What's down there that anyone cares about? No poaching, too few elephants . . . any ideas?"

Shaking his head, Tone answered, "Hell, there's all sorts of stuff in the papers about environmental destruction of old forests for new tobacco farms, but those outfits are mainly funded by Chinese holding companies out of Dar." Pero understood he meant Dar es Salaam, the former capital of Tanzania on the coast, five hundred miles away. "I can't see what that has to do with German interest. But you know, these may be excolonialists, German relatives left over from the First World War. But still, why armed?" Tone nonetheless promised he would put out feelers and report in. "At least it's something

I can sink my teeth into! And I might ask your friends, the Singh brothers in Dar es Salaam, if they know anything. All right with you if I use your name?"

"Brilliant." The Singh brothers ran some of the largest businesses in Tanzania as well as the secret police. "Mbuno's waving. Time to go. See you, Tone."

"Godspeed. Bring 'im back, Pero, bring 'im back."

Passing his wife, Pero hugged her close and kissed her full on the lips. Unaccustomed to public displays of affection, Susanna blushed with the love she felt for her husband and then, much to her surprise, burped. "Sorry Pero . . . still a bit of plane sickness."

"Rest at the hotel and ask Mary to keep an eye on you. Bye, darling." And he ran to climb aboard the aging but perfectly maintained Cessna 414.

CHAPTER 7

Wanyama—Wild Animals

The right engine coughed into life. Bob sat strapped in as Mbuno took the seat opposite and did the same. Pero climbed aboard, told the pilots to go, and sat in the row behind Mbuno. Pero was making the silent point that Mbuno was in charge.

Once they were "wheels up" and headed south-southeast toward Moyowosi, Pero unbuckled and sat on the floor between Bob and Mbuno, facing the tail of the plane so he could see their faces. He said, "I haven't been to Moyowosi before. Can you give me a rundown of what to expect?" Pero knew that East Africa contained virtually every climate and type of vegetation, terrain, and animal species in the continent. From snowcapped mountains to scorching deserts. From deep jungle to open savanna. From densely populated cities to areas the size of New Jersey where only a few tribespeople roamed. From the descriptions the tourists had recounted, the region they were flying to was likely to be wet and well-grassed, but Pero needed a producer's assessment, something he could use to shape his thinking.

Mbuno gave a rundown from memory based on official tourist information. "Moyowosi Game Reserve is very, very rich in animals. There are large populations of buffalo, the topi antelope with prized twisted horns like the larger hartebeest, who is also there, and the even larger roan antelope. There is also a few greater kudu, a very big antelope that is very rare, also many big prides of lion and giraffe—but no Rothschild's giraffe that I have heard of—zebra, and, in the marsh regions, leopard, waterbuck, sitatunga or marshbuck, hippo, and crocodile. Of course, the reserve is also famous with birdwatchers, especially British twitchers, to see wattled crane and the shoebill, which is a very large stork-like bird. Both are very pretty and can be seen near Lake Nyagamoma that feeds the Malagarasi River." Mbuno looked exhausted at remembering all that.

Bob's mouth was open. "Good God. That's almost word for word what Ube said on our way down." Mbuno smiled and nodded. Bob smiled back and said, "Yeah, I see it now. One expert teaching another. Gotcha."

Pero was still puzzled by the German angle. "Mbuno, what the hell is down there besides a few hunting campsites, maybe a tourist lodge or two, that would attract a military organization? Is there any industry down there? Mines? Gold? Diamonds? Anything?"

"I think, Pero, in all that mud in the rainy season, it would be very hard. Now, at the end of the dry season, until the rains come, the hunting and wildlife are very good, very wild." He went on to explain, haltingly, searching for the right words, that even in the dry season, the marshes are very large, though not as large as in October when the rains come. So, during this time, the animals are pushed together, which is better for hunters. "But I think it is not a very good place to hunt in Moyowosi as it is in Kigosi Reserve. Kigosi is very wild, very big, very dry right now. Hunting is easier." Mbuno explained that Moyowosi was safer for tourists with a camera because there is little hunting anymore. "It is why camera safaris go now to Moyowosi, not Kigosi. It is safer."

"Not anymore it ain't," replied Bob.

Pero felt it necessary to uphold Ube's honor. "Bob, Ube would not have taken you there if there was any known danger." Bob immediately apologized; he had only meant that going forward it might not be considered so safe. Pero replied, "True, but I still can't figure out why."

Mbuno put his head back and closed his eyes. "It does not matter. We must find Ube."

Pero, for once, did not agree with his friend. He felt sure that to get Ube back safely, they needed to know what they were up against.

The flight droned on with all three men strapped into their seats. They flew over the vast Maasai Mara, then the Serengeti plain, then turned sharply and headed straight over the southern tip of Lake Victoria, veered south-southeast to avoid Burundi airspace, and circled southeast to pass over the western tip of Lake Nyagamoma to line up on Moyowosi Airport, if it could be called that. To Pero, the airstrip looked even smaller than the one at Lake Rudolf.

The plane touched down almost silently on the dirt strip, and from his window, Pero saw only a single WWII steel hut for police who would be acting as customs control. They disembarked from the Cessna and asked the two pilots to organize sleep shifts to be ready to depart on a moment's notice, twenty-four hours a day. The pilots explained that Sheryl at Mara had already briefed them, and they would be fueled and ready. All signs of customs or police were conspicuously absent, so the crew said they would handle it if anyone showed up. "This was not an expected arrival, so our guess is that the customs guy is at home in this heat, asleep. But don't worry, we have all the paperwork."

Pero, Bob, and Mbuno walked through the safari client's waiting room. A bold sign declared it to be the "Transit Lounge." There was not a matching chair to be seen. An old bottled water vending machine for tourists with a Scotch-taped paper notice covering the coin slot demanded three thousand shillings per bottle: "Pay Cash to Agent." As he passed the machine, Pero noticed that the plastic of the bottles was yellowing in the heat. *And lord, it's humid*, he thought, comparing it to the dryness of Lake Rudolf.

Outside, two Land Rovers were waiting. The two drivers immediately recognized Bob, and he them. Bob made the introductions. "This here is Teddy, yep, named after our great President Roosevelt. Seems his great-great-grandfather was a porter for T. R. And this is his younger brother, Keriako." Bob put his hands on their shoulders. "Fellows, thank you again for saving us." The men looked amazed that Bob was back and had questions for him in Swahili.

Mbuno silenced them, everyone, with, "*Ukimya!*" (Silence!) Then he looked at the ex-Marine. "Mr. Bob, I need to talk with these men." Pero could tell by the way in which Mbuno had said *men* that he was unsure of them; something was not straightforward, not typical of Mbuno's friendly nature. Mbuno walked the men off to a distance and began questioning them, and Pero heard the word *Sukuma*, and the men began shaking their heads. *Nope, they're not Sukuma tribe*, thought Pero.

Pero knew the Sukuma people were the largest single tribal group in Tanzania, a warlike people whom Mbuno did not have much respect for. Years before, on a Serengeti shoot, it was campfire gossip that Mbuno had accused one of the hired guides of providing meat with wire-noose snare traps; it was not an honorable kill. The man had argued with Mbuno and then produced a spear and thrown it to attack Mbuno. Mbuno had simply plucked the spear from midair, broken its wooden shaft over his knee, and dropped it in the dust. The Sukuma man left in disgrace.

Pero could see Mbuno was pressuring the men, who were holding their hands up in defense. Eventually, Mbuno clapped the one called Teddy on the back, took hold of his upper arm, and guided him back to Pero and Bob who were looking on, astonished. Mbuno seemed relieved. "These men can be trusted. They pretend to be Sukuma to get work, but they are not." He spoke to the men, "*Kuwaambia kweli ambao ni.*" (Tell them who you are.)

Teddy spoke for his younger brother, Keriako. "*Tunasikitika bwanas. Mama yetu ni Sukuma, lakini baba yetu ni Okiek na Kikuyu.*" (We are sorry, misters. Our mother is Sukuma, but our father is Okiek and Kikuyu.)

Mbuno explained, "The Sukuma in this region, away from their homeland, are not to be trusted. Kikuyu are farmers and government people only from near Mount Kenya. But the Okiek are relatives of the Liangulu." He turned to Bob and said, "My people." Then he said to Pero, "I know the Okiek." Pero understood he meant that he trusted the tribe.

Mbuno looked at the men and told them they had upheld the honor of the Okiek in saving these tourists. Now he, a father Liangulu, needed them to help him find Ube, his missing nephew.

It was the younger man, Keriako, who asked, "*Wewe ni nani, baba wa Liangulu?*" (Who are you, Liangulu father?)

When Mbuno gave them his name, both boys, probably not much older than twenty and twenty-one, dropped to their knees and began keening. Mbuno reached down and pulled them to their feet. For Pero and Bob, observers in this strange encounter, the next few minutes were confusing and yet profound. Both boys told a story in Swahili, tripping over each other's sentences. Pero could make out the words for grandfather and grandmother, as well as the tribal name of Okiek, but most of the rest was incomprehensible. After a few moments, it was clear Mbuno was also startled, and he began hugging the boys. Mbuno turned to Bob and Pero and said, "These are the grandchildren of an Okiek man and a woman I saved from a terrible place near Nairobi. You know it well, Pero, the place you call a slum—Kibera. I put them on a matatu to go home. We became friends. They send me honey."

As Bob was looking completely confused, Pero added what little knowledge he had, "Wild honey. It's what the Okiek are famous for harvesting. Mbuno here is addicted."

Mbuno smiled. "I would not say addicted. I do like honey very much." And he laughed, still hugging the boys, one on each side, both taller than he was. "Now, we can work together . . ."

Mbuno was giving instructions for one Land Rover to be left for the pilots and for Keriako to give them the keys when the sound of a plane approaching made them all look up and scan the sky. From the east, a sleek red-and-white executive plane, twin pusher turboprop, roared just feet off the runway. Reaching the end, it zoomed upward, barrel-rolled, and circled the runway to reapproach from the east once more for landing. Their own two pilots and the five men watched, fascinated, as the racy-looking plane made a perfect landing. As it was taxiing back from the end of the dirt strip, creating a massive dust storm behind it, the Cessna pilot called over and shouted, "Avanti, bloody nice!" Pero knew that model of plane was very expensive and not really suited for dirt strips in the middle of nowhere.

Suddenly, from the jungle began to emerge the sound of trucks approaching. Pero quickly gave an order. *"Haraka!* Mbuno, Teddy, Bob—get into the Land Rover quickly, and Bob, lie down out of sight. Mbuno, you and Teddy sit up front, leave the back door open for me, engine running." Mbuno translated the order to Teddy, and they went at a sprint.

Pero stood his ground, waved goodbye to his pilots as they took the other Land Rover keys, and motioned to Keriako to hustle back. Pero wanted to give the impression that he was ready to leave.

A Unimog—a four-wheel-drive, off-road expedition truck— pulled up in front of the steel hut, followed by a Mercedes diesel SUV. Two men got out of the SUV and walked into the waiting room. They paid no attention to Pero or his Land Rover. However, the driver of the Unimog, who wasn't African, watched Pero intently. Pero waved at him. The man flashed a finger. Pero smiled and continued waving back, pretending to have confused the gesture as a simple greeting. As Keriako reached Pero, Pero patted him on the back and told him in broken Swahili to walk slowly to the Land Rover and get in the back while leaving the door open. Pero walked toward the hut.

Inside, he saw two men in jungle camo outfits, both with new jungle boots laced in the German fashion, taking water from the machine. Pero went up to them and asked innocently, "Excuse me, fellows, do you speak English?"

"Yes, I do," replied the taller man with blond hair, perhaps in his mid-thirties, very thin. "What do you want?" His English was flawless, the accent thick. Pero couldn't place it.

Pero explained, genially, that he was on a round-Tanzania flight looking for possible locations for the TV documentary series they were about to start filming. "Moyowosi has some special birds—cranes—that the head office wants to get. Either of you fellows know where a shallow pond or marsh location would be filmable? Oh, and hey, are you guys down here hunting or filming?"

"None of your damn business. Just make sure you stay away from our camp. You see a truck or any vehicle, turn around and stay away. Got it?" The threat was plain, sudden, and out of keeping with tourist bush etiquette.

Pero calculated the intent was to frighten him away pronto, perhaps preventing him from getting a look at the faces of the three men in suits who were then disembarking from the Avanti. He decided to give the two men some room and himself a little cover. He cranked up a Los Angeles accent, "All right, all right, jeez, I was just asking. I work for Ultimate Films, you know . . ."

"I don't give a damn who you work for. Now, get going."

Pero feigned fear and went, fast. The engine was already running and the wheels turning before he shut the Land Rover door.

CHAPTER 8

A Dirt Road along the Malagarasi River

It was Mbuno, up front with Teddy, who asked the brothers questions and then translated for Bob and Pero in the back. The long wheelbase Land Rover had two single seats up front and two bench seats on either side of the back. It was a noisy diesel, and Mbuno almost had to shout for Pero and Bob to understand. The road they were on would skirt the lake, then follow the eastern bank of the Malagarasi River. The askari assured them it would only take two hours to get to where they had left the Land Rovers yesterday morning before setting off on foot. There was a ranger checkpoint there.

Bob explained, "We parked and then filled in a piece of paper of how many were in our safari group and where we were walking. There is a main trail that is signposted . . ."

Teddy continued his description of where they had walked and driven with Bob, answering Mbuno's translation with "that's right" or "I agree" every once in a while. The story took a long time to relate. The group had proceeded along the path into the outer marshland surrounding the river and followed the stream of the river south to the lake. They never got all the way to the lake. Ube had spotted fresh leopard tracks, although he had been looking for greater kudu, which like the marsh edges and sweet grass this time of year. Ube asked Mr. Winter if he wanted to pursue the leopard or keep looking for kudu. Mr. Winter chose leopard because he had never seen one alive in the bush. As they followed the tracks, they left the marsh and were in light forest off the side of the road. The leopard was in the tree . . .

Mbuno told Teddy to stop, he knew that part. What he had not heard was the exact details of what had happened next. Teddy explained, "*Kulikuwa na kelele kubwa katika msitu ambayo alifanya chui neva!*"

Mbuno shook his head and translated for Pero and Bob. "There was a big noise in the forest, and the leopard became nervous." Bob looked puzzled. "You did not hear this, Mr. Bob?"

Bob raised his voice to be heard up front. "I may not have been able to. Ube and Teddy were in front. I was twenty yards or more bringing up the rear with Keriako. But, man, what's a big noise? What did it sound like, can you ask?"

Mbuno did so and was surprised when Teddy admitted he had not heard anything; it was Ube who had told him and everyone else to get down, as Ube had heard the noise. Mbuno questioned Teddy, trying to get the exact words Ube had used. It was Keriako next to Pero on the bench who responded, "*Nadhani yeye alisema ni ajali kubwa.*"

Mbuno explained, "He says that Ube heard something, a great noise of a great crash. Those are not noises you hear in the forest. They are man noises. That is why he sensed danger." Mbuno told Teddy and Keriako to continue. Splitting the recounting, they said Ube had made them retreat into the marsh grasses where they hid for a while. Finally, Ube told them all to be quiet. Both men put a universal finger to their lips to demonstrate and said, "Shhhh ..." They heard men's voices but could not understand what they were saying. Then Ube told Teddy and Keriako to lead the safari party into the muddy ditch and to take everyone to safety.

Pero knew something was missing. "Mbuno, ask them about the orange hat." He did.

Keriako answered that the *"kijinga mtu"* (stupid man) with the orange hat had stood up, and it was Keriako who pulled him down while Ube took his hat from him. Keriako added something about the hat until Mbuno, having heard enough, stopped him with a hand gesture. Mbuno seemed angry.

They were driving as fast as the road conditions would allow, swerving now and then to avoid larger potholes. It was bright daylight, and the road was clearly visible. As they rounded one sharp corner after another, following the meandering river to their left, Pero thought, *When they had driven the tourists to the airstrip in the near dark, they must have been driving slower. And it would not have been so damn hot.*

The humid, fetid air from the riverside made Teddy run the wipers now and again. The actual marsh ran seamlessly off to the left. Pero watched and allowed his mind to wander. *Green, thick, and impenetrable ... tracking kudu in that? Leopard? Nuts.* When the road climbed a few dozen feet and they could see over the grasses, the river appeared. Muddy and tree-lined, it lay maybe a hundred yards beyond. On the right of the reddish-tan dirt road, the forest was no more than seventy-five feet high, a solid canopy of eucalyptus and other trees, whose roots would all be reaching deep down into the water table below, replenished by the river. Beneath the forest canopy, Pero could identify the usual East African small wait-a-minute bushes, acacia-like plants with spiked three-inch thorns, and small clusters of euphorbia cactus trees, a favorite treat of rhinos.

Shaking his head to clear his thoughts, Pero returned to the questions he wanted to ask. "Had they moved the campsite, and if so how far away from the other site?" Teddy explained that they had followed Ube's orders and taken the men to safety at the original campsite by the baobab trees, where they picked up their luggage and boxes, and then the brothers drove them to the airport right away. The plane was there, but it took a while to find the pilot, who was not expecting them. Speaking over each other, Teddy and Keriako quickly explained that they wanted to use the airstrip's police radio, but since the policeman was home, they had to go and get him, and he charged them six thousand shillings for the call. They confirmed that they spoke with Sheila at Flamingo Tours, telling her that Ube was not back and conveying what had happened. They asked for instructions. Sheila told them to send the safari clients back to base, then return by themselves to camp and pack it up into the Land Rovers. Then she told them to go back to the airfield and call in. When they did, she gave them instructions not to drive home to base, but instead to set up camp at a new site away from the old one, and then drive back to the airstrip and await the arrival of a Mara flight. Pero knew those were the instructions he had given Sheila. It all fit.

Mbuno continued translating as they recounted how the two of them returned to the baobab campsite, loaded everything into the two Land Rovers, and drove away. Mbuno asked where the new campsite was. Keriako explained that he and Teddy had discussed it and felt that keeping it near the trailhead would not be a good idea. So, they continued up the road into the reserve another five miles and set up the tents in a small clearing, maybe three hundred yards off the road. They felt it was safe atop a small hilltop with acacia and giraffe in sight of the camp. No lions, they were very sure about that. Mbuno and Pero knew that the typically skittish giraffe being near the camp was a good sign that things must be peaceful in that area.

Teddy looked at the rearview mirror and spoke up, "*Kitu ni kufuatia.*" (Something is following.) Instinctively, Pero, Bob, and Mbuno looked back. They could see the unmistakable shape of the large Unimog truck moving fast, maybe a mile back. Teddy started to speed up. Mbuno put his hand on Teddy's forearm and patted it, telling him to drive normally. Mbuno asked Pero, "What did you tell those men at the airstrip?"

"That we're a film-scouting crew looking for suitable animals to film. We're from Hollywood. They told me to get lost." Mbuno nodded in agreement to the lie. Bob looked concerned.

As the Unimog closed the distance, Mbuno knew the road was wide enough for them to pass, but he wanted to avoid confrontation. He told Teddy to indicate left and look for a place to turn into if necessary. The Unimog came close enough to ride their bumper. Suddenly, passing the Unimog, the Mercedes SUV pulled alongside the Land Rover on their right side, and Pero was glad Bob was sitting on the bench opposite him, on the driver's side, his face out of sight. To be sure, Pero said, "Hey Bob, pretend you're sleeping, okay?" Bob lowered his chin and did not turn around. The front passenger of the Mercedes peered into the Land Rover cabin, making a mental tally. Pero waved hello and got no response. It was the same man who had told him to leave. In the back seat sat three men wearing suits and ties, all looking straight ahead. None of them were African, and, to Pero, they appeared not to be Asian or European, either. *Something about their thin ties and shiny suits*, he thought.

The Mercedes hit the gas and sped past, inches from the Land Rover's side, and was quickly followed by the Unimog, which forced the Land Rover to put two wheels onto the rough shoulder, bouncing it over some rocks and dips, and choked them in the dust from the huge truck's wheels.

Teddy had been very calm, keeping the vehicle straight and in the lane, if you could say that a washboard dirt road in the middle of nowhere had lanes. Pero saw that Mbuno had put a hand on the wheel, and he thought, *Imaginary lanes, a possible sideswipe accident; not likely the threat will go away. Something is very wrong here*. He looked at Mbuno and suspected that he was thinking the same. If the truck had been a reckless matatu bus, driven as those means of conveyance often were—a danger to all—it would have been a normal occurrence on such a rural road. But for two shiny, undented, professional vehicles to be driven that way indicated a strong disregard for others and, perhaps, authority.

All Pero could say was, "Where the hell is Ube? Let's find him and get the hell out of here."

Mbuno simply responded, "*Ndiyo*."

Not more than five minutes later, as they topped another small hill, Teddy said he could see a dust cloud coming their way from far ahead of them. He pointed through the windscreen. Mbuno peered forward and told Teddy to get off the road quickly to the right. As they hastily bounced down the side of the raised road, the wheels sank into soft earth. Teddy engaged four-wheel drive low and made headway, slowly, to where Mbuno was pointing, slotting them between two large eucalyptus trees, mostly hiding them from the raised road behind them. Mbuno gave the order to stop and got out.

Bob wanted to know if they should all get out, but Pero told him to wait for Mbuno's instruction. They watched through the dusty side glass as Mbuno crawled up the road embankment, grabbing tufts of tall grass and putting them on his head, camouflaging his whitening hair. Mbuno reached back and gave a signal to stay down in the Land Rover. He meant for them to stay hidden. Pero was fairly certain that, from the road, the Land Rover would not be easily spotted. It was too late to do anything more.

The dust cloud could be seen now, advancing quickly. When it was near enough, the top of a giant, eighteen-wheeler Volvo logging truck, engine roaring, appeared, coming and then going at speed. It was not empty—the giant eucalyptus logs still dripped sap. It was followed, one hundred yards behind, by an identical brand-new, shiny Volvo giant. Following those two was silence. Not a noise from any animal, no birds, no calls . . . nothing.

Mbuno was still. Pero knew him well enough that this meant something else was coming. Moments later, Pero saw Mbuno make a hand gesture to wait and stay down again. As the choking truck dust settled, two more vehicles appeared, following the giant trucks. Mbuno could see clearly. Pero could just see the tops of the cabs as they drove by, moving fast. One was the Mercedes SUV, and one was a flatbed Nissan—a half-ton truck of the type seen all over Africa, dented, repainted perhaps a dozen times, showing signs of past accidents. The vehicle seemed to crab down the road, with two locals in the cab and two men in the open back.

Only Mbuno's expert eyes could see that one of them was Ube, unmoving, but his gaze was alert. His body posture, one shoulder up and one down, his torso slightly hunched in the middle, told Mbuno he had been beaten. Mbuno, in that split second of recognition, observed that the man with Ube was looking at Ube, not at the forest. Mbuno raised his hand, made a circular motion, and then dropped down from any possible sight. Ube's eyes were, Mbuno noted, staring right at him. He would have seen.

As soon as they passed, Mbuno returned to the Land Rover. Pero could see the resolve on his face. Pero, having been through so much with Mbuno, knew that he had seen something troubling from the roadside. Pero asked, "You okay, brother? What was it? What did you see?"

"It was Ube." Everyone in the car started to speak, making suggestions that they chase them, but Mbuno held up his hand. "He is hurt but watching. I see his eyes. He will wait. We need to scout, then rescue. If they were going to kill him, they would have left him for vultures. They are taking him. I do not know where. We must scout."

Bob spoke up, "But surely we need to follow—"

"It is Tanzania, Mr. Bob. The trucks are new, the Mercedes is new. These people are new. They do not belong here. They cannot hide . . . how do you say it?" He paused, "Yes, they cannot hide in plain sight and not be known. All the local people will know where they are, what they are doing, where they sleep."

Bob nodded agreement.

Teddy and Keriako asked Mbuno to tell them what he was saying. He repeated his thoughts in Swahili. They, too, were pacified, trusting Mzee Mbuno, asking only where he wanted to drive to now.

He told them to drive to the camp, adding in English for Bob and Pero, "We will radio. Zanzi-Agroforestry is the name on the truck." Pero understood Mbuno needed Heep, Mary, Susanna, and Tone to find out who Zanzi-Agroforestry were. Pero knew that once they figured out what Zanzi-Agroforestry was really doing there and where they were located, then they could rescue Ube. Mbuno put a cap on it: "We will find Ube." It was a statement of assured fact.

Pero and the rest of the Land Rover's occupants took comfort in Mbuno's leadership and resolve.

Only Mbuno knew how little confidence seeing Ube that way had afforded him. Once, long ago, he had rescued a life-threatened, injured Ube from a gang of Zanzibari—men from the Arab-influenced island of Zanzibar off the cost of Tanzania. Those men had been elephant poachers led by Ube's corrupt biological father, Mbuno's wife's brother. Seeing Ube in a truck with the words Zanzi-Agroforestry on the side sent waves of worry through his body. Mbuno feared that this time he might not be able to get Ube out alive.

CHAPTER 9

*Wito Nyumbani, Kwa Makini*_Calling Home, Carefully

On arriving at what Pero immediately thought of as "Giraffe Hill," Teddy and Keriako were eager to be useful. Mbuno told them to make a meal and make up the cots in the three tents, one for Pero, one for Bob, and one for Mbuno and the two brothers. Teddy looked at Keriako and beamed. The prospect of the honor being shown them to tent with Mzee Mbuno was palpable. Mbuno patted them on their backs and said, his eyes smiling, "*Kutosha, sasa kupata Kwenda.*" (Enough, now get going.) The young men sped off to their tasks happily.

The camp had no water supply so Teddy advised that they ration water until they could get down to the river for more washing water. At the airstrip they had filled a ten-gallon plastic container, mostly for hydration. Mbuno thought that would do for drinking and rinsing sand-scrubbed cooking pots. The problem of food was another matter. Keriako explained to Mbuno that they had left the remainder of a bushbuck carcass at the previous site, hanging from a lower limb of the baobab. There had been no time to keep the flies off it previously when they had driven the men to the airstrip in a hurry. Mbuno said not to worry. He could see there were beans, as well as corn meal and sorghum, the two staple ingredients for making posho. He was also pleased to see a fresh sack of wheat flour and told the boys to make safari bread, to be cooked in the embers of a hot fire after making enough posho and beans for lunch and dinner; they may need to eat dinner cold.

Pero, meanwhile, had opened the hood of the Land Rover, placed the green canvas bag on the right fender, and connected the two battery alligator clips. The canvas case was clearly ex-military. There were two latches, more like clips really, on the front that Pero released to lower the front flap. He tipped the radio back, read the frequency on Wolfie's taped piece of paper, verified that the dial was still set correctly, and called Bob and Mbuno over. "Ready, let's call in."

Mbuno had seen Susanna put the Silke Wire microphone on Mary at Lake Rudolf, and he repeated the placement. He opened his small Swiss Army knife that he always treasured and made a small slit on the inside of Pero's button-down collar. This created a pocket for the half-cigarette-shaped piece attached to the wire, which he supported over the re-buttoned collar.

Bob asked, "May I? I had a set in the Corps—well, newer than this—but I think I can handle it." Pero said, "Why not." Bob flicked the power on, and nothing happened except for the dial illuminating. There was a small red bar light that read, "Standby." Bob looked at Pero, and Pero shrugged, reached behind the radio, and switched on the Silke Wire base transmitter-receiver. The radio sprang to life. On the set, like on the dash of every airplane, was the radio's call sign. Pero spoke, "This is Auxiliary Z4WD broadcasting in the blind. Can anyone read? Over." On the radio, the blinking lights of the LED bar showed that Pero's voice was picked up, modulated, and was now broadcasting. It was comforting to know the radio was working.

Susanna's voice came in loud and clear. "I'm here, oh, sorry"—someone was speaking to her—"Z86DF receiving. Over."

"Hi darling, we're here, safe and sound. Over."

A distant voice cut in, mid-sentence, "Z3WD receiving Auxiliary Z3WD. In the blind, receiving you four by five, will monitor and stand by. Over."

Pero responded, "Hey, Wolfie, that's great. Pressing matter. Please all assist knowledge on reverse spell Y-R-T-S-E-R-O-F-O-R-G-A dash island off Dar. Who-what-where details. Over."

As Susanna responded, Pero heard Heep's and Mary's voices also in the background. "Copied, understood, will work that out. News missing person? Over." Pero was pleased they did not mention Ube by name. Anyone could be listening. Wolfie was silent, and again Pero thought that was a sign of his professionalism.

Suddenly a new voice cut in: "8KN98 here, confirm Gibson and I arranged Hasaan for development, delivery tonight to hotel. Over."

Pero was going to say Tone's name, then thought better of it. "Thanks. Understood. Over." Then Pero waited to see if anyone else added anything. The crackling radio made him impatient. Pero then had to relay the news of Ube. Pero explained that the person they were looking for had been seen being driven and had gone by them in the opposite direction. "You-know-who was sure they had recognized each other." His friends said that was a good sign but wanted to know the connection to the name he had asked them to research. Pero didn't want to broadcast that and said simply, "Currently unsure."

Heep's voice came on. "Okay then, we're over and out until later. Always standby, please."

Before he flipped only the Silke Wire switch to off, he heard part of Wolfie's "Affirma—" and the radio went silent. Pero unplugged the audio and power feeds connecting the Silke Wire, and the radio sprang to life again, listening to the airwaves. They caught the Interconti signing off and Tone Bowman saying he would "get on it right away; I'll telephone you presently." Pero hoped he meant research into Zanzi-Agroforestry. Pero felt foolish for spelling that backward and for using the "island" description for Zanzibar, but he figured Susanna and Mary would figure it out quickly enough.

Pero looked at Bob and Mbuno and knew that they, like him, were comforted to have such good radio communication. However, similarly, they had learned nothing and would now have to wait. Mbuno always seemed to know what to say. "When tracking dangerous animals, it is always best to observe, be patient, then you find their weakness. We may have a long wait."

The ex-Marine slipped into battlefield mode and added, "Then we wait. Shifts?"

Mbuno said, "Food first." He told Bob he should sleep first after the meal, then Pero, then Mbuno. The radio needed to be left on receiving, with someone always there. Pero and Bob nodded.

Bob asked, "Four on, eight off, that suit?"

Mbuno smiled and explained that in the bush, the sky and the place you are in tells the time, not a watch. Mbuno pointed up at the sun behind a cloud and asked, "How long will the sun need to change? You watch, it tells you when it is time."

Bob had clearly had experience dealing with people other than Americans in remote places. "Okay, like the Tigris people

I spent time with. They never used a watch and did things at different times of the day depending on the season."

Mbuno did not know the people of Tigris, but he understood the concept. In the winter season, you rose later, worked harder, and prepared for an earlier sunset. It was cooler because the sun was not overhead like it was that day in equatorial Kenya. However, at this time of year in East Africa in the middle of the day, you planned your day differently. "Mr. Bob, here in Africa it is the same. You watch the animals, they tell you when it is time to move and when it is time to rest."

As Pero went into the bushes to relieve himself, it occurred to him that Bob's allegedly short Marine military experience might not be exactly accurate. The Tigris people were in southern Iraq, an area Pero knew was out of combat within days of the 2003 invasion. So what was this young Marine doing there half a decade later when he would have been just old enough to enlist?

As he settled some dust, Pero also wondered why Mbuno focused on just the Zanzibar name of the Agroforestry company. What was it about Zanzibar that seemed critical? He decided to ask rather than keep guessing. *This is no time to play mental games. Keep everything out in the open, discuss it all, and we'll work better as a team.* Zipping up his fly, Pero went back to camp to talk with Bob and Mbuno.

Teddy and Keriako were finishing erecting a second camp cot, putting blankets and pillows on top. On the floor, they spread rush matting. When Pero came over, Teddy said, "This your tent, *bwana*. I check cooking now. Okay?"

Pero could see Bob was unfolding his cot blanket in the adjacent tent. "Yes, sure." Then he called out louder, "Mbuno and Bob, can you come and join us here?" When they ambled over, Pero asked Mbuno to explain the significance of the Zanzibar name.

Mbuno looked pensive, and instead of answering, he addressed the two brothers, "*Yeye anataka kujua kuhusu Zanzibar. Wakati sisi kula, mimi nitakuambia hadithi ya Ube na majangili Zanzibari.*" He turned to Pero and said, "Bob may also want to know about Zanzibari. When we eat, I will tell the story of Ube and the Zanzibar poachers." The brothers went off, one to clean cooking utensils, the other to split the firewood collected earlier. Then Mbuno simply told Bob and Pero, "Later, I will tell a campfire tale." Already, the pungent smell of acacia and thorn-tree green wood and steam from cooking bread flavored the air.

Within half an hour, the hot meal was ready and the safari bread, already baking in the upside-down pot in the embers, only needed a few minutes more. Pero had to admit, he loved the smell of safari bread cooking. Bob agreed. "We asked them to make it twice a day. Never ate such good biscuits."

Seated cross-legged away from the fire and on three-legged camping stools, the five men each had a tin plate of posho and beans, heavily salted the way Mbuno liked it. Mbuno ate slowly, carefully savoring every mouthful. Bob finished before him just as the radio made a squawking sound. Bob ran over and listened but did not move the dial. A few moments passed, but there was nothing more. When Bob came back, Mbuno said, "I will tell you the story, and then I will tell Teddy and Keriako."

He launched into the tale. Many years ago, when Ube was a teenager, his father wanted Ube to prove that he was to be a great Waliangulu elephant hunter. All Liangulu are elephant hunters, though Mbuno himself no longer hunted elephant. The Liangulu are an honorable people who once hunted with bow and arrow, and they only approached the oldest, and what scientists usually call sterile, males and females. When they killed them, they ate everything and saved everything else, honoring the elephant. They never wanted the tusks, trading them instead for corn to make posho. With the old bull or cow gone, a younger, more virile bull or cow would become the leader and the elephant family got bigger. There were more new babies, and the herd grew.

"It is true—Ube's father was not a good man. He wanted to make money, he wanted to live in Nairobi." To get rich, Ube's father helped Arab poaching gangs from Zanzibar, and Mbuno considered Zanzibari vermin for poaching elephants. Ube tried to stop his father, and Mbuno came too late to prevent Ube from being wounded by his father. Fortunately, Mbuno had been taught first aid by a park ranger's wife and quickly put sulfur and dressing on Ube's stomach wound.

Mbuno continued, recounting how Ube was taken by plane to the hospital, where doctors saved his life. Since then, Ube had become like a son to Mbuno and his wife. Pero had heard the tale from Tone and others over the years. It was legendary—pure, honorable Africa—and Pero felt, in the spirit of openness, that Bob needed to hear what Pero knew, too. "Mbuno, *tafadhali*, tell Bob what happened to the father, what happened to you and why you live at Giraffe Manor. It is important for Bob to know."

"Ah, Pero, that was unfortunate." He turned to Bob and simply said, "To save the Liangulu people, I had to stop the poaching by Ube's father. He did not agree. He died, and because I killed him, the tribe made me leave, an outcast. I was not wounded, but I had cut my feet very bad on lava rocks."

Pero prompted, "And?"

Mbuno explained that there were some very important people who were also part of the poaching who wanted to arrest him for murder. But good friends of the elephants he had saved hid him and nursed him back to health. Finally, a very good client arranged for a small house with running water at Giraffe Manor for Mbuno and his wife, Niamba. "It is most generous."

Pero shook his head. *So typical of my friend; he'll never tell of his own incredible bravery.* Pero added, "Yeah, what you don't know is that Mbuno trekked ten miles carrying Ube with the help of one of the elephants he had saved. Then another elephant picked Mbuno up and carried him to safety at a Ranger's station where the married couple running the station were amazed that he and Ube were alive. They flew Ube out in their private plane, the bush radio full of their exploits and bravery. Everyone knows the politician responsible for allowing the poaching—he's untouchable—but if he tries to go after Mbuno, there would be an uprising, African and European alike, not to mention a few American billionaires. You see, Mbuno has fans."

Bob observed Mbuno looking down at his empty dish. Bob was staring at the top of his head, wondering if such stories were possible, if they could be real. This was the stuff of myth. He had been feeling the adrenaline rush of a rescue, the feeling of going into battle for a good cause. Now here he sat, under the primordial shade of a eucalyptus tree with a CIA spook or maybe an ex-spook—about whom rumors had rippled through the Navy and Marines two years ago—and a small, innocuous safari guide who had killed a poacher, walked miles with an elephant, and single-handedly saved Ube. A more-than-capable field guide he had great respect for. Humbled in this august company, all Bob could say was, "I lied."

CHAPTER 10

Yote Haijawahi Nini Inaonekana—All Is Never What It Seems

Seeing all eyes focused on him, Bob threw up his hands and began to explain, "Okay, if we're coming clean, here it is. I was assigned to travel with Mr. Winter to Moyowosi. He hired me as a medic, that part is true. But how he found me was arranged by my bosses at the ONSI. I work for the Treasury Department."

Pero felt the familiar cold hand of the world of spies on his spine and asked, "What the hell is ONSI?"

"It's the Office of National Security Intelligence. At Treasury, we're responsible for tracing illegal funds around the world derived from drug trafficking. Lately, some serious funds, all in gold coin, have been pouring in from Russia, into terrorist groups from Rwanda all the way up to Nigeria, where the money has been supplying weapons support to Boko Haram and others."

Mbuno calmly asked, "Mr. Bob, what you were doing here may not be anything to do with Ube. But it is important—did Ube know? Were you already going walking, safari, on your own, looking for anything?" Mbuno meant spying.

Seated on the three-legged stool, Bob clapped his hands on his knees and said, "Christ, man, I don't know if I had anything to do with it at all. I didn't tell Ube, that's for sure, and I didn't do a damn thing. I was going to wait until the safari was over and after Mr. Winter left, and then I was going to go undercover to see what I could find." He could see everyone was fixated on him, even the brothers, who were also watching Mbuno for his reaction, all clearly awaiting more of an explanation. "Okay, okay, I'll give you a full briefing—well, as much as I know or can say, anyway. Look, I was sent on this trip as cover to get into the region. I was—well, am, of course—a Marine. I was a medic, Iraq mainly. The ONSI has satellite imagery that we share with the CIA . . . well, we watch for trade shipments, to gather global shipping intel. That intel shows that enormous tracts of forest are being cut down in this region, mainly funded by farming groups who get their guarantee from Chinese companies—you know, guaranteeing to buy tobacco. The trade in tobacco from Tanzania has grown twenty percent a year for the past ten years. Environmentalists are furious about the loss of habitat and trees, fearing that Burundi and Rwanda will be next, and there will go the gorilla habitats." He paused. "Okay, so farmers here are getting paid for their tobacco, but they all use local banks—the Chinese are on the up and up here, like them or not. And my bosses can see no connection to the sale of tobacco and the illicit drug money pouring into the region around here from Russia. And when I say around here, this is only one region in East and Central Africa that we're checking out. Anyway, we know it is drug money because the oligarchs shifting money through offshore accounts that we have tapped into are strictly in the drug business. One of them, Mikael Petrov, is the main supplier of raw cocaine to China and Korea, even Mongolia. The

Russian authorities don't care about drugs going to China or Korea, North or South, as long as Petrov doesn't pollute Putin's Russia. So, here we are in Tanzania—how is the money coming in and for what? The first part is perhaps easier to understand. Gold mined in Siberia, coins and ingots, is easy to transport and easier to trade. We have tracked illegal gold shipments that are being loaded, mostly carried on Russian oil tankers docking all over the east coast of Africa and also in Dar es Salaam. That port is hardly secure, with sailors getting on and off and almost no customs. They trade vodka, containers of the stuff. It could all be hidden anywhere. We've traced two sailors to the Russian embassy, arriving with bags and leaving empty-handed. After that? Who knows? But why bring gold here? And in exchange for what? As far as we can see, nothing valuable is leaving the region by sea. Certainly not through the port at Dar that we can see."

Pero was angry. "Well, Bob, that's a sad tale. You were sent into a region you are not familiar with, inserted yourself into a tourist safari, and perhaps you did nothing outwardly, but your presence alone might have been a tip-off. And then Ube gets lifted. A bit of a coincidence, don't you think? And who chose Moyowosi, you or your handlers? And you planned to come back here and do what, fit in? The color of your skin doesn't matter a bit here. Your ancestry is not from East Africa; you have West African features, and you stand out like a sore thumb, as much as me."

Mbuno put his hand on Pero's shoulder. "Let him finish." He turned to Bob. "Me also, I am not from this area. Please tell us the rest."

Not answering, Bob rose and went to his medical bag, reached inside, and produced a satellite radio. Pero recognized it; it was the same issue the CIA had once given him with a series of coded buttons to push to make it inoperable by any-one except in an emergency. Pero asked, "You use it yet?"

Bob nodded and said, "When we landed at Wilson before you arrived. Only to say the safari was canceled, we were being held until a plane arrived from Loiyangalani, and afterward I was going to change plans." He handed it to Pero.

"Well, that really bothers me. We trusted you." Pero's use of the past tense was not lost on Bob, who genuinely looked miserable. "However, the missing piece of your story worries me more. You mentioned drug trafficking a few times. Yet you profess not to know where this Siberian gold was going to or to whom or for what. And yet you were here in Moyowosi." Pero paused, "The whole thing's bull. There's more, so spill it."

"I need clearance." He nodded at the radio.

Pero looked down at the folded antenna, raised it, and tossed it over. "Keep it on speaker. We have a rule, Mbuno and I and the team in Nairobi—we share everything out in the open. If you don't agree"—Pero pointed back at the road—"start walking; you're on your own."

As Bob started dialing, hitting 666, he said, "Fair 'nuff." He had decided that he needed their help and realized that per-haps they didn't really need his. He wanted to remain part of the team. The radio responded with two clicks, and Bob pushed the speaker button. "Bob Hines, developments, need clearance to share intel with one Baltazar, CIA."

"Standby." The satellite radio crackled at the same time Wolfie's TR unit squawked with, "Interconti here, over."

Pero walked over, plugged in and switched on the Silke Wire transmitter, and said, "Standby, ready to copy news from here. Patience. Over." He then walked over to Bob, pointed to his collar where the microphone wire was visible and said, "Let's have my team listen in as well. Tell your people, if they come back, that it is an open HF transmission so be careful with what they say on the open. Okay?"

Bob nodded just as the satellite radio came to life, "Hines, what the hell are you playing at, you're half a day over—"

Bob cut him off and asked if Pero would mute the RT for a moment, adding, "Look, man, let's not make this too cryptic. I'll have my people give me authority, and then I promise I'll tell you everything I know, and I'll call the Interconti and tell them too. Let's save the RT traffic only for things we can say in the open. Some of this stuff is too delicate, okay?"

Pero shook his head. "Be careful what you say, but the radio stays on for now. Later, if you're staying, we can call the Interconti."

Bob was resigned, "Okay, I'll do my best, but I need a DC contact for you. My bosses will never give me authority unless I make them understand your clearance. Got a name for them to call?"

"Lewis by name, they should know him."

Into the satellite phone, Bob said, "Unsecured transmission here. Get status, one Baltazar from Lewis at Central, and give me authority to open full disclosure mission. Over." Using "Central," Bob hoped to avoid saying CIA.

"Standby." It didn't take long, but Pero and Mbuno knew that Nairobi was listening and the wait must have seemed interminable for them. The voice came back on. "Playing with the big boys without our approval, eh?" Pero didn't like the tone of the man instructing Bob; he sounded like a desk jockey willing to order chess pieces around the world into danger. Pero had to give Director Lewis one thing—he fought to protect his field personnel. The voice continued, "Okay, authority granted. I've been given orders, but I don't like them. This Baltazar only, no authority for anyone else."

Pero was shaking his head. Bob said, "Sorry, Baltazar has a team, they're included."

The voice got angry, "Yeah, is that so? Well I was warned that might be the case and so here's a message from Lewis to Baltazar: you're responsible, in charge, so you're reinstated as of now. End of transmission." And he clicked off.

Pero, ashen-faced, ran over to the RT radio, as if by being closer he might convey his regrets to Susanna, Mary, and Heep better, but mainly to comfort Susanna who he guessed would be furious. "I'm sorry. I didn't do this. Over."

Heep's voice came in loud and clear. "Yeah, well, Lewis said you might feel that way when we spoke an hour ago. We were going to tell you. Talk it over there and then call us. Over and out." The RT set went silent. Pero clicked the Silke Wire off and unplugged connections.

Pero said to Mbuno, "Lewis already called them?" Then, turning to the Marine, Pero was furious. He asked, "Christ, Bob, what have you gotten us into?"

Mbuno, levelheaded as always, said, "It is not something to get very angry about." He stood, stepped over to Pero, and said, "You may be an otter"—making reference to Pero's childhood nickname—"but even the otter falls over a waterfall sometimes." He turned to Bob and said, "You, Mr. Bob, are like the mongoose. Trustworthy, quick, not always thinking. Wanting to kill the snake, but you may also bite the hand that feeds you. Why? Because you cannot help it; it is the way of the mongoose, sharp teeth and thinking later."

Then Mbuno spoke swiftly in Swahili to the brothers, who listened raptly. They nodded from time to time, and their eyes got very wide when Mbuno explained that Bob was a policeman of sorts from America. But they trusted policemen, especially because Mbuno said they should trust Pero and Bob.

Insofar as Teddy was concerned, that was fine with him. He spoke for the pair, "*Kama wewe imani yao, basi ndivyo sisi!*" (If you trust them, then so do we!)

CHAPTER 11

Ube Ni Wapi na Kwa Nini?— **Where Is Ube and Why?**

Deep inside, Pero wanted immediately to leave, to save his marriage. If it weren't for Ube he would have driven off. Mbuno was right; Pero felt as if he had fallen off a cliff.

Mbuno, sensing the team needed to regroup, asked Bob to call the Interconti on satellite phone speaker to explain everything he knew. Turned out, it was precious little and didn't explain Ube's predicament.

Pero turned off the RT completely and sat back down on the stool, waiting for the flow of fresh information—information he really didn't want but needed to have. *Christ, all we wanted to do was get Ube back. Now we're up against Russian gold smugglers and damn terrorists? Terrorists again?* Pero was feeling despondent.

The afternoon sun was waning; animals were waking to take advantage of the last hours of daylight before nightfall and the cooler air. The birds, especially, made screeching sounds in the canopy above. If there had not been such tension among the five men sitting in a half circle in front of the tents, it would have been a perfect naturalist's dream. As it was, Pero was still furious and, he had to admit, a little scared. In the past two years or more, he had been shot at, poisoned with radioactivity, landed in the hospital twice, and narrowly escaped major catastrophes that would also have affected his friends and hundreds of thousands of innocent people. He was proud of what he had helped achieve, but that did not diminish the terror he felt at the prospect of a repeat trial against an unknown enemy. *And*, he suddenly realized, *they are indeed an enemy because they have kidnapped Mbuno's son.*

Mbuno and the two brothers, emulating the Mzee, waited calmly. Bob, for his part, felt as if he were drowning in his own stupidity. He launched into recounting what he knew. From time to time, Mbuno explained to the brothers, but mostly, Mbuno only told them what they could understand or what he felt they had to know.

"The satellite images we have been collecting, especially the synthetic-aperture images, show that as soon as the forest is cleared—all trees cut down and taken away to be milled—the next step is that the soil is transformed, flooded, and an interim crop grown. After thirty to forty weeks, that crop disappears, overnight sometimes, hundreds of acres at a time. Normal imagery, when we can prioritize satellites passing overhead, shows the newly empty fields being bulldozed and then planted with orderly rows of crops. We don't know what the first crop was, but the vegetation signature indicates it is a tall bush, about six feet high. The second crop appears to be a variety of tobacco. The only guess on the first crop is that it is *Erythroxylum novogranatense*. You know it as the coca plant." Bob seemed to want to stop.

Mbuno, sensing his reluctance to carry on, pressed him, "Mr. Bob, you must finish."

From the satellite phone speaker, Heep said, "Finish it up, Bob. Some of this Lewis already told us."

"Okay, when we looked at the quantity being grown, we could not find processing facilities on satellite anywhere nearby. And no trucks or trains going anywhere outside of this region with hundreds of acres of dug-up bushes. And, man, we looked. There was no heat signature of anything boiling in any factory, so we assumed it was all small and local, like in Colombia, to keep the processing small, movable, undetected. But then we managed to put a tracer on a bag of Siberian gold, and it went here—well, nearby to here. That's when I was sent to join the safari—my office arranged for Mr. Winter's doctor to advise him to take a medic in case of a heart attack since he had had one a year ago. His doctor was told to recommend me."

Heep asked, "Where did the gold go, Bob? Where did it end up?"

Bob was chagrinned. "We don't know where it ended up." Pero shook his head in disbelief. Bob continued, "No, honestly, it got to the station in Kombe and then went silent. The man following the RFID signal said it was there one moment and gone the next. He was only certain the guy carrying it got off the passenger train in Kombe. That's when I was sent in. The plan was to accompany the safari, get them interested in going to the southern end of the Moyowosi or Kigosi reserves, learn the terrain, act like a tourist. Then, when they were done, drop them off and come back where I would be considered another tourist or maybe an itinerant village doctor and see if I could find clues."

Pero looked at Mbuno, who nodded. This told Pero that Mbuno had assessed that Bob was telling the truth. Pero was silent, waiting for Heep. He knew Heep would want to tell them about Lewis. It didn't take long.

"Heep here. Look this is clearly more than just Ube being missing—"

Mbuno interrupted, "No, we have seen him. He was in the back of a truck."

On the satellite phone, the voices of the three in Nairobi came through, jumbled, but they all had the same demand that Mbuno explain where Ube had been taken, and whether he was okay.

"He was beaten. I saw his eyes, he saw me."

Pero said, "One of the Zanzi-Agroforestry SUVs was leading a Nissan beat-up pickup, and in the back Ube was sitting with who we presume to be a guard. They were headed south, back toward the airfield. Well, in that direction anyway."

Heep asked, "Did you follow?" Pero looked at Mbuno.

Mbuno explained they needed time to research what this Zanzi-Agroforestry was, where it was located, and who ran it. And then he added, "I think nighttime is better for scouting."

Mary came on the line. "Okay, fellows, here's what we have on the Zanzibar outfit. First, it's Zanzi-Agroforestry; took us a while to get to that name."

Pero said, "Sorry."

"Understood. It's owned by a German outfit, registered offshore on the island of Zanzibar, has mainly ex-colonialist Germans running the show"—she paused—"and Pero, you're not going to like this one bit: The principal shareholders— over 60 percent—are your old friends at Treuhand Banking." Pero and Mbuno's hackles rose at the same moment. Treuhand Bank was staffed with the remnant of the East German Stasi, many of them ex-Nazis and not any of them to be trusted. Pero, Mbuno, and Heep had encountered them in Germany the previous year when Treuhand's director was trying to smuggle radioactive material to terrorist groups.

Mary continued, "The business of—let's call them Zanzi-Ag—is to, and I am quoting here, 'help terraform the State of Nyamwezi'—that's where you are—'and make it possible to cultivate cash crops for the benefit of the Tanzanian economy.' In short, they clear and plow the land, and then farmers, large and small, plant cash crops."

Bob added, "The crops are tobacco, and the farmers are legit insofar as we can tell. Chinese backers and buyers, mostly."

Pero interjected, "Yeah, but there's an interim crop while they so-called clear the land, likely to be coca plants." Pero thought of something. "When does Zanzi-Ag turn the land over to farmers?"

Heep delivered the answer in a rush. "Your powerful pals, the Singhs, especially the one with the fish on his wall that you two caught, remember? Well, I spoke with him in Dar on the phone—by the way he advises you to stay out of trouble because his brothers are investigating Zanzi-Ag and suspicious partners—and he said, with some disgust I might add, that there are almost weekly television PR events with one or another minister at a shovel and ribbon ceremony as the cleared land is handed over to a farmer. You know, it's the age-old good PR event: *Your ancestors lived here on the land, trapped by the trees; now we have freed you and cleared the land and will make you wealthy as you grow the crop we tell you to plant.* Oh, and the Dar papers are full of the articles exposing the corruption, the people displaced, the wildlife slaughtered; and, of course, after the new farmer fails, the usual conglomerate farming companies move in to get the land for pennies while the locals are made homeless."

Bob looked amazed. "How did you find all this out? We didn't know any of that."

Pero, for once, took pity on him. "Look, Bob, do yourself a favor. You can't just parachute into a place and find things out all by yourself. It takes a team—team effort, team resources, years of being in the region to have real contacts—not just satellite images." Pero had a thought. "Heep, can you call Singh back and see if you can find out where the Tanzanian authorities are looking and for what? There is no way Singh won't be on top of the corruption. Maybe that'll tell us what, who, or where the drugs go. And if they are not drugs but just the leaves of the coca plant, they must be selling them to someone who then processes them." Pero turned to Bob. "Look, Bob, Zanzi-Ag may just be harvesting and selling the raw leaves to someone else. The border is porous here, and Lake Victoria, just about fifty miles northwest, means you can ship a bunch of vegetation almost anywhere. That may be why you are not seeing smoke or processing locally." Bob was nodding agreement.

Pero wanted next to find out why Lewis had called them at the Interconti, but Mbuno held up his hand and asked, "And a question for the Singh brothers: Is there a coup?" Everyone fell silent. "It is not normal to cut trees in a park reserve. It means the government is all right with cutting trees."

CHAPTER 12

Hatari ya Uhusiano—
The Danger of Connections

After Teddy and Keriako pulled the safari bread from the embers of the fire and dished up more food, Mbuno told them to go to collect firewood for the night. They did as they were told, guessing Mbuno wanted them out of earshot. While Mbuno busied himself preparing the meal, Pero took the time to speak privately to Susanna, cupping the phone off-speaker, assuring Susanna he had had no idea. She called him their pet name a few times and made it clear she knew this was just really bad luck. All that mattered was that they get Ube and everyone back safely, including her *dummer Mann*, so they could return to their lives.

Pero assured her that was one hundred percent his plan. Anything larger or more than a rescue was not his involvement or intention. Her response was a simple "I love you," which sealed the moral deal between them. Pero hoped he could live up to it.

When Heep had the phone back, turned onto speaker, he asked, "Mbuno, why do you ask about a coup?"

"It is not unusual these days." Mbuno gave a flat statement of fact, and Pero realized that he was right. After Kenya's recent electoral troubles and the Arab Spring all over the region and the Middle East, change seemed to have infected everyone.

Pero continued, "The Singhs are very powerful. If they wanted to, they could have taken over years ago. That makes them not likely as fomenters. But they would hear things. You remember that one brother is the only Toyota dealer, and the more powerful brother. Another is head of the regular police and the secret police, and then the oldest one is a government minister."

Heep agreed they were powerful but asked again why Mbuno thought there may be a coup. Mbuno saw human dealings in the region as a wildlife food chain, complete with a pecking order, like animals. "You have warthogs digging up the land. Someone is feeding them. You have vultures scavenging off the land—someone is leaving them *nyama*." (Meat.) "You have the local animals, people, driven off by jackals from the government. None of these is in charge. Somewhere, there is a very large pride of lions permitting all this. And lions eat a lot of *nyama*. Someone, maybe the Russian bear, is feeding them. The truth about lions is that once they can get more meat, they become more hungry."

Finally, Heep prepared to sign off, saying, "Okay, understood. We have a lot to talk about and do here. We'll call later. Susanna has your phone's code and number." Bob said she couldn't have, and Heep assured him that she did. Pero cryptically explained to Bob that Susanna was a genius and to take it on trust. The truth was, Susanna had pressured Director Lewis to supply it, saying he owed her favors after nearly getting her husband killed in Berlin. Lewis had sighed and agreed.

The food was hot; the biscuits, as Bob called them, wonderful. They drank a glass of water each as the brothers returned with armloads of firewood. Joined by the boys, they finished their second plates of food silently. After a short while, Mbuno began to explain to the brothers what he could. They were nervous at the news of drugs and kept looking at Bob, the man they saw as a policeman. Mbuno assured them that Bob wasn't after them, just the men who took Ube.

Mbuno looked at Pero, who was finishing his last mouthful, and said, "You have to make the call." Pero nodded but did not move. Mbuno waited as Bob looked back and forth between the two men, thinking, *What call?*

Pero looked about. He could see three giraffe, maybe two hundred yards away, calmly feeding on acacia leaves, the sun setting slowly behind them with maybe two or three hours of light left. Pero knew that the small furry hyrax would begin their throaty call soon after, making noises as if they were giants. Here they were far enough away from the river not to have to worry about hippo or crocodile, but hyena and lion were a real danger. Leopard would likely stay away from a fire. Into this perfect East African late afternoon, Pero would have to inject the reality of Director Lewis and the CIA's vast resources. If it were just Ube and a logging company, they would reconnoiter, decide on a rescue, and go through with a plan. But Pero knew Mbuno was right—you didn't have this type of large quasi-industrial operation in Tanzania without some very top-heavy support. There was serious money involved even before you got to Russian gold and drug smuggling; that only made it worse. The brand-new, Volvo eighteen-wheelers told Pero that. Only the richest of operations had firsthand trucks like that in East Africa. And that level of support meant the support of factions of the military, guns everywhere, and the ability to bury everyone, literally and fast. If they were going to rescue Ube, they needed to know things the opposition could not know. And for that they needed eyes from above. And that meant Lewis.

Taking the satellite phone, he pushed the speaker on, then the sequence of buttons he knew to reach Lewis. He heard two clicks, meaning they were listening. "Baltazar here. Get me Lewis."

Lewis was waiting. "Expecting your call. Go ahead."

"How did you know to call Interconti, over."

"Skip the over. Your arrival in Kenya was being watched. Hines of ONSI on daily sheet. Same location, same time, Mara Airways. Too much coincidence. Knew your usual hotel. Asked for Baltazar, got your wife."

"Yeah, okay, but I object to being reinstated."

"This dance again? Look, I had to tell ONSI you were in charge and that meant reinstatement. You make the calls, not their field agent; he's not experienced enough. And besides, he doesn't have an improper private team as you so rightly like to remind me."

"Okay. But all we want to do is rescue Mbuno's son, Ube. Zanzi-Agroforestry has lifted him, and we do not know why."

"The why is an interesting question. The secrets and activity they have are more interesting. The cloak of terraforming for economic stability with tobacco crops covers a route and trade of drugs and gold in return. If you happen to find out how, we'd be most grateful."

Pero knew Lewis was being solicitous. No orders, only appreciation, which was more likely to keep Pero from quitting—again. "Okay, Lewis, that's unlikely because, as I said, once we find Ube we're out of here."

"Understood. Now what can we provide to help a quick in and out?"

"We need a satellite look-down in our vicinity—suspects somewhere near or between an airstrip at Mgwesi, called

Moyowosi Airport—and any town north or south of here, probably a rail town: real time, continuous, today. The map shows the road to the airstrip continues south. Maybe there's access to the main artery there?" He meant transport artery: rail, road, commercial plane.

"Looking for?"

"Mercedes SUV followed by a Nissan pickup, two men in the flatbed. Where'd they go?"

"Time?"

"Between three and five hours ago."

"Standby."

"Okay, also how trustworthy is the ONSI man here, Bob Hines." Bob started to protest, but Mbuno told him to be quiet.

"Look-down evaluation wait is plus two hours. I'll call back then. Hines is Marine, capable, not operative"—he meant not a field agent with operational authority—"but record shows he's able and trustworthy. He's to take orders from you and, I assume, Mbuno. He listening?" Pero said they both were. Then Lewis broke with protocol. "Good. Hello, Mbuno. Oh, and Bob's office, on the other hand, are rank amateurs."

"That was my impression, too. Thanks, Lewis."

"Yeah, well I promised that wife of yours . . . over and out."

Bob mumbled mostly to himself, "Great, I work for an amateur outfit, and I am demoted in the field, more likely fired. Second time it has happened. Guess I'll resign when this is over before they can fire me."

Pero laughed. "Demoted? Hell, that's the nicest I've ever heard Lewis describe anyone other than CIA people and, of course, Mbuno there, who he thinks can walk on water."

Mbuno said in his most subservient manner, "Not walk on water, *bwana sahib*. I ask the water gods to carry me." The three of them laughed together, easing the tension. Mbuno continued, "We now must rest." He turned to Teddy and Keriako, telling them to keep watch and to wake him if anything or anybody came near. He handed the phone to Pero and went inside his stifling tent with three cots to sleep. Pero and Bob looked at each other, shrugged, and went to do the same. As he drifted off to sweaty sleep, Pero thought, *Was it only this morning that we were happy at Lake Rudolf?*

Bob, for his part, dreamt that he was a lamb staked to the ground, and lions were closing in. His boss was supposed to be ready to shoot before the lions got the sacrificial lamb, but they were too busy talking about how wonderful their jobs at Treasury were. Bob died over and over again.

The satellite call awakened Pero, who found he had it in his right hand, which was pinned underneath his chest, his arm tattoo of his deceased wife Addiena once again touching his heart. It took him a moment to realize where he was, but then he pushed the sequence of buttons to answer.

"Lewis here; two hours ago, thirteen thirty-two Zulu, SUV and Nissan used truck with two in open bed passing over small lake on boat then entering compound of logging company, perhaps sawmill, southeast side of train line near Kombe."

Pero thought, *Thirteen thirty-two Zulu; that'll be local time four thirty-two.* "Copy that. Distance from Kombe to Moyowosi airstrip at Mgwesi? Size of lumber yard or mill?"

"Distance as the crow flies, twenty or twenty-five miles. Approx. six acres, perimeter wired fence. Two entrances, one for railcars taking logs and cut timber away, one facing lake. No road access, only rail is visible. Six semi tractor-trailers in compound, all log carriers. Three flatbed trucks, all similar. One Mercedes SUV and one utility truck, specialist type."

"Unimog?"

"Could be. Also, train schedule shows expected pickup freight sixteen hundred hours Zulu coming from east but currently no rail cars in mill compound or seen loaded. Second freight train expected from west, leaving Kigoma and Ujiji, arriving oh-eight-hundred hours Zulu, may be carrying empty cars as computer manifest shows collecting timber. No visual on incoming train yet. Schedule shows same train type leaves westward from Dar for Kigoma every day at approximately five a.m."

Pero made a mental note. *If the Kigoma train arrives on time, they are planning to load lumber and logs within two hours.* "Who runs the train company? How accurate are those times?"

"German rail technicians, so should be reliable times, plus or minus."

Pero paused. "Lewis, if anything happens, you'll take care of Susanna, won't you?"

Without hesitation, Lewis responded, "I'll have to fight that sister of hers and probably Heep and Mary, but of course I will." Pero was pleased that he said *I* and not *we*. "Look, get Ube out of there and run, run like the wind."

Run, a command to run from Lewis? Pero thought. *What does he know that we don't?* "Lewis, what are we really up against. This is not like you."

"Just do as I say for once, and I'll explain after. The less you know . . ."

"Yeah, the less I can tell if I'm not lucky." Pero knew the risk of working in the field. If you were only doing something simple and had no other knowledge, you were more likely not to be a threat worth killing if captured. "I'm not happy here, but I'll run like hell once we get Ube back." He avoided saying *if we can get him back*. He disconnected the phone and went to talk with Mbuno and Bob, giving them the update on the lumber mill.

Mbuno asked Teddy to fetch the rifle he carried on safari. Mbuno knew Teddy probably could not shoot very well; askari were hardly ever given live fire practice. Teddy handed the aging rifle to Bob along with the only two shells the safari had been issued under license and Pero told Bob to dry practice with the rifle and be ready. Bob looked happy to have something to do as he cycled the rifle's bolt action. "Thirty-aught-six, good rifle. Old, but it'll do man, it'll do."

Pero said, "Now we eat again and break camp. Get everything into the Land Rover on the top, and we'll head to the airstrip to the plane. It is time for them"—he pointed to Teddy and Keriako—"to leave."

CHAPTER 13

Njia Moja Pekee, Mji Mmoja—
Only One Road, Only One Town

At the airstrip two hours later, the pilots professed their surprise to be taking the two askari to Nairobi alone with all the equipment. Bob retained his medical kit and rifle; Pero, the RT and a good pair of safari binoculars the brothers had handed him; and Mbuno, the extra biscuits and the refilled water container. Pero gave the pilots instructions that, on landing, they were to turn the two brothers over to Tone Bowman and Tone Bowman only, then they were to stay with the plane and be ready to fly and pick them up, no matter where. They agreed, happy to be getting overtime pay.

As soon as the Cessna departed, Mbuno told Bob to park the Land Rover, now empty of the camp equipment, deep in the forest at the eastern end of the runway. Mbuno and Pero drove behind him on the airstrip in the other Land Rover that was still full of fuel, with an extra jerrycan on the back. When Bob emerged from the forest, he climbed into the back of their Land Rover and raised his eyebrows upon seeing that Mbuno was not driving. Pero explained, "He sees and knows better than I do. He'll tell me where to go."

They set off for Kombe. The graded two-lane dirt road ended a half mile from the airstrip, petering out to a single track with twin tire ruts, deeply gouged, some filled with mud and water. Mbuno seemed satisfied. "It is well traveled, see the sides?" He pointed to the cut into deep ruts. "Something very big, not long ago."

"Surely those Volvos couldn't navigate this road, could they?" Bob asked.

Pero had recognized the trucks for what they were and explained. He had seen the same models in Alaska, all-wheel-drive behemoths, six-by-eight axle configurations, capable of traversing thirty-degree inclines while hauling over twenty tons. Dirt roads were no match for their thirty-eight-inch tires. Mbuno commented, "Two passed here; see tracks." He pointed, but neither Bob nor Pero could see what Mbuno's sharp eyes had discerned. It didn't matter; they both knew Mbuno would not make a mistake. Mbuno continued, "It has not rained since. They were very heavy when they went."

Pero asked, "Could they be the same ones we saw this morning?" Mbuno thought they could; the heavy load gave them away. Pero concluded, "Logs, freshly cut from up alongside the Moyowosi."

"*Ndiyo.*"

As they drove along, bouncing from one rut to the other, Pero tried to straddle the ruts and often failed, slipping and sliding in and out of them. He bottomed out the Land Rover on the packed earth hump in the middle. He knew the vehicle was built strong and that the fuel line and brake lines would be tucked up into the chassis. What he was more concerned about was ripping off the exhaust and releasing the diesel's raucous sound. He slowed to decrease slippage and hard contact.

At one point, as darkness began to fall, Mbuno unlatched the observation hatch that all safari vehicles have cut into the roof and stood on the front left seat to get a better view. After a few moments, he squatted and told Pero to pull into the bush off to the right and cut the lights and motor. Pero turned the wheel, advanced a dozen yards, knocking down small bushes and grass, turned the key just enough to silence the engine, and pushed off the headlight switch.

Mbuno stood again. Bob and Pero sat silently, waiting, listening intently to the surrounding wildlife sounds and calls. Mbuno kept watch unmovingly. Suddenly, he flopped back down on the seat, whispering, "*Ndovu*."

Elephant! Here? Pero recognized Mbuno had used the Liangulu word instead of the Swahili word *tembo*. He stared out the windscreen into the gloom. The early stars illuminated the bush, but there was no moon yet. Pero could see nothing resembling an elephant and whispered, "Where, Mbuno?"

Mbuno made a circle, just barely visible in the glow of the Land Rover's instrument panel. Pero looked from side to side and could see nothing except vegetation. Suddenly, a thin tree trunk moved six yards to their right, its uppermost branches sweeping the night sky. Mbuno popped up through the hatch again just as the herd surrounded the Land Rover, passing by, jostling the chassis that was clearly in their way. Once they were past, Mbuno sat down in his seat again and simply said, "A good family, twelve, two *totos*." He made a gesture to Pero spinning his finger in the air.

Pero started the engine and looked at Mbuno as he touched the headlight switch. Mbuno shook his head and said, "Follow, *tafadhali*, no light." Pero did as he was told, slowly in first gear, the bush now flattened before the Land Rover, the elephants' passage easy to follow slowly. When the elephant reached the rutted road, they turned right in the same direction Pero had been driving. Pero glanced at Mbuno who nodded, just visible in the dark.

From the back seat, Bob said, "Oh my God, man, I could've touched them! Real elephant, man, this is so damn cool." Even Pero grinned. In Africa, even with the wildlife all around, nothing was as unique and wonderful as elephant. The spirits of all three men rose as the miles went by, the Land Rover slowly following the herd.

Pero was aware that compared to the massive bodies in front of them, one Land Rover should not be easily spotted. It was like moving camouflage. But he had to ask, "What'll we do when they turn off this path?"

Mbuno knew elephant; more than anything, he knew elephant. Elephant marching with determination, not feeding when there was food all around, meant only one thing—a need for water. They were headed to water, to bathe and drink in the cool of the night. So he gave Pero his best guess. "Mr. Lewis said there was a lake. Then the mill. They head to water. We will follow. We will see the water from the forest, or we will see a marsh. I do not know, but we will be hidden. That is good. The elephant will help us."

Pero and Bob thought Mbuno meant that the elephant were useful, getting them safely out of sight, nearer the mill. But Mbuno had other plans.

CHAPTER 14

Kuoga na Tembo— Bathing with Elephant

The half-moon was finally up, and the road through the forest was widened by the herd, their giant feet pounding the soil to become almost a level roadway. Briefly looking up through the open hatch, Pero could see the stars and even the Southern Cross framed by mature trees on each side of the Land Rover. The driving was slow, steady, and the elephant did not seem to mind that the men were driving along, a few hundred yards behind.

As Mbuno predicted, once they came over a rise, they could see a little lake below, not more than a mile long by half a mile wide. The forest ended at the top of the rise, replaced by dense bush and then tall grasses for the half mile downhill to the edge of the water. A quarter mile before the lake's end, train tracks stretched from left to right. Next to the train track was a dirt road following the tracks.

The elephant wasted no time, plunging straight ahead, over the railroad ties and dirt road, oldest elephants first, followed by the totos, entering the water with playful glee. Mbuno made Pero turn the Land Rover off into the shimmering water before the last elephant disappeared. They stopped, hidden by rushes and tall marsh grass, some taller than the vehicle itself. Mbuno told Bob and Pero to join him through the hatch.

Pero was the tallest of the three, and he could just see through the rushes above the grass across the lake. He scanned with the binoculars and saw nothing, just some industrial yellow lights about a half mile away across the lake. Even with the half-moon, there was not enough light to make anything out. Besides, clouds were scuttling across the moon now and then. He explained what he could see to Mbuno, who merely said to wait. Bob wanted to know where they went from here as the truck tracks ended at the lake, turning neither left nor right, and didn't follow the train tracks or service road.

Mbuno pointed to a rock outcrop fifty feet to the right of where the elephant entered the water. Pero trained the binoculars but did not know what he was looking for. As he swept left to right, he watched an elephant that seemed to trip and tumble over in the shallow water, immediately righting itself and moving away from the place he had tripped. Pero saw a glint of metal. He peered intently through the binoculars and said, "Wire."

Mbuno nodded.

Bob said, "What, where?" Pero pointed at the rocks and then moved his finger down to the water. He handed over the binoculars. Bob focused and leaned forward, trying to see what was possibly there. "Ah, got it. Big, thick cable. What's it for, man?"

Mbuno answered, "It is a ferry cable." He pointed to the flat beach. "It goes from here across the water to the other side." That was half a mile away. Bob wanted to know why they needed a cable; there was no current in the lake and you could simply drive a boat across. Mbuno explained, "When there is no bridge for trucks, you need a strong boat—"

Pero interrupted, "A barge?"

"Yes, a barge, *tafadhali*. A barge cannot have a motor in the water, it is too shallow. It has a motor that pulls along the cable."

It appeared simple and effective to Bob and Pero. No propeller to get tangled in the weeds or rocks in shallow water, the barge would simply winch itself across. Pero asked, "So I guess the barge is over on the other side, right?"

"*Ndiyo.*"

"So we drive around, or walk around the lake?"

Mbuno shook his head. Pero was worried. Pero guessed what Mbuno was going to suggest. He was unfortunately right when Mbuno explained, "We must swim. There is no path we can take without lights to drive. On foot there is great danger from hippo. No, we must swim."

Bob was alarmed. "What about crocs?"

In the starlight and moonlight, Mbuno's smile was radiant. "It is why we need the ndovu. The crocodiles will be in shallow water, but not"—he pointed at the frolicking herd—"anywhere near ndovu. They would be trampled." He patted Bob on the shoulder. "It will be all right."

Pero said, "What do we need?" They compiled a list of what they had and what they would take. Bob volunteered a plastic bag for the satellite phone. Each carried a knife, and they found a flashlight in the Land Rover that appeared waterproof. "What about telling Nairobi?"

Bob suggested a quick call on the phone, but Pero had an idea and quickly opened the Land Rover's hood and connected the alligator clips to the battery and powered up the RT set. "This is Auxiliary Z4WD broadcasting in the blind. Come in Nairobi."

"We're here. Go ahead." Pero heard a groggy Tone responding, and Wolfie as well.

"Okay, we've left the campsite; we're proceeding to the airstrip to meet the plane coming to pick us up. No sign of the person we were looking for. We'll have to wait and see if he's lost and turns up somewhere. Over." He heard the disappointment from everyone listening and signed off without any further discussion. Then he asked Bob for the satellite phone and dialed Lewis. "Baltazar here, need to speak to Lewis."

"Standby." Moments later: "Lewis here, go ahead."

"Please call Interconti and have them carefully contact Tone Bowman and also Wolfgang in Loiyangalani and tell them I told them a lie. We are not returning to Nairobi yet. Instructions: One, call Sheryl at Mara Airways and have her dispatch our Cessna after it lands, or if it has already landed, as if we ordered its return to the airstrip. Once airborne, have them divert to any airstrip in Kenya and await next command. Two, investigate Zanzi-Agroforestry if we do not return. All roads lead to them; no other location for missing Ube is possible. Three, we are going to cross a small lake, enter the compound, and rescue Ube if we can and then, as you said, run like hell. Please wait . . ."

"Standing by."

"Bob, there's a map in the glove compartment. Haul it out, will you, and let's see if there's an alternative airstrip we can use in daylight." Bob quickly pulled it out and folded it to the relevant section. Pero spotted it almost immediately. "Tabora, do you copy, Lewis?" Pero heard two clicks, meaning affirmative. "Good. Tabora has an airstrip—actually, an airport. Have the Cessna also file a flight plan for Tabora but only once they are out of Wilson radio range. We'll meet them in Tabora tomorrow afternoon. Copy?"

Two clicks and then: "Be careful, Pero. Get him, get out."

Lewis is being unusually emotional, Pero thought as he disconnected. He checked the battery level on the phone, and it showed more than half full. He turned it fully off, and Bob put it in the plastic bag and sealed it, twice, with rubber bands.

Mbuno, Bob, and Pero discussed the plan that Pero had laid out. Pero knew he was being paranoid about someone tracing the plane or listening in on the RT transmission, but, as he said to Bob, "Look, better be safe than sorry, right?" Bob agreed. Pero explained the Tabora idea. "If we get Ube back, we return here, drive the Land Rover away from the lake, and pick our way east. The rail line is a few miles south of here, but too near the mill. But it loops north after a while"—he pointed at the map—"and we should run into it if we head due east through the forest." His finger traced the route of escape, perhaps eight or ten miles until the train tracks. "Then we drive the railroad ties until we come to the main road, drive to Tabor, get on our plane, all in daylight. I figure by the time we cross the lake and then cross back, the sun will start to come up so we won't need headlights, and the forest up there"—he pointed back up the hillside—"will hide an army, let alone one forest-green Land Rover."

Mbuno agreed it was a plan. Bob saw nothing to contradict or suggest so he just nodded, checking the satellite phone in the plastic bag, carefully wrapping it one more time, tightly, with waterproof wound dressing tape from his medical bag. Once satisfied, he made sure his two companions saw where he put it, in case they needed to retrieve it—inside a money belt beneath his shirt. Mbuno added, "Take off your shoes and leave them here. People here do not have shoes. We must be like them."

After they put their shoes in the Land Rover, the three men walked over to the boulder standing next to the two-inch-thick cable. Mbuno whispered, "No talk, ever." The elephant were still bathing, splashing water, the totos rolling in the shallows. Mbuno started making a noise, what seemed to Bob to be burping. The sound became more like a stomach-rumble belch. Two of the elephants turned to stare Mbuno down. Mbuno increased the belching rumble, and the elephant flapped their ears, and in the moonlight, Pero was certain he saw them quizzically cock their heads. Mbuno waded into the water, motioning for Bob and Pero to stay behind him. Mbuno grabbed hold of the cable, signaling the other two to do the same, and lowered himself into the water, deeper and deeper until only his head was visible. The elephant stopped paying any attention to them.

Soon they were beyond the elephant, and Pero was suddenly worried. The cable was getting deeper, already at their naked feet, and soon it would be beyond reach. What were they going to follow? Bob, on the other hand, was treading water as he looked back at the elephant and whispered to Mbuno, "How did you do that? What was that noise?"

"I was saying hello; it is all right."

Pero interjected, having already heard about Mbuno's ability to communicate with elephant, "Later, Bob. We're going to get lost quickly out here; the cable's getting too deep!"

"Ah, Pero," responded Mbuno, "see the rock where the cable is attached?" He pointed. "Now see the line it makes to here?" He spun in the water facing away from the rock and the shore. "We follow this line to the other side." He could see Pero was doubtful. "And I will cheat a little." He pointed up at the Southern Cross hanging in the sky. "It is a good marker, do you not think?" He paused to smile.

And so they began to swim. Bob was a strong swimmer, crawling, dragging the medical bag, and, occasionally, pulling alongside Mbuno. Waliangulu men know how to swim, but many would call it more like staying afloat rather than actual swimming. Mbuno was doing a cross between a dog paddle and breaststroke. Pero, trailing the two, swam sidestroke, keeping an eye on the elephant behind them and watching for water ripples that could spell an attacking croc or, worse, a hippo. Pero, intent on not being surprised, began falling behind. Mbuno whispered, "Wait a moment." And the three men tread water together. To Pero, he said, "It is night; the hippo will not come—they are feeding on land." Pero nodded. To Bob, Mbuno said, "Please not to swim that way; swim like Pero or I do, no splash." Bob also nodded, and Mbuno resumed swimming.

Pero realized that, Southern Cross or not, he would have been hopelessly lost by now. They were halfway across the lake, and a faint shimmer off the water prevented him from making out any landmark or mill lights on shore. For all he knew, they could be headed into a crocodile den. Already swimming for over an hour, Pero's mind wandered. Some people he knew would say what they were doing was brave. But Pero thought, *Bravery doesn't stay; it comes and goes quickly. It's like a wave, coming and then receding. I hope I can hold on.* Pero had to admit to himself that he was now frightened in the black water, so far away from land. He was equally sure Mbuno wasn't. *Mbuno is used to danger, living so close to raw nature. I'm not, really.*

So why am I doing this? In his fear, Pero had asked the unanswerable question, perhaps as a means of finding an escape in an answer. He recognized cowardice in his thought process. So he spoke to himself, to strengthen his resolve. *Pero, you're a good person. A good person through and through. Good never leaves you; long ago it permeated your soul and can never leave. Good people do good. It is who you are. Hang tight, hang tough . . . you don't have to be brave, just resolute.*

Meanwhile, Bob did what trained military men do—he followed a leader and cleared his mind of question and doubt. Since teaming up to help find Ube, everything Mbuno had done or said had impressed Bob. Not since his time in a war zone had he felt such confidence in a natural-born leader. That the man was nearly half his size, lithe, and gray-haired did not shake Bob's respect and trust in Mbuno. Mbuno led; Bob was content to follow.

Mbuno was aware that his mind was filled with doubt. Doubt in his ability to find Ube. Doubt in his ability to explain to Niamba, his wife, if Ube could not be rescued alive. Doubt in his age and diminishing physical abilities. And, finally, doubt that they would be able to get ashore safely, for Mbuno knew there were no ndovu on the far shore to give them cover from crocodiles.

CHAPTER 15

Kambi ya Magogo—
The Logging Camp

When they were a hundred yards from shore, Mbuno motioned them to stop and tread water. He swam back and forth, feeling with his feet until he reached the cable. He motioned the two over and whispered, "Feel the cable. Now we be quiet." He started to inch forward, gently paddling and keeping the cable in touch. The moonlight was sufficient to see large objects ahead, even with the increasingly overcast night. There was no dock anyone could see, but the barge appeared, seen from the water surface—gigantic, over ten feet high on the side. The barge bow facing them had a twenty-foot steel ramp sticking straight up.

Mbuno held up a hand. He looked at Bob and Pero and made a snaking movement with his hand, making sure they understood. He then gave them the wait signal again. He began paddling forward, following the cable up to the right side of the barge. Standing on the cable, he inched upward, palms against the hull. He motioned to Pero and Bob to follow. There was no alarm, no noise from anywhere, just the oily lapping of the water against the barge's hull.

Pero had seen the crocs wake on the left side of the barge, and then, going past the vertical ramp, he lost sight as he reached the barge's right side. He wondered if the crocs would come around and pick them off. He inched up the cable as fast as he could, as Mbuno had done. Bob followed Pero, more athletic and sure-footed.

The winch for the thick cable consisted of two truck rims, four feet off the water's surface. The bottom rim consisted of a truck rim with a rubber tire that slotted into a wider truck rim above, pinching the cable. Run the motor one way and it would pull the barge across the lake; run it backward and it would pull the barge back. Farther along the side of the barge, Pero could make out a duplicate winch setup, giving the barge directional stability. Once Mbuno stepped over the first winch, he tightrope-walked the cable, clear of the water, to the second winch and waited there for Bob and Pero to catch up. He whispered, "I will go ahead to see if there is askari. Wait here." Both men nodded.

A few minutes later there was a sound akin to a huff, and then Mbuno's head appeared above them. "There was one, not local, very strange tribe. He is sleeping. Follow the cable. There is a door. Go through."

As Pero went through the hatch in the side of the barge, Mbuno was there, finger on lips. Bob saw Mbuno's gesture, too. Mbuno started a hunting run, semi-crouching, sound-less, across the steel deck. Pero and Bob saw him stop at the bulkhead next to the steel ramp that was deployed onto the beach. From their vantage point, they could see there was a hundred and fifty yards of open beach before the entrance to a chain-link gate. The gate was slightly ajar, topped with barbed wire. On either side of the gate, a permanent ten-foot fence disappeared in the gloom. Pero thought there was something wrong with the fence and whispered to Mbuno, "The fence, it is wrong . . ."

"*Ndiyo*, it faces in, not out."

Bob made a gesture to say he did not understand. Pero explained as quietly as he could, his lips inches from Bob's ear, "If you want to keep people out, the fence faces out with barbed wire. This fence," he pointed, "has the top facing in. It is to keep people in, not out." Pero asked Mbuno, "How are we going to get across and through that gate?"

Bob had a suggestion, whispering, "The truck ruts are maybe two feet deep; we can crawl." Mbuno nodded and, looking carefully for any signs of movement, quickly ran down the ramp, his wet bare feet not making any noise, and dove into the truck rut.

From his vantage point, Pero thought Mbuno looked like an eel squirming forward. Bob followed, and so did Pero immediately after. Ten minutes later, exhausted after the long swim and crawl, the three found themselves inside the compound, lying prone under a giant logging truck, hidden from view, just inside the fence. They were all breathing hard. The harder mill ground was no longer pitted with tire tracks. Anything they did from now on would be visible.

Not that Pero could see anyone keeping watch. Machinery sounds were coming from somewhere far ahead, but where the men were, in a garage and service area, all was silent. Pero asked as quietly as he could, "Anyone have a plan?" He was looking at Mbuno.

Mbuno's voice held resolve. "We must search and find Ube."

Bob responded, "Do we separate or stick together?"

Mbuno answered, "We go together, one house at a time. We go now."

The first building was empty of people or living quarters but full of machine parts. The second through tenth were the same, often revealing their contents with each of them taking turns looking through windows. Some of the houses were stacked with what looked like hay bales, hundreds of them. As they advanced, in crouching runs across the yard, they saw no one, and no alarm was raised. *This is going well*, Pero thought. *Too well* . . . And he remembered the old Wild West trooper movies and the standard lines from a protagonist awaiting an Indian attack, "It's quiet tonight, Sarge . . ." "Yeah, too quiet."

All across the expansive compound, the sounds of rhythmic machinery got louder but never enough to disguise a sudden noise, should they make one. Pero and Bob crawled when needed. When speed was necessary, they placed their running feet carefully, eager to maintain stealth. Mbuno, the professional hunter, took smaller steps, seemingly gliding across open ground, always silent. Arriving at each building, they flattened themselves against the walls and listened before inching along the sides and peering through dusty and rain-streaked panes.

They approached the last two buildings before the giant milling plant—there was one long hut without windows and one with windows beyond it. Suddenly the end doors of the nearest building opened, spilling blinding light across the open space to their left. Two men emerged, engaged in an intense argument that Pero could not understand. Pero looked at Mbuno, who shook his head. *What language is that?* Pero wondered.

The arguing men walked off, still almost yelling at each other.

Mbuno tapped Bob and whispered, "Pero, stay. Bob with me." And he ran, crouching to the side of the hut as the doors automatically shut via hydraulic closers. When they reached the full closure, there was an audible click from the latch. The men were out of sight, and again, everything was silent. Mbuno inched around to the doors and tried the handles. No luck. Locked. He peeked down the other side of the hut and motioned to Bob to follow. Bob quickly went to his side. Mbuno gestured to Pero to go around the hut from the other side.

Pero watched Bob and Mbuno disappear from view and quickly ran to the near side of the hut and turned right, following the flat windowless wall to the far corner. On his knees, sneaking a look around the side, he saw a pair of doors and, this time, two windows spilling faint light. Off to his right there was only one larger building with many windows down the side, some illuminated faintly, others dark but, Pero could see, not blacked out. Beyond that stood the towering mill in total darkness, gantries and scaffolding glinting in the moonlight. Pero looked over at the windowed hut, which had a lived-in feeling to him. It looked like a dormitory.

He refocused on the building he was next to. Inching around to the windows next to the twin doors, Pero peered in. What he saw was a long room with tables and chairs, obviously a dining area. At the far end, light was coming in from twin open doors, perhaps to a kitchen. Pero could see pots and pans hanging.

Pero nearly jumped out of his skin as Mbuno and Bob came around the hut quickly and furtively. Bob said, "Men coming . . ."

Pero heard the door at the other end of the building open and close. He looked in the window and saw the shadows of someone moving in the area he had assumed was a kitchen. There was noise and shouted commands. Again, Pero did not recognize the language. The empty hall reverberated with their yelling, now quite clear. Mbuno motioned them to crouch down. Mbuno's face showed deep concern. "It is Hausa, I think. That is very bad."

Bob wanted to know, "What do we do now?"

Mbuno whispered, "We must scout quickly; this is most serious."

Pero asked, "What is a Hausa? From where?" Almost in answer, the three rescuers froze deep in the shadows of the dining hut and watched two more men emerge from the lighted hut with windows. They were carrying automatic rifles with tan butts. Pero instantly recognized them as Russian AK-47s. The men wore threadbare camo outfits, appeared unkempt with very long dreadlock hair, and their posture said they were cocky, ready, strong, violent.

When they passed behind the hut and from view, Mbuno whispered, "Hausa, Nigeria, maybe Boko Haram."

Pero felt a steel-cold shiver run up his spine. His head began to fill in frightening details, women and girls kidnapped and enslaved, victims tortured, terrorist killings of whole villages—his mind reran newsreels he had watched of their atrocities, and for once he wished he didn't have such a mind for details. He asked, "Are you sure?"

Mbuno nodded. "Vultures." To Mbuno, the immediate danger made perfect sense. Hausa-speaking people from northern Nigeria had no reason to be in Tanzania. Their very presence here meant they were vermin—dangerous and evil. Mbuno looked at Bob and saw he was wide-eyed, almost in shock.

Bob said, "Look, man, we need to leave here right away. I need to call this in. If these guys are Boko Haram, we need the real army, not just us. We have to call this in."

Mbuno put his hand on Bob's sleeve, instilling confidence. "Yes, we will go. First, we must help Ube escape."

Pero thought that was a strange way of putting it. But if Mbuno said to follow, Pero would follow him to hell and back, so he said, "You lead, we will both follow, right Bob?"

"Man oh man, you guys are nuts. Okay, okay, I'm with you, but man alive, this shit is getting crazy."

The only building left was the lighted one, perhaps a dormitory. They ran as fast as possible to the side and peered into the side windows, one at a time. The first four windows were all part of the same room. Pero glanced in and shock took his breath away. He turned, put his back against the wall and slid to the ground. Mbuno gave him a questioning look and peered, carefully, into the next window along part of the same room. Mbuno's face showed steely anger.

Bob was about to try the next window, still part of the same room, but Mbuno waved him past and pointed to the next room's window.

Taking a very quick peek, Bob copied Pero's action, putting his back to the wall and sliding to the earth. He pointed up at the window. Mbuno scooted over and put one eye over the sill. Inside was a table and chairs, and tied to one chair was Ube, head hung down. At the table, playing dice, was the guard, idly shaking and throwing the cubes. The guard was facing Ube and the door, not the window. A pistol was on the table next to a cup.

Mbuno looked up at the roof and whispered, "I go up, Bob." Bob laced his fingers and gave Mbuno a leg up strongly and quickly enough so that Mbuno was able to swing onto the roof silently. The pitch was very shallow, so he crouched and frog-walked up the roof to a three-foot galvanized ventilator. Gripping it in a hug, he twisted and lifted it off silently and put it to one side. Then he slipped in and disappeared from Pero's view. A moment later, glimpsing through the window,

Pero saw the ceiling tile behind the man's chair being lifted without noise and Mbuno dropping down onto the guard. He placed his arm around the man's neck and tightened. He did not let go until he was sure the man was silenced. He picked up the man's pistol, a Beretta M9, and stuck it in his trouser belt. Quickly, he untied Ube's wrists and legs. He slapped Ube's face and shook him to wake him up.

Pero and Bob, watching intently, could see that Ube was not coming awake; he looked drugged. "Bob, get up there and lend him a hand." Pero laced his fingers and hoisted Bob up. He clambered as silently as possible onto the roof, went to the open ventilator, and carefully leaned over and extended his hands as far as he could.

Inside the room, standing on the table, holding Ube upright, Mbuno gave Ube's hands one at a time to Bob, and then, taking hold of Ube's thighs, the two of them lifted Ube up through the ceiling. Mbuno followed, holding onto the drop ceiling rafter to pull and swing himself up. Then he pushed and Bob pulled, and Ube popped up through the open ventilator hole onto the roof. Ube did not make a sound.

Mbuno aligned Ube's body across the roof and simply rolled him down and off the roof into Pero's arms below. When the three men were reunited, Mbuno said, "You two carry him—Bob first, over your shoulder. Go back the way we came. I must leave tracks"—he looked down at his bare feet and then at Ube's, which were also shoeless—"make people think he escaped, on land. I will come, but go now." He pulled out the pistol and then ran off toward the giant mill before either man could protest.

Bob looked at Pero, shrugged, took the silent Ube over his shoulder, and started back exactly the way they had come, carefully scouting and listening for anyone that may be outside in the compound. No one appeared. When they got near the gate, they dropped into the truck ruts again and between them jointly dragged Ube, face up, toward the water. Pero really didn't want to risk the crocodiles again, but he nevertheless mounted the ramp, headed for the side hatch, and then slipped through, stepping onto the winch cable mechanism as they had when they entered. Crocs or not, he knew he really had no choice.

Bob motioned him to stop and said, "We wait here."

Pero said, "No, Mbuno said to keep going."

"Look, I agree, but give me a moment, will you? I can't figure out how to get Ube across that water without drowning him."

Pero understood but suspected that even Bob was feeling frightened, simply because Mbuno was not there. Suddenly, Mbuno appeared in the hatchway.

"One moment, we need decoy for crocodiles." He savored the new word, *decoy*. Then his head disappeared from view. Seconds later they heard a distant splash, and when Mbuno came back through the hatch, he said with confidence, "We go now."

As they made their way down the cable into the water, Bob carrying Ube and Pero helping to steady them, Pero's fear of the inky black water and the crocs that may be waiting rose up, and he tasted bile in his throat. Slipping into the water, Pero said to Bob, "I need something to do. I'll tow Ube like a lifeguard, face up. Leave him to me. Mbuno, you lead the way. Okay?"

"*Ndiyo*," Mbuno said and took the lead, following the cable and taking readings off of the Southern Cross that appeared from behind clouds every now and then. Bob kept looking around them, wondering if they would see an attack if it came.

Mbuno saw his agitated state and said, "They will not come now. The water is too deep, and they have food. Not us."

Pero wondered what he could mean and then remembered the barge guard. Croc food, no traces. It could, indeed, look like Ube had killed his guards and made good his escape.

Good our escape? Long way to go. Pero kept up his single-handed sidestroke, kicking his legs in scissor fashion, breathing hard. He knew there were maybe hours to go and wondered if he had the stamina. Ube slept on, his breathing shallow but regular. Pero could feel it under his fingers as he cradled Ube's chin.

CHAPTER 16

Kupata Kuzimu nje ya Hapa—
Get the Hell out of Here

Near exhaustion, Pero inwardly rejoiced when he heard the word, "Ndovu!"

The swim had been uneventful even as it had built steadily to a climax—a climax of Pero's physical ability to tow Ube and the impending doom of certain crocodile encounters if the elephant were not still in the shallows.

When Pero could hold the cable with one hand, Bob came next to him and said, "Hold onto my belt, I'll pull us along the cable to shore." They glided past the slumbering elephants in the shallows who paid them no heed. Mbuno was too tired to speak to the ndovu. He hoped they would remember him as being no threat. Elephants have a long memory.

All three men dragged themselves up the shore and to the shelter of the boulder. Ube had been tugged by his shirt collar like a sack of rice, and no one had the energy to pick him up. It was Mbuno who spoke first as he lifted the pistol and made sure it was drained of water. "We have little time to get back to the forest. They can see this place in the daytime with binoculars. Come!" It stirred them into action. Bob put Ube, with Pero's help, back on his own shoulder and stumbled up the beach and through reed mud to where they had left the Land Rover. Pero ran ahead and opened the rear door. Mbuno got in, and Bob passed Ube to him. Pero jumped into the right-hand driver's seat and started the diesel, astounded at the engine's noise in the predawn quiet. He glanced around at Mbuno cradling Ube in the back and Bob getting into the front passenger seat. Seeing Mbuno's nod, Pero started off.

Before the first rays of the sun illuminated the beach, they were well into the forest along the truck path. Pero stopped the Land Rover and said, "Bob, first-aid time, I think."

Opening the back of the Land Rover and climbing in, Bob could see Ube's face properly for the first time. He had been beaten, and his nose was clearly broken. Then he felt along the jaw and recognized swelling and bruising. He pronounced, "Jaw's not broken, but I think it may be a hairline fracture." He continued to check Ube all the way down his body, even to his feet. "There's some bruising on his sides, possible kidney issues—we'll know when he pisses—but the bones, ribs, legs, arms don't appear broken." He went back up to Ube's head and felt his skull carefully. "Doesn't seem to be any contusions or bumps here."

Pero asked, "So why's he asleep?"

Mbuno responded, "Not asleep; bad medicine."

Bob raised Ube's eyelids and saw the pupils were dilated. He put his head on Ube's chest and listened to the heart and lungs. "I don't like this, his heart is thready..." he felt Ube's carotid artery with his finger. "Too damn thready. He's been overdosed with something."

Pero asked, "What? What do you think it is?"

Mbuno asked, "What did you say the Russian people sold?"

Bob nodded. Then, almost talking to himself, he began a narrative, repeating his training instructions. "First, it is important to assess the general conditions of the patient, airway first." He opened Ube's mouth and plunged his fingers in, peering down Ube's throat using the flashlight. "Okay, that's clear. Now temperature . . ." He put his cheek on Ube's forehead. "Christ, he's hot. Leave the cold, wet clothes on him. He's hyperthermic."

Mbuno looked at Pero, who responded, "It means he's hot and cannot control his body temperature."

Bob continued his survey, mumbling, "Rhabdomyolysis and hyperthermia, got to find out if he's got rhabdomyolysis." He felt Ube's muscles—arms and legs. "Christ, I have no idea if he's losing muscle tissue."

Pero asked, "What would that mean?"

"In cases of severe cocaine overdose, patients have rhabdomyolysis and hyperthermia. But usually the rhabdomyolysis— sorry, muscle deterioration—follows extreme physical fits and muscle spasms. The muscles break down and flood the system with, well, muscle garbage, sewage, that overload the kidneys. If he's got that, I can't see it. If he already had those fits, my guess is he'd be dead." Bob looked at Mbuno. "Look, man, I really don't know what they gave him. I am thinking cocaine, in some form." he turned Ube's arm over and showed Mbuno the telltale signs of where Ube had been injected. "I guess they were questioning him. But man, if I treat his . . ." he paused. "Give me my bag." Pero reached over and grabbed the wet bag off the front seat. Bob opened it and extracted a plastic box. "Let's hope this thing still works." He opened the box and took out a pressure cuff, wound it around Ube's upper arm, and pushed a green square button. The device sprang to life, pressurizing the cuff, measuring Ube's blood pressure.

A few moments later: "Christ, one-eighty-five over one-ten. Pero, empty the damn bag and find a pink-cross plastic pill bottle with the word *BP* on it." Pero searched. "Mbuno, I only have Mr. Winter's medications with me. I have a calcium blocker called Nifedipine, and I intend to give it to Ube to reduce his high blood pressure. I don't have it in injectable form, but we need to get it into him. I need you to help me open his mouth. I'm going to crush the pills, two of them, and put it under his tongue. That's the fastest way into his system, I think." Pero found the pill bottle, opened the container, and took out two pills and offered them to Bob.

Mbuno reached over and took them. "Mr. Bob, I will help." With that, he put the pills in his mouth and chewed them, then opened Ube's mouth, lifted Ube's tongue with his fingers, and spat the saliva and pills under Ube's tongue. Bob was astounded. Mbuno explained, "It is how my wife, our tribe's doctor, feeds little babies who are sick."

Bob said, "Okay then, now we have to keep an eye on Ube until he is no longer in danger, neither tachycardic nor hypertensive." He pumped up the pressure cuff again, listening, ear on chest, to Ube's heart. For a worrying few minutes, Bob kept shaking his head. Then, listening again, he said, "The heart is steadying down, I would guess ninety beats or so, no longer racing."

Mbuno asked, "Can we move?"

Bob nodded while he inflated the cuff one more time. "The sooner we get him to the hospital, the better." Pero took the hint and climbed over the front seat bar and dropped into the driver's seat just as Bob called out, "Phew, one-sixty over ninety-five, pulse still thready at around eighty-five, but at least the BP is coming down. I'm going to give him a sedative—"

Pero called back as he started the Land Rover, "Hey, he's sleeping already . . ."

"Yeah, but we need to keep his heart rate down, lower still, and the BP, too. It'll help the kidneys as well if he's already got rhabdomyolysis. All we're doing here is getting him stable. He needs to get to the hospital; that's all I am doing. Wish I could do more."

Mbuno patted Bob's arm. "First aid, it is a good thing. I learn very much, *asante sana*." (Thank you very much.)

All Bob could think was, *What an extraordinary man.* He searched the medic bag for Mr. Winter's pill bottle of Valium. He shook his head when Mbuno held out his hand. "I don't want you falling asleep, Mbuno. One of these will knock you out if you are not used to them. I'll put one under his tongue and let his body do the work."

Mbuno, cradling Ube's head in his lap, suddenly lifted his chin and said, "Ndovu come. We must go, now."

Pero engaged the gears and low four-wheel drive and turned east into the forest of eucalyptus trees. He began picking their way through the dense jungle just as the rain started.

CHAPTER 17

Muda Mrefu wa Kukimbia— A Long Time to Run

Pero's estimate of ten miles on the forest road to the railroad tracks was fairly accurate. What was not very well assessed was the time it would take. The Land Rover got stuck in the rain-washed forest floor and the marshes they crossed so many times that Pero lost count. Each time he would leave the Land Rover and drag the free-spooling winch wire, slog ten yards to a large tree, and hook up the winch cable. Then back into the Land Rover, bringing clumps of mud into the cab, activating the winch, dragging the Land Rover further along in the forest and marsh. Repeat the process, again and again. Some hours they only traveled a mile.

Pero was reasonably confident that if any pursuers tried to discover where they went, the Land Rover would have left easy-to-follow tracks until the morning's rain turned the forest floor to a sea of mud after the first mile. That and the elephants' reappearance should, he felt, help cover their tracks.

Every once in a while, exhausted as he was, Pero asked for an update on Ube. Bob said Ube's pulse was down to eighty-five and his blood pressure was still a little high at one-thirty over eighty. There was also that one continuing worry for Bob. "I still have no idea of kidney function. So let's hurry if you can, Pero." He went back to ministering to Ube.

Pero, on his own, forged ahead, pushing the Land Rover, knowing the world's best off-road vehicle would, somehow, make it through. *Yeah, well, it depends if I have to get out and winch the damn thing one more time* . . . Then, at that moment, through the trees on a downhill slope, he spotted the railroad tracks—a sight that raised his spirits. "Hey guys, the tracks!"

Getting on was easy. Driving along the rails and over the wooden railroad ties proved no contest for the Land Rover. Yes, it was a little bumpy for the three in back, but no one was complaining. They were making progress.

Tabora and the longed-for airport and, hopefully, a waiting Cessna were perhaps an hour away when Pero saw a bright light on the rails in front of them. "I've got a train coming; I've got to drop down off the tracks, so hang on." He spotted a less steep side on the left of the raised single-rail roadbed and bumped the Land Rover over the last rail, starting the slip and slide down the embankment. "We need to hide. There's a thick wait-a-minute copse over there . . . I'll drive into it. Keep your hands in." As the Land Rover's sides were scraped by the half-inch thorns, Pero selected a lower gear and battered the Land Rover deeper into the bushes. The rainy season had started so the bushes were all green and lush, and after a few moments, Pero was sure the Land Rover was well hidden. He cut the engine and turned toward the back. "Well, I got us here, but I doubt I can back up and out the way I came."

At that moment, Ube stirred and started shivering, and his limbs started shaking. Bob warned, "If he starts convulsing, it's a bad sign. We need to get him to a doctor."

There was nothing else to say. Either way, they had no choice but to sit still and wait for the train's passing. With the Land Rover engine off, the rumble of the freight train was palpable, shuddering the sides of the Land Rover as the train rumbled along. Pero stood on the driver's seat, flipped open the hatch, and cautiously popped his head out the top of the cab. The locomotive was already a quarter mile past them, towing empty freight flatcars. Pero could only see one faded blue-and-white locomotive, diesel fumes belching out of the top, followed by—he counted them—ten flatcars, all empty. No caboose or guard's van. The only signage Pero could see, beyond the typical Tanzanian livery of the locomotive, was on the sides of the beam of the flatcars. It read *Siagwa-Bagir* in blue lettering.

As soon as the train had passed, Pero started the engine, backed out of the bushes, and contemplated the embankment in front of him. It looked steeper from the bottom. "Hold on back there; I'll try and keep it straight so we don't tip over." Pero had been driving four-wheel vehicles for decades. Other than Mbuno, there was no one more capable in the car. That and with the Land Rover's low gear range and the car's good tires—*thanks to Tone as always*—Pero thought he would make it. They slipped sideways once, but Pero corrected, and they reached the top and continued on their way.

An hour later, a little after three in the afternoon, they reached Tabora and headed for the airport. There was a guard at the airport entrance who wanted papers, driver's licenses, and vehicle permits. Pero opened the glove compartment and handed all the documents to the guard who walked off toward a building with the words *Airport Security* on the side in green letters. Pero said, "I've got no driver's license with me; it must be in Nairobi. You, Mbuno?" Mbuno shook his head.

Bob said, "Quick, climb back here and switch with me; I have mine." Clumsily, the men swapped places just as the guard came out to talk with them. He looked at Bob, now in the driver's seat, and asked for a driver's license. Bob produced it.

The guard compared it to the vehicle's paperwork and nodded. "Only persons allowed to drive is on this paper." He tapped the paper again. He looked at Bob. "You are American?" Bob nodded. The guard continued, "Then keep that *mzungu* away from driving unless his name is on this list."

Pero objected to the use of a slur. As they drove into the airport, Bob asked, "What's a mzungu?"

Pero explained, "It is racial. It means European but is also a slur for white man."

Bob shook his head. "Man, I'm really out of my depth here." He slowed. "Any idea where the plane is?" Ube began shaking and shivering again. The three watched him until it subsided.

Pero said, "Bob, drive down the flight line, around that hanger there. We'll spot it; they'll be here." And the plane was—exactly where they expected it—outside the main terminal getting refueled. They drove up; the plane's cabin door opened immediately and steps dropped down.

One of the pilots that Pero recognized, a big burly man, hurried down and over to the Land Rover. "Ready to leave within ten minutes." He glanced into the Land Rover and broke out into a broad smile. "Good show! Let's get you all on board and out of here. There have been some strange questions asked by a couple of locals—police types—why we're here with no clients. We said we're waiting for safari clients."

Pero asked, "Any idea what we can do with the Land Rover?"

The pilot answered, "That's easy. What's not so easy is getting your friend there onto the plane without letting anyone else know." He paused and turned toward the plane. "Hang on a moment, be right back." He sprinted back up the stairs into the plane. A few moments later he was back with a pilot's navigation case that he put inside the rear door of the Land Rover. "Listen, get him into those overalls, then use the case for all your things"—he spotted the pistol in Mbuno's waistband and pointed—"including that."

As Mbuno and Pero worked to get a nonresponsive Ube into aviation service overalls with the words *Mara* in red on the front and back, Pero asked, "What do you have in mind now?"

"As soon as he's dressed, drive to the other side of the plane and put him in the starboard cargo hold along with any luggage." He pointed to the black case. "There's a door we'll open just aft of the wing. Once inside, you can undo the cargo net in the cabin and pull him forward. Is he okay?" The pilot looked worried. Pero explained that someone had drugged Ube, but that he was stable. "Good. Then as soon as you put him on board, drive over there"—he pointed to a building next to the security building—"and park and honk. Honk loudly. That'll piss 'em off. Keep their attention drawn while we button up. As soon as you drop the keys with the attendant, run and get aboard. We'll be in the air before anyone can say anything."

Pero asked, "You worried about something?"

The pilot responded, "Yeah, we heard that someone was waiting by a phone to see if men in a Land Rover would come here. We ain't going to wait for nobody to arrive." Pero appreciated the double negative; it mirrored how he was feeling after more than twenty-four hours of near terror and perhaps more to come.

Less than ten minutes later, they were safely airborne on the way to Nairobi.

CHAPTER 18

Hospitali na Ubalozi, Nairobi—Hospital and Embassy, Nairobi

Their almost two-hour journey before touchdown at Wilson Airport allowed a napping Bob, Pero, and Mbuno to have a momentary sense of relief. From the air, they had radioed Tone with news that they had rescued Ube, but that he was in a bad way, perhaps having been given a drug overdose. On landing, they pulled up to the ambulance that Tone had ordered, and Ube was loaded in and driven away to the best medical facility in Nairobi, the Aga Khan University Hospital. Bob traveled with Ube to inform the doctors what he had dosed Ube with. Pero and Mbuno assured Bob they would follow momentarily.

Pero said, "We'll wait for Tone and drive straight over. If there is any trouble at the hospital, use my name, all expenses, anything Ube needs, okay?" Bob nodded as the ambulance doors closed and the siren began.

Pero had spent time in the Aga Khan Hospital as a result of a thorn infection some years ago, and the previous year, Mbuno's wife had been hit by a matatu bus, and Pero had had her moved there for care. Mbuno was almost a local celebrity at the hospital, especially with the nurses who all seemed to love the aging Mzee. Pero was sure Mbuno's adopted son would get first-class treatment.

Pulling up as the ambulance sped away, Tone greeted them warmly but avoided asking questions. He knew he would learn all, in time. He offered to give them a lift, sliding the minivan door open. Inside, Pero could see that Tone still had the two askari, Teddy and Keriako, with him, waiting anxiously in the third row of seats. Tone explained they had slept at his house in Langata, the garden suburb ten miles outside of Nairobi where Karen Blixen of *Out of Africa* fame had her tea plantation. Seeing Mbuno's expression of contentment, Tone explained further, "I wanted to keep an eye on them; they've never been to the big city." Although Mbuno initially said nothing, Pero knew Mbuno would feel relief. Pero was aware that Mbuno felt responsible for them. As Okiek young men of familial acquaintance, Mbuno would take that family bond of responsibility seriously.

Getting into the minivan, Mbuno greeted the two brothers, who were openly welcoming and happy that Mbuno was back safe. They peppered Mbuno with questions, who answered in short bursts, the fatigue still affecting him. Finally, Mbuno held up his hand and said, "*Kutosha kwa sasa.*" (Enough for now.)

As they pulled onto Langata Road, turning east and heading into Nairobi, Pero said to Tone, "We need your help, Tone. There's a problem."

Pero's serious tone of voice caused the van to swerve a little and Tone Bowman to exhale. "Okay mates, but let's get Ube settled and then go to my house?"

"No, we need to regroup at the Interconti with the whole team, and I'm including you, if you agree."

From the back seat, Mbuno said simply, "*Ndiyo*, Mr. Tone." Tone nodded his agreement and pressed on to the hospital in silence.

As they approached the center of town, Pero asked to be let out. His clothes were thoroughly filthy from the hours winching in the muddy forest. He explained that Mbuno could take care of the Aga Khan, reminding Mbuno that any bill should come to Pero, money was no matter. Tone briefly argued that since Ube was on his safari, Tone would cover all costs and had already instructed billing at the hospital. In the end, Mbuno understood that Ube would get the best care possible. Tone further explained that Sheila from his office was picking up Mbuno's wife, Niamba, from Giraffe Manor, where she and Mbuno lived, to take her to the hospital directly.

Giraffe Manor was a charitable giraffe sanctuary in Langata that had some very serious international patrons. Some of those patrons had gifted a small house on the estate for Mbuno and Niamba to live in, complete with running water and an inside toilet. Although Mbuno would have preferred to live among his tribe, the Liangulu, way past Tsavo on the way to the coast, he could no longer return since, as he described that night at camp, he'd been banished for disobeying the tribal chief and killing his wife's brother in self-defense in his fight to stop an elephant slaughter. What Mbuno had done was also recognized as having saved his tribe from being branded as poachers, but tribal rules were rules, and he accepted his banishment. Niamba, who was the chief *liabon*, or doctor, for the tribe, stayed with him, forcing the tribespeople to have to call on her to ask, politely, if she could make a village-call. Dutifully, Mbuno often drove her down, staying in the car while she administered to the sick and needy once every few weeks. While he sat in the car, often a borrowed Giraffe Manor Land Rover, for hours, one by one the villagers brought water from the river and simple traditional meals to the Mzee. Soon after, the elders were always followed by most of the village children coming to hear the tales of their ancestors and the fables of East Africa and how the Liangulu became elephant hunters and the elephant's protectors. Mbuno was loved, Niamba was respected and somewhat feared, and life continued, village honor upheld.

The van arrived at the first roundabout, skidding around, and went straight on. As they entered the outskirts of Nairobi, Tone said, "Just another ten minutes; not much traffic today."

Pero borrowed Tone's cash, whatever he had. As they reached the inner ring road in town, Pero asked to be let out, promising to meet them all at the hotel within the hour, if that was not too soon for Mbuno. Tone slowed the van, and Pero opened the door and exited before the vehicle came to a full stop. He waved them on and then hailed a taxi and asked for United Nations Avenue. The US embassy had been rebuilt after the previous one was bombed in 1998. It was now located miles away from the center of Nairobi in the northwest part of the city—easier to protect, set back away from street traffic. When Pero saw the building a hundred yards off, he told the driver to stop, gave him cash, and exited. Walking up the avenue, Pero made sure the video cameras spotted him approaching, muddy clothes and all.

By the time he reached the gate, the Marine on guard was turning away visitors, pointing at the sign that clearly said, "Opening Hours, Nine to Five." When Pero stood silently before him, arms at his side, the Marine listened to his earpiece, glancing up at Pero, and then waved him through. Pero was met at the main door by a uniformed officer with a pale-blue blouse who directed him away from the main lobby and through a side door leading into waiting room. Pero sat at the small, nondescript Formica topped table, folded his hands, and waited as the woman officer watched his every move, scowling at his filthy clothing. She watched clumps of baked mud fall off his trouser legs, tracing their descent to the linoleum floor. Pero shrugged his shoulders apologetically.

Less than five minutes later, a door opened and she was summoned away.

Pero remained sitting alone, waiting. He heard muffled voices, then the door opened and a young man entered. He looked along the skirting board, spotted a receptacle, and plugged in a phone. He put the phone on the table in front of Pero and left the room. The phone immediately rang.

Picking it up, Pero listened. "Standby." He kept silent. Then again, "Standby." Pero responded by pushing the star key twice.

Director Lewis of the CIA came online. "Pero, all safe?"

"Yes and no. Ube has been drugged; we're hoping nothing permanent. He's been taken with Bob Hines, the ex-Marine, to the Aga Khan Hospital, along with Mbuno."

"Congratulations."

"Well, it was mostly Mbuno's doing. There is another issue. Secure line?" Pero was aware this was a telephone, not a satellite connection. Telephones can easily be tapped.

"The line you are on is the Ambassador's, scrambled. We insisted. Local One"—which was diplomatic speak for the top local diplomat, in this case the Ambassador—"well, Local One has ordered full assistance. Seems your previous exploits in Berlin and Kenya stand you in good stead."

Pero thought he detected a hint that the current "exploit" might not be seen so favorably and wondered why. He pressed on with the questions he had been mentally preparing. "Any local station around?" Pero meant CIA top staff at the embassy.

"Local station is in New York. Deputy station is in Kenya, whereabouts unknown. Need further assistance?"

"Depends on two things: one you will not like, and one I suspect you knew and withheld from us."

"Proceed." Lewis' voice wavered, seeking to calm Pero's anger that he believed was coming. "And nothing was withheld; it was simply too dangerous."

Pero was, indeed, fuming. What only he and Mbuno had seen at the lumber mill was deeply troubling. "Okay then, the thing you knew. Boko Haram."

Silence from Lewis. Pero waited him out. Lewis gave in. "Okay, yes, we suspected they are involved. NSA cell phone traffic picked up hints of Boko Haram personnel traveling to the region. It tied in with illicit funds traveling to and from the region that ONSI tracked."

"Oh, really? That all?" Pero was getting angrier.

"Need to know."

"Lewis, do not play that game with me. I'll walk out of here straight to the press and tell them everything I know if you play that game."

"Oh, stop it," Lewis responded, getting angrier himself. "There are things you do not want to know, Pero, really dangerous information that would require you never to travel to places where you could become a target. Even to places like where you are. I can't tell you everything; how we get information, what sources we have . . . that would make you have to live behind a desk like me."

Pero thought for a moment. What Lewis was saying was true, but . . . and then Pero realized what was bothering him. The risk to himself didn't matter. What mattered was that because he had a relationship with the CIA, he always seemed to place his friends in danger. He had taken Mbuno, Teddy,

Keriako, and Bob into harm's way based on classified secrets from the CIA, satellite imagery, special coded phones. Any one of these sources made him—and by extension all of his friends, even those at the Interconti—targets of dangerous enemies. It was, he realized, once again, all his fault, all his meddling. *But what was I supposed to do, wait? Wait for what, for whom?*

Lewis seemed to read his thoughts and said, gently, "I warned you not to involve your friends."

"Can I get out? Can they ever be safe again?"

"Look, this will all die down. You rescued Ube. Hopefully, he'll be fine. But, listen to me, leave well enough alone and move on."

Pero shook his head. "I wish it were that simple." He knew, right then, that there was no waiting. Mbuno was, he was sure, already planning, ready to move.

In Africa, danger was always a step away, like a ticking bomb. Pretending it wasn't there could get you killed. Foolishly mishandling nature and the men that threatened savage harm could be suicide. The only way to survive in Africa was skill and knowledge. He knew Mbuno had more than enough skill for them both. Now he, Pero, could use his resources to get the knowledge they needed.

Lewis wanted to get the conversation back on track. "Can you give me a verbal report on exactly what you did and saw? That intel would help us plan next events."

"Yes, but before I do, I need to order information. I need an assessment of the mill plant after we rescued Ube—changes in vehicles, train traffic, movements, anything different."

"Different than what?"

"Oh, come on, compare satellite images for the past month and then tell me if there is an ant swarm of people suddenly after our escape, around zero-one-hundred Zulu this morning."

Lewis was on his guard. "What the hell do you need that information for?"

Pero concocted an excuse. "Look, if they are coming after us, if they think we're a threat to their whole operation, they would be bugging out, and that would mean they would come after us. If they resume normal logging operations, then a few investigations may be had, why and how Ube escaped, and they may not know who we are or where we are." Pero knew that was a lie; the warning at Tabora Airport that someone was asking about them told him they at least suspected who was involved. Pero was not going to tell Lewis that. Pero also knew the Zanzi-Agroforestry men at the Moyowosi airstrip would remember the film producer they encountered—they would recognize the man they told to get lost. However, Lewis would, Pero hoped, believe Pero's simpler reason for needing the intel.

Lewis relented. "Okay, I'll find that out for you and pass it along. You need a secure phone, not the ONSI unit. I'll have the Ambassador's security detail—you met her already—hand you one. Keep it hidden. Same codes as before. Give me a few hours for your intel. Now, can I have that briefing?"

Pero complied, telling Lewis everything about the forest track, the lake, elephants, the logging mill, the approach, the train access, the buildings, the bales inside the buildings, the dining hut, and the dormitory where they rescued Ube. He told him there were men armed with AK-47s, likely Boko Haram as they spoke Hausa. He told him that the guard on the barge was probably unconscious when dumped overboard to waiting crocodiles. He told him that Ube's escape might appear real—there had been no gunfire, and the man guarding Ube was silenced. He did not say by whom, thinking, *No point in implicating Mbuno.* Lewis knew better than to ask for names anyway. In the end, Pero summed it up with a promise to supply a progress report on Ube when he knew more.

Lewis responded professionally, "Excellent job. We'll take it from here. You're clear."

"Well, we still have film to assess, and if they are coming after us, we'll have to deal with that . . ."

"Agreed, but limit yourself to that. Within the month we'll have better intel to deal with Boko Haram in Tanzania and forces in place. You stay clear."

A month? Pero wanted to change the subject, so he asked a question. "What do we do with Bob?"

"He's leaving tomorrow night; his flight is being arranged via London. Tell him to call in."

"Is he in trouble? He really was instrumental in the rescue. I'd stick by him anytime."

Lewis laughed. "And make him part of your team? No chance. He's finished at ONSI, but I have an interest . . . if you think I should."

The thought had not occurred to Pero before that moment. "Hey, now that's an idea, Lewis, thanks for the suggestion . . ."

"What suggestion—oh, God, no, that's not what I meant—"

Pero cut him off with, "I'll expect your call in two hours, please. Signing off." He hung up the phone. Almost instantly, two people entered. One was the phone guy who had unplugged and removed the phone; the other was the officer in light blue who gave Pero a small cardboard box with a stenciled *1* on the lid. She gave a salute and even a little smile as she opened the exit door. Pero walked through and out of the embassy, past the Marine on guard, and whistled a cab ambling down the avenue. Minutes later he arrived at the Interconti, dreading the reunion, the questions, and, not least, his wife's possible fury at what he was more than ever sure was to come.

CHAPTER 19

Timu Pamoja—The Team Reunited

Pero's first stop at the Interconti wasn't with his friends and wife but with Mr. Janardan, the under-manager in the backroom offices, which were devoid of any glitz or glamour—paint peeling, air conditioning barely working. They had known each other for years. Unlike the usual Swiss manager whose bearing and dealings were precise like a Swiss watch, Mr. Janardan was Asian, warm, open, and helpful. "Mr. Baltazar, how very, very good to see you again." It was his standard effusive, singsong greeting, which he gave whether Pero had been away for just a few days or months.

Pero's reply was always the same; it was their ritual: "Keeping the whole hotel together I see, Mr. Janardan." He extended his hand. "I'm glad to be home."

They cleared away money business, which was plaguing Pero's producer's conscience. Mr. Janardan assured him there was no issue. "We know Mr. Heeper very well, very well. He offered his credit card, but I refused, knowing you would regulate accounts in the usual manner." Pero knew they preferred a bank draft, saving the credit card commission. "I hope the rooms on the fourth floor, all adjoining, that we were able to secure were satisfactory? Yours and Mr. Heeper's, of course—small suites as normal."

Pero told him he was sure they were. He signed the bank draft order for the local bank where he kept their production funds and thanked Mr. Janardan for the loan of the shortwave set his team had been using. Mr. Janardan again expressed the hotel's pleasure in serving a long-standing customer, but had to ask, "Will you be needing it for much longer?"

"No, I think we're done for now. I expect we're going to go on safari, more filming, more crocodiles—probably Tanzania, Pangani—maybe tomorrow." Pero didn't like lying to Mr. Janardan, but he was already covering tracks in his mind. "As you can see," he indicated his filthy clothing, "I really need a hot shower and some clean clothes."

"I will alert the laundry staff to give your rooms priority service. Cleaned and pressed within two hours, if you will just call them." Pero stood, they shook hands again, and Pero walked back into the lobby toward an open elevator and asked for the fourth floor. Staring into the nearly empty lobby from the elevator as the doors shut, he was aware of two men, both with blond hair, sitting on the lobby couch and hardly reading the local paper. Their eyes were tracking Pero, of that he was sure.

On the fourth floor, he stepped out and was stopped by the askari guarding the residents and rooms. "Key, sir?"

"I have none. I am joining my friends and wife."

"No sir, you must have a key. Please go down and get a key." Pero chose, instead, to call out to Susanna, Heep, and Mary. Two doors quickly opened, and Susanna and Heep assured the askari that Pero was with them. "Ah, very good." Then, addressing Pero, he said, "Please, *bwana*, next time have the key, please."

Pero was impressed at the efficiency of the fellow and told him so. "Mr. Janardan will get a report from me about this. I am very pleased, thank you. Good job." The askari beamed.

When he reached Susanna, she fell into his arms, her cheek pressed up against his muddy shirt, and he held her tight. Heep was patting him on the back while Mary, exiting the room, peppered him with questions. "Some of what happened we know from the Mara Airways people—Sheryl, actually, who told us you had Ube and were en route. But where is he and Mbuno? And that ex-Marine, Bob?"

From two rooms down the hall, Nancy and Tom appeared and rushed over, babbling that it was good to see him.

Pero motioned them all into his room, to the little ante-living room area. Susanna was still hugging him as he shut the door. Then he told them all he knew, leaving out what he called the dangerous detail—"For later," he explained. When he was through, he quietly said, "Look, when we know more about Ube . . . maybe Tone will call from the hospital, then we can have a discussion on what's next. For now, I'm dead beat. I stink." He indicated his mud-caked clothes. "And, well, to be perfectly honest, I am not sure what's next. Mbuno needs to be here for me to explain further."

At that moment, Heep spied the cardboard box Pero was clutching and asked, eyes squinting with premonition, "What's that, Pero?" Pero handed it over. Heep opened it and held the radio in his hand, knees buckling, sitting on the bed. "Yours or Bob's?"

"Mine. I do not know if I need it yet." Pero hoped Heep would not open it in front of Tom and Nancy who, so far, could not be sure of Pero's connection with the CIA, or especially if it was current.

His wife looked up into his eyes and saw only concern and worry. She took charge. "Out, out, everybody out. I need time with my husband alone. When Mbuno is back with Bob and Tone, we can discuss. Heep, you make sure we have more rooms, please? One for Mbuno nearby and Bob, too, if possible." Heep nodded. "Okay, so, no more discussion. Everyone out." She started shepherding and pushing the team toward the door, saying, "Later, later . . ." They went reluctantly, but they understood her authority and concern for Pero.

Fatigue, and a relief to be back safe with the one he loved, caused Pero to want to avoid a discussion, just wash up and rest with Susanna while she held him tight. He was, he realized, still frightened and suffering from a post-adrenaline hangover. Susanna looked into his eyes, put her fingers on his lips to silence any thought of revelation, and walked him into the brightly lit bathroom. She turned on the shower, helped him undress, put him under the strong water stream, and flipped on the shower stall lights. Then she put the back of her hand over her mouth to stifle a scream. Shocked, Pero turned and loudly exclaimed, "Darling, what's wrong?"

She waved at him. "*Ach mein schatz, stay, wash, ich komm gleich wieder.*" (Oh, my darling, stay, wash, I'll come right back.) She ran out of the bathroom and out of earshot, opened the door into the corridor, and banged on the door of Heep's room. "Leeches; his back and legs are covered in leeches." Heep went to his equipment bag and grabbed a tiny screwdriver and a butane lighter. He followed Susanna back to her room and into the bathroom, and Susanna opened the glass door of the shower.

Pero was surprised to see Heep there, and a little embarrassed. Then he saw Heep heating the screwdriver to red hot, coming closer. He looked down at his thighs, saw the black slugs, and responded how everyone else usually does—shiver from head to toe. "Oh, God . . . okay, Heep, carry on."

Heep stuck the red-hot screwdriver tip into each leech in succession, watching them release their hold, each leaving two small rivulets of Pero's blood that dripped down his legs and was washed away by the shower water. Susanna was simultaneously checking parts of his body that Pero could not see. "Lift your leg . . . yes, see, Heep? There's one up there."

Having a friend stick a red-hot poker into a leech hiding in your crotch was not something Pero ever thought he would have to endure. *At least I'm awake now!* He thought. Then he asked Susanna, "Do you have any Alcide made up? I guess it might help stave off infection." Alcide was a two-part liquid formula, an antiseptic, antibacterial, anti-fungal solution that Pero had gotten from a NASA doctor. He'd used it for years and swore by it. He had even prevented dysentery once by swallowing some after a suspect meal left the rest of the crew violently ill the next day. Susanna opened her bathroom case, pulled out a bottle of previously mixed yellow liquid and some cotton balls, and started cleaning the leeches' punctures with the stinging Alcide. Pero thought, *The more it stings, the deeper it goes.*

Heep worked away, reheating the point of the screwdriver, pulling the leeches off Pero's legs and torso, dropping them into the toilet. Finally, he said, "I can't see anymore. Their nerve toxin really kept you from feeling them, eh?" Heep prattled on, "But you had more than thirty, Pero, more than that. Maybe you should take some antibiotics to be sure . . ." Susanna thanked Heep as he turned away.

As Heep left the bathroom, Pero heard him say, "It's okay, Susanna, we've known each other a long time. Not a worry. But that's a record amount of leeches! He'll have bragging rights." Pero heard Heep's laughter clearly, then it cut off when the door to the corridor closed.

Susanna returned to the bathroom and continued applying the Alcide. Then she handed Pero her shampoo. "You smell. This will help." He lathered up and washed his hair and then his whole body. After he rinsed, she handed him a large towel as he stepped from the glass enclosure. As he dried, she inspected the leech bite marks, some still bleeding a little. She dabbed more Alcide, and one stung more than the others did. "This one may be deeper. Hold still . . ." she dabbed more antiseptic on the punctures. "*Ach*, okay it is as good as I can do. But they might get infected. Heep may be right about the antibiotics."

Pero nodded, yawned, and realized that fatigue was rolling over him again. Susanna escorted him to bed, tucked him in, and went around to the other side to lie next to him until he was asleep. Soon Pero was breathing deeply, out cold. Susanna got up, went to the phone, and said quietly, "Heep, bring the walkie-talkie in here, please." Moments later, there was a knock at the door. Heep handed her a walkie talkie, holding another one in his other hand. She turned one on, clicked the transmit switch to on, held it in place with two strong rubber bands, and motioned Heep out the room, following along. "Turn yours on, please, channel three." Heep did so. "Good, now we go into Mary's room and talk. We wait for Mbuno. He will know what is wrong."

Heep looked at Susanna, wondering what she meant exactly. *Was it the satellite phone?* Ube was safe; Pero, Mbuno, and Bob had clearly done their part brilliantly. *Yes*, he thought, *there may be a risk of retribution, but surely we are safe here, no?* His thoughts turned into wishful thinking. *We're done, aren't we? Please, God, let us be done.*

Susanna, hugging Mary, sensed Heep was still worrying that something was wrong. Holding Mary's hand, Susanna said, "I know him, so do you. The satellite radio doesn't tell me; his worry does, his sad eyes. He is not content at their success in rescuing Ube. There is more." The three friends held their concerned expressions. Susanna added, "It can wait. We have to wait for Mbuno."

CHAPTER 20

Kuja Nyumbani—Coming Home

From a deep and troubled sleep, Pero woke and called out for Susanna. She was not there. He started to get up when the door opened, and Heep, Mary, and Susanna hurried in. Pero had woken with one thought. "Make sure Mbuno and Bob do not come into the hotel, not the front entrance. Ask Mr. Janardan to let them in through the servants' entrance." Then, he had an afterthought. "And if Ube has recovered, maybe he should not come here at all. Well, maybe the back entrance would be okay."

Heep sat on the edge of the bed. "What's up?"

"Two men, blond hair, were watching me arrive and saw me take the elevator. They were sitting in the lobby."

"It might be nothing, you were filthy . . ." said Heep, but then he realized it was foolish to argue.

Mary said, "I'll go down and see Mr. Janardan right away." She turned and left.

Pero relaxed. "Any news?"

Heep replied, "Not yet. I called the hospital, and Ube is still unresponsive but stable. They have given him something to counteract the drug he was given. Tone Bowman, Mbuno, your two askari, and Niamba are with him. Tone made sure I was to tell you that he also has the two askari standing guard." To change the subject, he added, "We have the films, all developed. I've been through them—nothing I can see. Just the usual tourist stuff."

"Maybe we can look at them later when Mbuno is back. Then he and I need to tell you all the real story—maybe, if he wants to, and if you want to know." Heep and Susanna started to protest. They wanted to share, to see if they could help. "No, really, I am not sure you would want to know." Pero sat up, changing the subject. "How are Nancy and Tom doing? They want to bug out yet?"

Heep understood Pero's diversion to normal business and answered, "I think we should release our assistants if you have other plans. No point in involving them. Want me to arrange it?"

Pero wasn't sure. For some reason he clung to the idea that they could continue filming, get back to a normal life. "No, they're safe and being paid. Let's wait a day." He hung his head. "I dunno what to think or what the next step is."

Susanna and Heep had never seen Pero indecisive this way. They looked at each other, and Heep raised his eyebrows in a look of concern. Susanna took charge. "Okay, look, *Liebling*, you are no use to anyone so tired. *Schlafen* while you can, and we'll wake you when Mbuno gets back." Susanna and Heep left the bedroom after they showed Pero that the walkie-talkie was on and they could hear him if needed.

Once back in Heep's room, Susanna said, "Do you know how to work that thing?" She indicated the cardboard box. Heep said he thought so. "Good. Maybe it is time for Mr. Lewis to be helpful for a change."

"Okay, but let's wait for Mary to get back. We're a team; let's keep it that way as much as we can without telling everyone. I am sorry we cannot talk safely with Wolfie; he's been a rock."

Although Susanna knew that Heep had radioed Wolfie to say that the three were back with "the missing party," she wasn't sure if the shortwave radio broadcasts to Oasis Lodge in Loiyangalani were a good idea anymore. She looked at the box. "Do you think they would have another one of those we can borrow?"

Heep smacked his forehead. "No, not this one, but a satellite phone? Sure. They're illegal here in Kenya without a special permit, but I'll be damned if I can't get one to Wolfie by tomorrow morning. I'll handle it." He went to the phone and made two calls. Within the hour, the brother of Sheryl at Flamingo Tours who was the head security man for the United Nations Missions in East Africa drove his personal satellite phone to Mara Airways, and Sheila handed it to the two pilots, still on standby. They would take off at first light, about five hours later; there was no way to land at Loiyangalani in the dark. While Heep had Sheila on the phone, he begged her to call Tone to make sure that he and Mbuno did not enter the lobby. They were to go to the servant's entrance and ask for Mr. Janardan. Sheila was concerned, but Heep assured her it was just Pero being overly cautious. Hopefully.

Heep told Susanna a satellite phone was being arranged just as Mary came back. Mary confirmed that Mr. Janardan was posting hall porters around to watch the two blond men who were still there and, within the hour, make them go away. Mary said, "Germans, if I ever saw any. Blond specimens, good tans, though. Sorry Susanna, but that Aryan look always bothers me."

Susanna understood. "Me too, it is what we all fight against, to stop it happening again. It is what Tacitus said . . ."

Heep said, "Who?"

"Tacitus, the Roman historian. He said in fifty-six AD that such Goths are like a bramble across the path of civilization that, every once in a while, needs to be cut back." She laughed, and Heep and Mary joined in. "Okay, now let's get some food up here, many sandwiches and fruit. He will be hungry when he wakes. And when Mbuno comes, we better have toast and honey, too. I hope I get to meet Niamba."

Mary dialed room service, Heep turned on the TV to listen for news, and they waited. No one tried to use the phone in the cardboard box.

The news that Ube was awake, speaking, and sitting up came as a great relief. Tone explained that it was Niamba who had woken him. First, she had thrown stones from her ceremonial *enkidong*. Tone and Bob had watched, fascinated. In a whisper, Tone explained, "An enkidong is simple—just a gourd, filled with bits of stone and glass. Some of these spiritual gourds are hundreds of years old. But, Bob, all are very serious mystic medicine. Each is personally chosen for qualities only a liabon— the tribal doctor like Niamba, powerful people—can be trusted to divine. They know the power of the casting of the enkidong is determined by the gods who act through the liabon." Bob was watching, rapt, as Niamba chanted and swirled the gourd over a hide painted with symbols and markings she had spread on Ube's bed. Nurses also looked on, fascinated. Tone continued, "The gourd is filled with stones, little pebbles, marbles, bone chips—anything the liabon feels will help her read the signs."

Niamba had poured the stones out steadily, not daring to lose her magic connection with the gods. She could feel power flowing through her. The stones rumbled out of the enkidong, rolled around on the hide, and made a straight line, the only quartz stone and the only pink stone pointing to her left. She had gasped.

Only once before had she seen such a thing. The stones and beads were individually uneven, not totally round, and yet they had perfectly aligned themselves, pointing directly at Mbuno. All saw it. There was not a sound in the room.

Niamba then moved them, one at a time, flicked this bead and that pebble, choosing those that some premonition told her to touch. The multicolored beads and stones rolled randomly on the smooth reverse side of the hide and one by one came to rest with the flicked pebbles and bits of glass, forming a cluster that circled seven bright blue beads that were grouped together—the only blue beads on the hide.

Niamba knew what this said in her heart and mind, but she had to impart the mystic reading to her husband and for Ube's benefit. She proclaimed, "Only Mbuno and the *wanaume na wanawake*"—(those who help rescue)—"*peke yake.*" (Can stop the killing.) "*Wanaume saba na wanawake.*" (Seven men and women alone.) "Only then will people be saved." She then took one of the center pebbles and placed it on Ube's chest, pressing it into the skin, making a dent, then took some power from her medicine pouch and blew it over his face and torso.

Awakening, suddenly, Ube's voice trembled as his head fell back on the pillow, eyes darting around the room, "*Niko wapi mama, Laiboni?*" (Where am I, mother doctor?)

"*Wewe ni Salaama, kuamka.*" (You are safe; now wake up.) "Aga Khan Hospital, Nairobi," she whispered to him. Nurses ran to get the doctor.

Ube looked toward Mbuno and Tone and spotted Bob standing there. Bob had been his client. Ube wanted to stand, but Niamba and a nurse forced him back. "I am so very sorry, Mr. Bob, for the trouble. I am pleased to see you got back to Nairobi in safety."

Bob was grinning. "Thanks to you, man, thanks to you. And a little help from the Mzee here."

Mbuno waved. Ube bowed his head. "*Nasikitika, baba.*" (I am sorry, Father.)

Mbuno replied, "*Hakuna. Wewe kufanya mimi fahari, nasikitika ilichukua sisi kwa muda mrefu.*" (No. You make me proud. I am sorry it took us so long.)

As the doctor entered to examine Ube, Ube looked at Tone and suddenly had a thought. "The brothers, Teddy and Keriako, they are safe?"

Hearing their names and guessing from the nurses' and doctors' commotion that something was up, both men poked their heads around the door. Seeing Ube awake, Teddy started keening, his wailing sound echoing off the hospital corridor walls. Keriako called out, again and again, "*Furaha! Furaha!*" (Happy! Happy!) Ube beamed, which made his broken nose hurt, but he still waved to them both.

Aware that they were making a ruckus in the normally quiet hospital, Tone decided to take charge and ushered everyone except Niamba out, though he kept the door open. The doctor went over Ube, checked vital signs, and discussed possible treatment. Everyone crowded in the doorway, awaiting news.

Tone was not sure what the hospital should treat Ube for, so he asked, "Doctor, any idea what he was given? What can you do?"

The doctor, an Italian, said that the lab tests had come back and it was clear that Ube had been given a dose of unprocessed, raw, cocaine resin. Without the excellent care that Bob had administered, Ube could have soon gone into convulsions, shock, and certain death.

Ube understood some of it, especially the part about Bob treating him. *But where, when?* Ube thought. He looked perplexed, and Tone came over and patted his arm, saying, "Take it easy. They'll tell you everything, but wait until the good doctor here says you can get up."

The Italian doctor laughed. "Get up? As far as I can see, he's fine. He needs to rest for a day or two, watch that broken nose, eat carefully"—he looked at Niamba—"and I'll leave his medical care to my fellow doctor here. Clearly, she knows more than I do." Niamba nodded her agreement. "Let's have him stay here only until I can get a urine sample for analysis." He checked the saline IV and saw it was nearly empty. "Should be any moment now." He reached into his white smock and handed Niamba a yellow plastic jar with a green lid. "In this please, doctor. Just hand it to the nurse when full." He glanced down at his medical clipboard. "Anyway, the blood work looks fine." He shined a pencil light into Ube's eyes. "Eyes clear." He took Ube's head in his hands and gently moved it about. "Any dizziness?" Ube said no. "Okay then, urine sample first, get dressed, and go home. Your private doctor is in charge," he said, smiling. The doctor's enthusiasm was infectious. "Now, stop bothering me. I have sick people who need me."

In under an hour, the brothers, Tone, Mbuno, Niamba, and Ube, who rolled to the curb in a wheelchair, piled into the Flamingo Tours van. Tone's cell phone beeped. He read the text message and announced, "Seems we may have observers at the Interconti. The back entrance is where we are going. All aboard."

Twenty minutes later, Tone pulled the van into the service bay at the back of the hotel, told the guard to close the door, and asked for Mr. Janardan. Mr. Janardan was waiting and immediately whisked them up the service stairs to the fourth floor. Tone knocked on Pero and Susanna's door and was surprised when a sleepy Pero in a hotel towel robe answered. Tone asked if Mr. Janardan knew the other room numbers where the rest were located, and Mr. Janardan pointed to the doors opposite and next to Pero's. Tone tapped on them all. People came out and started hugging everyone, even the still-filthy Bob and Mbuno.

Mr. Janardan looked at the ex-Marine, saw the state of his clothing, and said "Welcome to the Interconti, Mr. Hines. It is Mr. Hines, I presume?" Bob nodded. "Ah, good. At least you are not, I would say, quite as muddy as Mr. Baltazar was, but we shall have laundry service all night should you require. Your room is four-oh-six, just there." He pointed further along the corridor. "I will have a key sent up immediately." With that he turned and left, taking the service stairs down. The askari still on duty saluted as he went past.

Niamba and Susanna were greeting each other warmly, and Niamba was stroking Susanna's hair in comfort, turning some of it on her finger. When Pero looked at his friends gathered together and the genuine happiness they shared at Ube's safe return, his spirits rose again. But he was worried about Bob and Mbuno. As he hugged Niamba, he whispered, "I had many leeches, you know the bloodsuckers?" Niamba nodded. "Maybe you can check Bob and Mbuno?"

Niamba called Mbuno over and lifted first his trouser legs and then his shirt and ran her hands over his stomach and torso. "*Ruba . . .*" (Leeches.) Mbuno's eyebrows went up. She gently slapped his stomach. "*Kitu.*" (Nothing.) Niamba pointed at Bob, who came over to her. Everyone watched, even Ube, fascinated but not surprised at her authority. She pulled up his trouser legs and then his shirt and ran her hands over his skin as she had done with Mbuno. "*Pia hakuna kitu.*" (Also nothing.) Bob asked what she was looking for. Someone said, "Leeches," and Bob flinched.

Niamba looked at Pero, glanced down at his legs, and shook her head. "*Ngapi?*" (How many?)

Susanna answered, "Heep got them off—over thirty."

Heep added, "More like forty."

"*La ema . . . la ema . . .*" (Not good, not good.) She reached into her medicine bag and pulled out a packet made of banana leaf. She handed it to Susanna. "Rub powder. Good." Susanna said she would.

Pero had had enough of standing in the hall. "Can we all go inside? I for one am hungry!" Mary explained the food was already in their room, and everyone packed in, including the two askari brothers who had to be encouraged by Tone. People sat where they could in the little sitting room and on the bed, sandwiches were gobbled up, and bottled water and mineral water were handed all around. Everyone ate, smiled, and kept glancing over at Ube, who amused everyone by looking thoroughly perplexed. Every time someone tried to start the conversation on how, where, and what had happened, Pero cut them off. He explained with a big grin on his face, "We need to celebrate; we need to know we're together and that Ube is back safe. For now the only thing I can tell you is that if Teddy, Keriako, Bob, and I had not helped Mbuno, he would have managed it all alone and then probably smacked us for deserting him."

"If Mbuno hadn't, Tone, Mary, and I would have!" Heep chimed in.

Susanna added, "And Wolfie, don't forget Wolfie!"

Teddy and Keriako had no idea what the conversation was about, but the air of victory, food, and friendship was infectious. The two boys clapped and laughed with everyone else.

The only person not laughing was Mbuno. He glanced at Pero, who gave his head a quick shake, telling Mbuno he had not said anything more about what they had seen. Mbuno knew the information they had to share would change the mood quickly. It was past midnight; everyone needed sleep. Tomorrow, early, would be soon enough. Mbuno walked Pero aside and asked, "The Mara plane, does it wait?"

"No, it leaves at first light for Loiyangalani. I'll explain. For now, the hotel has a room for you and Niamba. Let's talk, first light, and decide what to do."

Mbuno nodded. "*Ndiyo.*"

A knock on the door and the hall askari presented Mary with two sets of keys, each in a folder with Mbuno's and Bob's names written clearly. When he was handed his, Mbuno held up the key folder and simply said, "Ube will sleep here also."

Pero turned to Tone and asked, "Can you and the boys be here at eight for breakfast, in this room?" Tone nodded. "Good, then we can discuss events past and, if needed, future."

People drifted out of the room, Nancy and Tom had said almost nothing the entire time. Their roles had been those of onlooker and employee, but they were visibly moved by the bravery and success of rescuing Ube. Dangerous real-life events didn't cross their paths every day. Once in the corridor, Nancy turned to Tom and said, "You know, this is like being part of the news. Strange feeling. Exhilarating, but somehow I feel like an intruder—and I feel useless."

Seasoned international traveler that he was, Tom responded quietly, "Careful what you ask for in East Africa. I think they got lucky, and they know it."

CHAPTER 21

Alfajiri—Early Morning, Interconti Hotel, Nairobi

Pero awoke early in the morning in the arms of his wife. There was no way he could move without waking her, so he whispered her name until she woke, causing her to hug him closer. She mumbled, *"Mein dummer Mann,"* and snuggled. Pero smiled and tried to squirm out of bed. His head was clear; the solid five hours of sleep had refreshed his thoughts.

He needed to talk to Mbuno before everyone assembled for breakfast. He noticed the cardboard box with the scrambled satellite phone on the table by the television and knew that Lewis would have the intel he desperately wanted to know. If the lumber mill had been evacuated, Mbuno's and his decision would be, in one way, easier. If it was not, that meant that the danger was still present but also that they had to do something. What, he was not sure.

It was Susanna who opened one eye and, seeing what she called his "thinking face," said, *"Ja,* make the call. You look silly wondering." She smiled at him and released her grip.

Pero sat up and swung his legs off the bed. What he saw was ugly and worrying. His legs were covered in welts and scabs—his stomach, too. *At least nothing is leaking*, he thought. Standing, he made his way into the bathroom.

Susanna yawned, checked the time, saw it was six-ten, and frowned. Naked, she got out of bed and followed her husband, saying, "Let me see the one between your legs, and the one on the back of your thigh." He let her examine him. "All fine. That Alcide is good. But we watch, okay?" Pero nodded. She opened Niamba's packet and dusted his punctures once again, then said, "Make the call now, *ja*?"

He agreed, put on the towel robe, took out the satellite phone from the box, and went to open the window, lifting the phone's antenna and pointing it skyward. He pushed the buttons and said, "Baltazar here, awaiting intel from Lewis."

"Standby." Pero gave two clicks. He waived Susanna over, who had put on a bathrobe. He pushed the speaker button.

"Lewis here, where have you been?"

"Busy recovering. All the team have been exhausted. Could not think. Sorry." Pero felt that Lewis deserved an explanation. He had, after all, demanded a report within two hours, not eight.

"Well, seems your inactivity paralleled theirs. Mill is quiet, normal activity, normal truck traffic; logs in, logs and lumber out, all stacked inside rail yard. Small twin-engine plane, likely Avanti type, new model, landed at Moyowosi met by SUV, likely your Mercedes request, cannot confirm how many got on board, then departed. Tracking, landed Dar, refueled, no passengers alighted. Note that." He paused, "Departed flight plan for Tirana, Albania, estimated arrival twelve hundred Zulu today."

"Did the Avanti pick up or drop off passengers anywhere?"

"Cannot say for sure, we suspect a pick-up, as the SUV is still at Moyowosi Airport four hours later. Unmoving, no target in proximity." He meant no one had been seen near the vehicle. "More?"

"Please."

"Okay. Shipment on eastbound train, six flatcars loaded with cut timber, no passengers seen boarding, no passenger cars." Pero thought that was in keeping with the schedule he had been told about. "Then ten flatcars arrived and were loaded with great big logs. No passenger cars. Currently heading west toward dock at Kigoma on Lake Tanganyika."

Pero remembered there was no caboose or guard's van, either. That must have been the train they had hidden from. Then he remembered that the flatcars' sides had read, "Siagwa-Bagir." He interrupted Lewis. "The cars that were loaded going west—we saw that train as we were going to Tabora. They were marked 'Siagwa-Bagir.' Can you get me information on that company, if it has any significance? The flatcars were all new, and only one company, too." Pero knew he was clutching at straws. All train transport was on mixed freight and flatcars, rental being the norm. But there was something too new about those flatcars and unusual about them being from the same company.

Lewis responded, "Siagwa-Bagir. Got it. Chinese shipping and freight company. Logs, not cut lumber, shipped to satisfy Chinese demand for export manufacture of goods. Siagwa-Bagir is the largest shipper in China." He went silent for a moment. "Our intel is that Siagwa-Bagir is not, repeat, *not* involved in any illegal activity. We'll probe further."

"Advise you watch train schedules and traffic. Whatever is there at the mill comes out hidden under the lumber or logs by train. If any train has passenger cars, I need to know.

Also, keep watch on the mill compound and advise on any bus, truck, or possible transport of multiple people that comes or goes. Track any transport of people. Confirm?"

Lewis replied tersely, "Yes, yes, we know our job. What you have to do is advise us on what you are going to do, where you are going. We'll monitor any threats at your new location. And as I said, we'll take matters from here."

"I'll tell you when I know what we're doing, later this morning. And yes, I know you are right, I should not involve them anymore, but Lewis, I don't think I can handle anything like this on my own."

As Pero hung up, he heard Lewis ask, "What do you mean handle . . ."

Until Pero had a chance to talk with Mbuno, he was not going to commit to promising Lewis anything.

Hearing the whole exchange, Susanna looked at her husband and stared intently into his eyes. Neither said anything for a moment, and then, sensing it was not yet time to discuss it further, Susanna went over to Pero's shirt from the day before that had been dumped in the corner of the bathroom, picked it up between two fingers, held it out in front and away from her body lest any part touch the white toweling robe, and said, "And did you not think to remove the Silke Wire before you got so filthy?"

Pero apologized. He really had forgotten it was there. He had no doubt it was ruined, between the swim to the mill and back across the lake, not to mention the hours spent deep in mud. "Oh, I am sorry, darling. I really am—"

She cut him off. "*Nein, nein,* it is a good test, no? Let's see if it is working still." She pulled the wire and small cigarette-like tube from the collar slit and went over to her case underneath the coffee table by the couch. She opened it, flicked a switch, and the battery light came on. She read the number on the Silke Wire and changed the receiver to correspond. She spoke into it, and Pero could see the decibel LED lights dance. "*Ja, Ja*, the signal works. Now let's test quality." She tossed a Wi-Fi headset to Pero who put it on. She turned her back to Pero and said, "*Mein dummer Mann*, I see you have a decision to make. But you are not alone anymore; I am pregnant."

A dumbfounded Pero ran over, picked up his wife, and kissed her passionately.

Mischievously, Susanna said, "*Ach, gut*, the microphone, it works."

For Mbuno and Niamba, having never slept in a soft European bed together before, the night was surprisingly comfortable. The bed covering was too hot for Niamba, but with just the sheet covering them both, they fell asleep holding hands. Ube slept on the couch cushions Mbuno had arranged at the foot of their bed. Niamba wrapped him up in the bed cover and told him to wake her if he felt dizzy or too hot or too cold. Ube slept, soundly, and when he got up in the morning, he asked for permission to shower. Mbuno told him to go ahead. Mbuno then realized that he had no clean clothing, and neither did Ube. Field guides, especially safari guides, travel light, taking only the clothes they travel in. Being in the hotel, especially the one he had stayed in once before with Pero, Mbuno knew his way around, but at six-thirty in the morning he was also acutely aware that he was not dressed properly and certainly not clean enough after their swimming adventures. Then he remembered Mr. Prabir Ranjeet, Nairobi's oldest and most reputable cloth and clothing merchant. He picked up the phone and asked the operator if she could find a number and call Mr. Prabir Ranjeet at his home. The operator said she would call back. Niamba marveled at her husband commanding the phone operator to do his bidding.

When the phone rang, Prabir clearly sounded like he had been woken up by the operator's call. "Yes, who is it?"

Mbuno apologized for calling so early and explained that he and his wife, his son, Ube, and Mr. Baltazar were at the Interconti hotel. Mbuno liked Mr. Ranjeet. He was on a first-name basis with him, so he asked, to be polite, "How are you, Mr. Prabir, and your *patnee*, Acira?" (Wife, Acira.) "And is your son, Amogh, doing well?"

In his singsong Indian accent, Prabir responded, "Ah, Mbuno, thank you, everything is just fine, just fine. Can I help you with any little thing?"

"Do you remember you sold Mr. Pero a safari outfit for me?"

"I do. Let me see . . . a fourteen-collar shirt, a thirty-two-inch waistband, and sandals, say English size ten or nine. Something suitable for Pangani, hot and humid as I remember." Ranjeet's emporium was known for excellent service and memory of customer specifications.

"*Asante sana*, yes. May I ask you to supply the same for me and my son as soon as possible? Here to the hotel Interconti?"

"Of course, my pleasure. And I will add a sweater for each." All locals always had a sweater for morning or evening. They felt the chill at anything lower than eighty. "May I suggest that I get my cousin, Petam, to send you over two real pairs of sandals?" Petam Bogota's were world-famous, leather cross-over sandals with tire retread for soles. All the rich and famous sported them if they came to Kenya. They were strong, until the glue gave out or the cotton threading rotted, but most important, they were impervious to thorns underfoot.

Mbuno agreed and thanked him again. Prabir promised to send over brown pairs, not black—that was for city folk along with the clothing. "Shall I send the bills to the hotel as before?" Mbuno thanked him once more, and each said their goodbyes.

Mbuno suddenly thought that perhaps Pero would need clothes, and possibly Bob as well. Putting on his spoiled trousers, he left the room and went over to Pero's room, putting his ear to the door to see if they were awake. The floor daytime askari came over. "It is not allowed."

Mbuno stared at the man, who was many inches taller. The facial features told him the tribe. "Kikuyu?"

"*Ndiyo.*"

"*Jina langu ni Mbuno Waliangulu.*" My name is Mbuno of the Liangulu.

The askari took a step back, bowed his head, and said, "*Sikitika, Mzee. Sikujua.*" (Sorry, Mzee, I did not know.) Then he knocked on the door, much to Mbuno's annoyance. Susanna opened the door, dressed in a towel robe. Mbuno explained why he was knocking, that Mr. Ranjeet was sending over new clothing and was there anything Miss Susanna wanted for Pero and, perhaps, Bob?

Susanna smiled and gave Mbuno a lingering bear hug, which greatly surprised him. "In case I forget to thank you, every day, for keeping *mein dummer Mann* safe." She called back over her shoulder to Pero, asking if he needed anything in the way of clothing from a Mr. Ranjeet. He answered in the affirmative, and Mbuno nodded. Susanna added, "Can you take care of this for him and Bob?" Mbuno nodded again. His silence came as a direct result of the embarrassment he felt in such close physical contact with a woman in a bathrobe who was not his wife or child. Susanna was having none of it.

"Mbuno, I consider myself your sister after all we have been through. Can you not think of me that way, too?"

Mbuno's eyes crinkled. This was an honor he had not expected. He and Pero had a pact as brothers, and here was a woman openly professing the same attachment. He wondered if she understood the real implication of sisterhood in his culture and tribal custom. This was serious, and he needed to be sure. "You make a great gift. It means my life is yours, and yours mine to protect. There can be no wall between us." He watched her face.

A tear formed and rolled down her cheek. She knew emotions were running high, and yet she also knew that this man, this wonderful man whom her husband loved as family, was, for her, the embodiment of honor and trust that she needed in her life. She needed it now more than ever because she felt more danger was to come. "Mbuno, I ask you, please, allow me to have you as my brother, too."

And so Mbuno hugged a European woman for the second time that day, calling her *Dada* Susanna. (Sister Susanna.) Then turned her around and, as an older brother would, pushed her gently into her room and told her to please get dressed, before walking back to his room to call Mr. Ranjeet again.

Susanna skipped over to Pero and told him what Mbuno had called her. Pero hugged her, happy for her and for them all as a family.

When Niamba heard what Susanna had asked, which would make Niamba her sister as well, she clapped her hands. "*Ajabu! Nami nitakuwa na mpwa!*" (Wonderful! I will have a niece!)

Mbuno knew better than to doubt his wife, but still he had to ask, "*Una uhakika? Mpwa?*" (Are you sure? A niece?) In response, Niamba put her hand on his cheek and patted it. Then Mbuno was sure. Pero and Susanna were going to have a daughter.

Smiling, for even he was always amazed at Niamba's powers, he called the operator again and, when put through once more to Mr. Ranjeet, placed the order for Pero and Bob. As an afterthought, he asked Mr. Ranjeet to send over one of his finest kangas, with knotted ends so he could present them to Susanna as a gift, from her new brother and her new sister. "Please, Mr. Prabir, may I ask if you have the kanga with silk thread?"

"I do, woven into cotton thread so the kanga will glisten in the moonlight."

"May I have one, please? It is for a pregnant lady."

"Ah, then I will make sure the silk is a color . . ."

Mbuno asked Niamba if she had a preference for the color of the silk thread.

Niamba smiled. "*Ni msichana, wanawake European kama pink.*" (It is a girl; European women like pink.)

"Pink it is, Mr. Prabir. Do you have one with pink?"

"I do; it is the finest in the store, even with real gold thread. It will be my honor to send it to you, and we will wrap the kanga as a most beautiful gift. The pink one is very expensive. Would you allow me to offer a discount?"

Mbuno thought hard. A discount would mean the kanga was also from Prabir Ranjeet, at least a little. He felt that was fair. "I accept if you will allow. I want to share the gift so it will be from Niamba and me, as well as you and *Bibie* Acira." (Lady Acira.) "It is for Mr. Baltazar's wife, Susanna, who is with child."

Prabir was clapping, the phone on speaker. Mbuno could hear him telling his wife the good news. He replied, "I am most honored, Mzee Mbuno, most honored. It will be an equal sharing gift, most welcome, most welcome. I will bring it personally within the morning."

Hanging up the phone, Mbuno suddenly wondered if Pero even knew. Niamba saw his face, guessed the dilemma, and began laughing. Mbuno shrugged, looking uncharacteristically sheepish. Niamba loved her husband now more than ever.

CHAPTER 22

Kifungua kinywa na Ukweli—
Breakfast and the Truth

Mary called room service for quantities of pastries, toast with honey, croissants, pots and pots of coffee and tea, a fruit assortment, and a dozen glasses of freshly squeezed orange juice. Meanwhile, Pero was calling each room and checking that everyone could get together at eight. Heep called Tone, who confirmed he was on his way. Mr. Ranjeet's clothing selection arrived, delivered to Mbuno's room, but not the sandals yet. Once dressed, Mbuno dropped off Bob's clothes at his room. Bob was surprised, and on seeing what was in the package, responded, "This is great, man. How much do I owe you?"

"Nothing, Mr. Bob, it is the least we can do for you. Pero says breakfast at eight." Then he went to deliver a similar package to Pero.

He knocked and Susanna answered. She smiled at Mbuno and reached out for a hug. Mbuno smiled back but shook his head. "Dada Susanna, I cannot be hugging every time I see you."

She paid no heed and grabbed him and hugged. "Well, maybe you cannot, but I can."

Pero came to the door, and Mbuno handed him the parcel. Pero tore open the brown paper wrapping and said, "Great, thanks." Then he looked at his watch—it was seven forty-five. "Can you come in? We need to talk before everyone gets together." Mbuno entered. He was going to ask Susanna if Pero knew she was with child but decided then was not the time.

Pero started. "Okay. You and I, and only you and I, saw what was in that first room." Mbuno nodded. Susanna looked on quietly, knowing all was to be finally revealed and that her patience had not been in vain. "Now, I called Lewis"— he pointed to the satellite phone on the windowsill, antenna still extended—"and got information on the logging camp. Nothing dramatic has happened since we left, no movement of people, no people transport in or out. Just the Mercedes SUV that went to Moyowosi Airport and stayed there after that plane—you know, the modern pusher prop we saw?—landed." Mbuno nodded, "Well, seems someone got out of the camp— I'll assume it was the boss, what you call the lion—boarded the plane, and left, bound—so far—for Albania. The only other thing that has left the camp were two train shipments. One eastbound with cut timber and one westbound with the uncut trees. No possibility of passenger transfers."

Mbuno was pensive. "They may feel Ube escaped alone."

Pero thought Mbuno did not sound confident, adding, "True, but there may be doubt. I am worried about the pilot who said there was a query about our people leaving Tabora airport. And then, last night, two people who looked to be German were interested in my arrival here at the hotel."

"*Ndiyo*, it is like baboons. They believe a thing but check to make sure they make no mistake. Baboons are very clever.

Baboons are meat eaters, too; they pretend to be afraid but are very good hunters. Baboons are very clever, brother. Never trust baboons."

Pero agreed. The problem he was facing was what to do. What did Mbuno advise? There was no way around the issue, so he asked bluntly, "How do you want to handle this? The discussion with our team?"

"Is there any help from Lewis?"

"He says leave it to him—Boko Haram, that is." Susanna's eybrows shot up and Pero took her hand to calm fears. "He doesn't know about the room." Pero held up the other hand and raised one finger at a time. "One: He knew Boko Haram was there, but not what we saw since I didn't tell him. Two: No one has any idea about the cocaine leaves or resin, where they are going, or what they are being manufactured for; all that cocaine stuff is a mystery. He wants time to find out. I told him we did not find out, either. Three: The drugs are helping fund Boko Haram; he made that connection. Four: Why the lumber mill? As cover? Seems that cover will evaporate when the local forests are cut down; hardly seems worth the expense to build a mill for just the timber in that one area. Five: The Singhs in Dar know something is going on there, at least they intimated as much to Heep. And six"—he held up the other hand—"and I did not talk to Lewis about this—why hasn't one of the Singh brothers stopped all this . . . gold in, drugs out, Boko Haram? All on their doorstep? Doesn't make sense."

"*Ndiyo.* But you are right." Mbuno smacked his hands on his knees. "It does not matter." Pero was silent. "The room." Mbuno's quiet statement sent shivers down Pero's back. Susanna, still sitting on the end of the bed, looked from one man to the other, seeing the conflict in each, trying to calculate who would give in first.

"Look, Mbuno, I know, I know," Pero was almost pleading. "But if Toyota Singh and the policeman are already investigating, and if Lewis and the CIA are already planning something, if we try and do something now, we may ruin their whole operation and allow the leaders to get away. And if they move their operation anyway . . ."

"The room." Mbuno, the hunter, had his eyes on a target.

Pero realized he would not shift Mbuno from his focus. "Okay, I understand. But do you understand the risk? Not just to ourselves, but to larger events and evil leaders in some far-off land?"

"It is as I said, brother. Lions, once fed, are always hungry. They can be killed, or they will move on and kill somewhere else. Vulture always follow lion. Hyena are happy with lion killing. Carcasses become too many; the land dies. The lion moves on. Lion are not interested in small game. Hyena and vultures are. It is why they stay when lion leave. And when the meat is gone, only the baboons remain. Always it is baboons who survive. It is baboons who take over." The word *coup* popped into Pero's head again.

So, Pero, looking at Susanna, asked the same question again, "Mbuno, what is your plan?"

"We tell everything, you produce. We rescue. We go rescue *wasichana duni.*"

Pero, disheartened, translated for Susanna: "The miserable girls."

Breakfast, once Tone arrived, was friendly enough. The hotel staff had wheeled in three tables and extra chairs. The suite was packed when the room phone rang and Mary picked it up.

"Yes, they are here . . . uh-huh . . . yes, please ask Mr. and Mrs. Ranjeet to come up to the Baltazars' room."

She hung up the phone and explained to Susanna. "The Ranjeets are on their way up. It was their son, Amogh, who flew the plane that saved everyone before." She was referring to the Nairobi al-Shabaab attack. "It seems they want to see you, and Pero, of course."

In that room, only Pero knew that Prabir Ranjeet was also a Mossad agent in place. There was no reason to suspect that he knew anything about their plans, but Pero was instantly nervous. He could maybe use Prabir's help, as before, but he was more worried it would complicate the quick-in, quick-out plan he needed, without CIA or certainly without Mossad intervention. Pero understood Lewis's reluctance for his maverick behavior; there may well be greater fish to catch on a different timetable. The image of the frightened, half-clad girls outweighed, for him and Mbuno, other considerations.

Susanna took his hand and pulled him toward the door, followed by Mbuno and Niamba. As they stepped out into the corridor, the elevator doors opened and Mr. Janardan and the Ranjeets exited. The askari saluted the hotel under-manager. Prabir exclaimed to Pero and Susanna, "Ah, so wonderful to see you, so wonderful. It is wonderful news!"

Pero was thoroughly confused and looked at Susanna, who was similarly perplexed.

Mbuno and Niamba stepped forward to stand next to the Ranjeets. Mbuno nodded to Prabir. Formally, he lifted a yellow, silk-wrapped present with both hands and tendered it to Susanna. Prabir explained, "Mr. and Mrs. Mbuno explained the wonderful news, and we decided, together, to congratulate you on the growth of your family."

Susanna blushed and looked at Pero. He said, "I didn't say a thing! I promise." Susanna started laughing. She looked at Niamba and instantly knew.

Mbuno took Susanna's hand and said, "Dada, no one keeps secret from Niamba. You do not mind?"

"Mind? Honestly, I am thrilled! Of course, my brother." Then she went over to Niamba and put her hand around Niamba's waist. "And sister probably knew before my husband, no doubt!" The Ranjeets looked on, amazed but happy. Pero was still smiling when he heard a sound behind him. He turned to see Heep, Ube, Mary, and Tone.

Mary exclaimed, "I knew it!" She looked at her husband. "Didn't I tell you?" Heep patted Pero on the back and kissed Susanna's cheeks.

For the next ten minutes, everyone piled into Pero's room. They unwrapped the beautiful party-quality kanga, and Susanna went into the bathroom with Niamba to try it on. When she emerged, she received a round of applause because the kanga was so beautiful and she looked radiant. Pero could not have been prouder. His mind, however, was drawing him away. *She looks lovely, but I have to get moving. We need to concentrate on the job at hand . . .*

Mbuno knew Pero would be worried about the timing. He raised his voice and asked everyone to leave the couple alone. There would be time for celebrations later, in a few days when they were not so busy. "We eat now. *Tafadhali.*" The mood changed, and people drifted back to breakfast in the other room. The Ranjeets said goodbye, and Mr. Janardan escorted them to the elevator. Pero called after them, "Thank you, thank you both!" Prabir waved as the elevator doors closed.

Pero's room phone rang—it was Sheila from Mara, calling to say the satellite phone had been delivered. Business instantly returned to matters at hand. Susanna ran to the bathroom to change back into day clothes. Moments later, coming into Heep and Mary's room, Pero asked Heep for the number of the United Nations' receiver. He dialed, put the phone on the windowsill, pushed connect, and Wolfie answered immediately. He pushed speaker, telling Wolfie who was in the room. He then asked Heep to repeat the rescue story while he took Bob aside into the corridor.

Keeping his voice low, Pero said, "Bob, look, you did a good job. You get your flight information yet?" Bob nodded. "Okay, good. Now listen. I don't know what's in store for you back in the USA, but I owe you the truth here, and then you need to make a decision. Okay?"

"Somethin's up man? I thought something was weird last night. You weren't too happy."

"That doesn't matter. Mbuno and I saw something at the mill. We can't overlook it." He quickly added, "That doesn't mean you need to get involved. But what I am saying is this: We're about to explain everything to our team, and, yes, I consider you part of the team even if Director Lewis has forbidden that already."

"You don't take orders very well, do you?" Bob said, smiling. "Look, I'm done with ONSI; they are amateur. Your guy was right. And when we saw Boko Haram there, well, it really made me mad because I wasn't trained by ONSI for that type of solo action. No way, man. So, whatever you saw there that makes you think you need to go back down there again, I'm in. I trust you, okay, and, sorry, Pero, but honestly? I'd follow the Mzee anywhere. I know a leader when I see one. My sarge got court-martialed after an incident in Iraq . . ."

"Near the Euphrates?"

"Yeah, near there. Anyway, he was like Mbuno, moral high ground, if you know what I mean, coupled with skills, man, deep-shit skills. I'll tell you some other time."

"Okay, for now I'll include you in the conversation. But when you know what we saw, and when we make a plan, you can bow out any time you want, agreed?" Bob shook Pero's hand, and they went back into the room as Heep's tale of the arrival at the hotel last night was winding down.

Ube stood up and said, "I thank all of you, you save me. *Asante sana.*" People were clapping.

Pero asked for silence. "You still there, Wolfie?" His voice came through loud and clear. "Okay then, Wolfie, you may want to leave us now. But, as you were so helpful in Ube's rescue and coordination, I wanted you to know the outcome . . . it is a big but, and what comes next may be something you"—he looked around the room—"and others here may want no part of. All I ask"—Mbuno touched his arm—"sorry, all Mbuno and I ask is that you keep secret everything we are about to say and discuss." From the phone came Wolfie's agreement and everyone around the room was nodding as well.

Mbuno held out his hand to Susanna. She rose, and he pushed her toward Pero. Niamba rose and stood next to Mbuno, her hand on his shoulder, giving him confidence. In a clear voice, Mbuno said, "We go back. We find girls." There was audible shock from everyone.

Pero explained. "In the first windows of the hut where we found Ube, we peered in carefully. Inside there was one lightbulb hanging from a wire. I could see maybe twenty or thirty young girls, most without clothing, some with skirts or ripped blouses. All wore the same uniform. It looked like a school uniform."

Mary stood up and screamed, "The kidnapped Boko Haram girls!" Heep stood, grabbed her, and made her sit, comforting her.

Pero squatted before Mary. "Sorry, sorry. I forgot, your uncle has been leading efforts to find them, to have someone rescue them. I should have warned you." Pero explained to everyone else, "Mary's uncle is Reverend Jimmy Threte." Some people gasped—Reverend Threte was a world-famous evangelist.

From the phone came Wolfie's voice, "The guy al-Shabaab tried to shoot and blow up two years ago?"

Heep answered, "Yes, the same. Mary was a target then, too."

Mary looked at her husband, who had thrown himself in front of the assassins' bullets to save her. She hugged his arm hard. But Mary wasn't sad. She was suddenly angry at Pero. "You took a day to tell me? Why?"

Pero stood again. "Look, everyone. We needed to make sure Ube was back safe and well. And we needed more information from Director Lewis. We needed to regroup. This ain't easy."

Nancy asked, "Who the hell is Lewis?"

"Sorry, guys. I was a CIA runner, small stuff, while I traveled. Then there were those two big events that we all"—he looked around the room—"managed to take care of. Director Lewis is at the CIA; he's useful for information when we've needed it. This time, he wants me to stop and go away, leave it to the authorities in Tanzania and, I suppose, the CIA. But Mbuno and I saw those girls. We can't wait for someone else to decide what to do maybe a month from now. These are young girls . . ."

Bob spoke up, "Yeah, that's about what I was supposed to do, too—find out what I could and leave everything alone. I didn't know about Boko Haram being there at all."

Tom asked, "And who the hell are you, really?"

"I was ONSI, the Treasury, tracing drug money pouring into the region. Seems it's for Boko Haram."

"You *were* ONSI?" Nancy asked.

"Got fired yesterday. Now freelance. I'm staying to help."

Mbuno said, "Good man, Mr. Bob."

From the telephone came the voice all the way from Loiyangalani, "Always knew there was something fishy about you, Pero, after the Nairobi al-Shabaab thing. *Scheisse*, this is a bad thing, these Boko Haram devils in East Africa. Okay, I help, too. What do you need?" Wolfie's commitment sounded firm.

Tone spoke up, "Nothing you can send us from there, Wolfgang, but I can help here and now." He faced Mbuno. "Old man or not, Mbuno, count me in. I'm still a crack shot. Bloody bastards in East Africa? Not on my turf. And some of the old white hunters, one of them will join up in a second." Then Tone realized that Teddy and Keriako were still in the room. "Mbuno, should they leave? They haven't understood very much so far . . ."

Mbuno was decisive. "They are Okiek. They are warriors, they decide." He turned to the two young men, placed a hand on each of their shoulders, and brought them into the picture in rapid Swahili. Their eyes got larger and larger, they started to raise fists in anger, and finally it was clear they were in. Mbuno patted each man on the back and said, "*A heshima mpiganaji.*" (Honorable warriors.)

Teddy answered for the brothers, "We rescue, yes?" Mbuno nodded. "*Ndiyo, sisi kukusaidi; kutuambia nini cha kufanya.*" (Yes, we will help; tell us what to do.)

Heep stood. "Hold on, hold on. All this is like a riot beginning. We need a plan, we need . . ." He stopped. The room went silent. He said, "Pero, *ja, moet je een werkbaar plan te maken.*" Mary tapped Heep's leg, reminding him to speak English. "Oh, sorry. Yes. You, Pero, need to make a workable plan . . . or people will get killed for nothing. Produce this rescue."

Pero knew it would come to this. All his life, he was the organizer. It was what made him an excellent producer, keeping on budget and on time, dealing with governments and regulations around the globe. It was, as Director Lewis had once said, what had helped him prevent two world disasters—planning ability. This time, however, Pero knew they were having to plan an attack, not merely prevent an attack or terrorist threat. It was one thing for him to plan to stop evil forces before they did anything, but it was another thing entirely to plan an attack to overcome an enemy. Then it occurred to him. "Hold on a second, what are we trying to do?" He looked around the room. Everyone said the same thing, that they must rescue the girls. "Does anyone here care if we do not stop Boko Haram in Tanzania, if we do not stop the drug trade, if we do not find out who's behind all this? The girls come first and foremost?"

Everyone was shrugging or shaking their head. Mbuno simply said, "It is the girls."

Pero felt better, more confident. "Okay then, a rescue mission is what we'll mount. We need a way in and a way out. Coming out will mean transporting every girl, talking to them to help calm them." He looked around the room. "And when we get them out, we need a place to go that's safe for them and for us." Pero's enthusiasm was growing, and it was infectious to those in the room, even Teddy and Keriako, who only understood enough to know plans were being made. "The best way to slip in and out of that mill is across the lake—but that doesn't help take the girls out safely. And there is no road leading from the mill, right?"

Bob agreed.

Pero summed it up. "So—we need to steal a train."

CHAPTER 23

Mipango Yote ambayo Inaweza Kukosea— All the Plans That Can Go Awry

Pero knew that any decision by committee was a sure-fire way to have this rescue fail. He was determined to get the girls out by using his planning skills and always relying on Mbuno's abundant abilities in the bush. The previous dangerous adventures of the past few years had ultimately been his responsibility. Now the link to Lewis and the CIA made him responsible for this mission's success or failure. He was determined to avoid the latter. He had spent much of the night going over possible plans in his head. Now he needed to talk them out, get feedback, and improvise. All good producers must improvise. It is how they stay on time and budget. He would take charge. No committee decisions. Of course, he knew he would still defer to the experts, and thinking of that, he looked at Mbuno.

Mbuno saw Pero watching him in the middle of the crowded room, where seemingly everyone was talking at once about what they had heard on the news about Boko Haram. He could see breakfast dishes, cups, saucers, and empty orange juice glasses littering every surface. Mbuno decided to take charge of setting the tone of what was to come. "Mr. Heep, call for this"—he waved his hand around the room—"to be taken away, *tafadhali*." Heep reached for the phone. Mbuno continued, "Mr. Tone, Pero is a producer. He is good producer, he is in charge." It was a statement, not a question. Tone immediately agreed, as did Wolfie over the speakerphone. Mbuno turned to Pero and said, "Good. Now give instruction." Then he sat down, leaving Pero the only man standing. Niamba watched her husband in awe. He was ordering everyone around, including Pero.

"Okay then, some of the simpler matters first." Pero held up his hand and raised one finger at a time as he enumerated. "One: safety. Assume the worst. Those two Aryan types in the lobby, whether they are there today or not, may be part of the mill operation. Mr. Janardan is shooing them away, but they will be watching the hotel. So, we need a safe base where no one can get in or out without us knowing." He called out, "Wolfie, can we take over a wing at the Oasis?"

Wolfie responded, "Guests leaving this morning; I'll have eight rooms. I'll shift things around, take no new bookings. How many nights?" Pero said a week would suffice. "Good, no problem. Can I hang onto this phone or will we be using the radio?"

"The satellite phone is more secure. Can you charge it?" Wolfie said he already was. "The strip at Loiyangalani can take a larger plane—I even saw a DC3 there a few years back—so we'll aim for everyone to end up at the Oasis. Only one way in and one way out. Easy to keep watch. Okay then, Wolfie is our safe base. Fine with you, Wolfie?"

"Depends." He made everyone wait, then chuckled. "Depends if I have use of the generators to keep the pools full." Those who remembered the pool draining, just a few days ago, smiled or laughed.

"Thanks, Wolfie. Now, two: the team to effect the rescue. Volunteers please. Me, Mbuno—"

Niamba spoke up forcefully, "*Kuna watu tisa ambao wana-taka kwenda.*" (There are nine who will want to go.) Niamba had seen nine when she threw the contents of the enkidong at the hospital.

Pero asked, "Why nine, Niamba?"

In response, she did not answer but instead pointed around the room, starting with Mbuno, Pero, Bob, Ube, Teddy, Nancy, and Tone, then added, "*Polisi jijini Dar rafiki ambaye ni waw-indaji na Tone.*" (A police officer from Dar and hunter friend of Tone.)

Pero was about to ask how and why she had thought of those choices, but looking at Mbuno nodding vehemently, Pero decided to accept Niamba's verdict. "Let's assume that's the team going to Tanzania. Everyone okay with that?"

Nancy stood. "You are assuming a lot. You have to ask me."

Mbuno answered, "Niamba says you want to go. She does not tell you."

Nancy felt suddenly out of her depth and explained, "Look, I've been to Nigeria. Maybe it's that. I went with my parents on a mission for our church. But this is a whole lot different..."

Mbuno asked, "You speak Hausa?"

The realization hit Nancy hard. She sat next to Mary on the bed. "I do, a bit." she looked around the room. "I take it none of you do?" Everyone was shaking their head. "Okay, I get it. Jesus Christ protect us. If I go, my parents will kill me if anything happens. If I do not go and something happens to those girls, my parents will kill me anyway."

Mary asked, "What does your faith tell you, Nancy?" Everyone looked on anxiously. They saw it was a tough decision, one demanding bravery, the type of bravery more commonly reserved for soldiers.

Nancy looked at Mary and asked, "What would you do?" She saw it in Mary's eyes. Then she looked at Susanna and saw the same determination and commitment. Lastly, looking at Niamba, she nodded her head and said, "I guess you knew already. I'll go. I was in Nigeria when I was their age—young, thirteen going on fourteen—and I loved everyone I met there. I cannot forget that. I'll go."

Pero and the others in the room congratulated her. Pero repeated the question, asking if everyone on Niamba's list was in.

Tone spoke up. "I will be when I make a call. Stephen Pritchett is who I had in mind, son of a great white hunter, crack shot. Was in the Territorials in Britain for ten years, staff sergeant. Solid. He'll want in. Who's the policeman she's referring to?"

Pero explained that during the last troubles in Tanzania, one of the Singh brothers had come to their aid. He was pretty sure he'd want in. "I'll make that call shortly."

Mary spoke up. "You mean that sweet little roly-poly man who tried to defend me from my mama crocodile at Pangani with only a popgun? Commissioner Madar Singh? Him?"

At one point during their filming in Pangani with a seagoing monster crocodile, Commissioner Singh had felt Mary—the crocodile expert—was in danger, so he ran down the beach with a small .22 pistol to defend her. There was no need, but his bravery made an impression on everyone there.

Pero smiled. "Yes, that's the one. Heep, you talked to his brother Virgi the other day. As soon as we're done here, I'll call Commissioner Madar Singh—he has an Interpol scrambled phone like the one I have there. I'm sure he'll help." That left Bob and Teddy. Niamba's premonition or not, Pero needed to be sure they were volunteering. "Bob?"

"I'm in, man, I'm in. Don't hold with kidnapping."

"Teddy?"

Mbuno responded for the brothers. "They are Okiek warriors, and I will guide them. We need them." He turned to the boys, especially Teddy, "*Yeye anahitaji kujua kama wewe kukubaliana kwenda kwenye kuwaokoa.*" (He needs to know if you agree to go on the rescue.) The men nodded. Mbuno added, "*Ni hatari!*" (It is dangerous!)

Teddy looked at his brother and nodded, then Keriako spoke for them both. "Ube *alituokoa. Lazima tuwahifadhi wasichana.*"

Mbuno translated, "Ube saved us. We must save the girls."

Pero asked Mbuno to explain that he was leaving the protection of his crew in Loiyangalani to Keriako, under the orders of Wolfie. He nodded at the radio. Mbuno explained, and Keriako stood and proclaimed, "I protect!"

Pero was pleased. He held up another finger. "Now, three: the bigger the city, the more chaos to hide in. We're going to need to steal the train in Dar and ride it all the way to the mill and pick up their cargo. The hijacking of the locomotive may be easy. The schedule of when a train is expected is harder. I'll get the Singhs working on that when we're sure about them." He paused to make sure everyone was following. "Four: Susanna, Heep, Mary, Keriako, and you, Tom, I need you up at the Oasis by this evening. Set up base there. Susanna, you're communications. Can you get ahold of Lewis securely with Wolfie's satellite phone?" She said she could. "Heep and Mary, I need you to prepare for the arrival of the girls. They need help, Mary—"

She interrupted, speaking to the satellite phone, "Wolfie, can my uncle stay, too, please? He'll bring a team of experts, maybe four. We can all squeeze in two rooms."

Wolfie responded, "He can have my quarters. I'll take the hammock—nicer this time of year."

Mary looked at Pero. "I'll need the phone"—she pointed at Pero's satellite phone—"to call my uncle. I do not want anyone here knowing." She meant the hotel operators. Jimmy Threte was the personal savior of thousands in Nairobi. If anyone knew he was coming, they would walk to Loiyangalani for the chance to see him.

"Okay, Mary, that's great, and thanks, Wolfie. Mary, make sure he brings that giant bodyguard of his for security, Kweno Usman." Kweno Usman had saved Mary's life years ago and was devoted to both Jimmy Threte and his niece. Pero felt better if Kweno could be around—to protect Susannah as well. "Now, Heep and Tom. Get set up, video cameras, buy anything else you need today here and take it with you. Think Shoa Project . . . an unfiltered, stream-of-consciousness recording while it is fresh in their minds. We want these girls' stories down on tape. It'll be critical for the World Court if anyone is ever arrested." People started to complain that that was not the purpose of the rescue. "I know that's not our goal, but if we do find out anything, the taping would be critical evidence while details are fresh in their minds. Agreed?" Everyone seemed to understand.

"Now it gets harder. Five: Assuming we get into the mill, assuming we have the capability of releasing and putting the girls on the train and then leaving . . . the direction we can take is limited to the track being clear. It is a one-track rail system. Back to Tabora and fly out? Or onwards to Kigoma and the airport there? We'll know more after we go to Dar. And that's where I need you, Tone. You know all the flight operators at Wilson Airport. We need planes to carry fifty in all, waiting at both airports without attracting attention, without staging an air armada. Ideas?"

"Having that many planes might be hard to keep secret. It will, I am afraid, attract a lot of attention at Wilson just by me asking. What do I tell them?"

Pero wasn't sure. He didn't want leaks or to worry people of the danger already afoot. It was the danger that keyed a memory. "Can everyone hold on? Wolfie, can I cut you off and make a call? I'll call right back." Pero ended the Oasis call and pushed the buttons for Lewis' sequence. He heard, "Standby," and responded, "Baltazar for Lewis, urgent."

"Lewis here. Baltazar, you leaving Nairobi yet? No, wait, am I on speaker?"

"You are. I am talking to my team on where to go next. Suspect surveillance here." He put a finger to his lips to tell everyone to be quiet. "May need transport, non-local. Can you arrange?"

"What about civilian flights out of Nairobi? I can clear seats . . ."

"Negative, non-civilian flights. Anything Navy in Mombasa we can borrow?"

"What are you up to? I told you—"

"Lewis, listen, and listen carefully. You made me operational, you said my CIA articles are still active. So, I am the field agent here in control. I am instructing you to arrange military airlift capability, multiple aircraft, on my command. To be available within two hours within the next thirty-six. Maybe three tons max load. Pickup may be open ground. Flight distance under one thousand five hundred miles. No air-to-air hostility expected. We do not know where we can go yet to effect safe egress. Copy?"

"Yes, yes, okay, copy." He sounded too tired to argue. "Is that wife of yours there?" Pero looked at Susanna and nodded.

"Hello, Charles." Susanna used his first name. "How can I help you?"

"Since it is obvious your husband won't listen to me, can I at least ask you to keep me informed? He's playing God again, and it might be better if he didn't try it alone."

"God has nothing to do with it. Being a good man with good friends does," she said. Then she raised her voice. "And that includes you."

From the speaker they all heard the exhausted voice. "Oh, Lord, this is a mistake. Here we go again. Lewis out."

CHAPTER 24

Kusonga Haraka, Kusimama Bado—
Moving Fast, Standing Still

As the initial briefing wound down, Pero asked Heep, Bob, Teddy, Keriako, and Ube to come to his room. "Heep, you have the photos?"

"Yeah, Sergeant Nabana left them with us when we didn't see anything useful. What do you expect to find?"

Pero shook his head and thought, *Probably nothing, but maybe the four who had been there will recognize something.* On the coffee table, Heep spread out the color prints Nairobi Labs had made from the slide film Mr. Winter had used. "Seems there were thirty-two rolls, only four from that day. They printed every shot that wasn't blank. I am afraid the order has gotten mixed up. Sergeant Nabana has the original slides in safekeeping. The originals are numbered if that helps. I did have the lab make a fast, digital copy of every slide."

Pero immediately saw nothing of interest. The usual long-range shots of a leopard in a tree, a carcass or two with flies, and vultures. Lots of grass, bushes, and trees. He turned to Ube. "Can you put these in order?"

Ube started sliding the images around on the glass top. Eventually he seemed satisfied. "Early"—he pointed and ran his hand over the images to the end—"to late."

Heep asked, "Anything? Ube, Bob, you see anything that would account for what happened?" Everyone peered closely and then shook their heads. Heep said, "That's what I thought. I could not see anything significant. Only Nancy thought the color of the grass in these shots was weird, but then again she's only interested in color balance." He indicated three shots of the head of a bushbuck moving in the marsh. The shots were out of focus.

Ube said, "Just after this, there was a loud noise—maybe ten minutes later when we were seeing the leopard."

Pero peered closely at the images. The head of the bushbuck appeared almost glowing. He couldn't see what Nancy was talking about. He decided to find out. He opened his door, went across the corridor, and knocked, asking, "Nancy, can you give me a hand here?"

Nancy followed Pero into his room and over to the coffee table. Pero asked her what was strange about the shots. She was apologetic. "Really, it's nothing. I was asked if I saw anything unusual. See, the shadow here and here?" She pointed. "The sun is behind the camera. See how it illuminated the grasses? So why is there a glow coming from behind the bushbuck's head? It looks yellow. Weird."

Pero asked Heep, "Can I see the digital image? Let's blow this up."

Heep ran and got his laptop, selected the images while walking back, and when he put the laptop on the table, he said, "Zooming in . . ."

When the bushbuck's head filled the frame, they all saw it—yellow paint with part of the letter Z. "That must be a

Z from Zanzi-Agroforestry. One of their damn trucks." Pero asked Heep to move around the image, see if there was anything else. When he moved to the left they saw the bottom of another letter. "Can't be," Pero said. "It's upside down. It's a letter A. Heep, pan to the right. There should be no more letters." Pero flopped down on the couch. "What the hell? They crashed the truck off the road? It's upended. You would have heard that. And who would give a damn? Ube, how far off the road were you?"

"About two hundred yards, Mr. Pero. But where that is, is deep mud off the raised road."

"Okay, let's figure this thing out. Bob, you would have heard a truck crash from that distance, right?" Bob said he was sure they would. "Okay, the truck had crashed long before you got there. So what were they worried about and what did you hear?"

Heep suggested, "Maybe what you heard was the truck being put back upright?"

Pero nodded. "That seems likely, but how? Those trucks are massive. It would take a crane—"

Bob interrupted, "Nah, man. I've seen this in Pennsylvania. You get a heavy tractor-trailer stuck in the mud, even turned over, then you get a bigger truck, put on a four-inch nylon cable about three hundred yards long between the two trucks. Rev and run the solid truck full tilt; the rope stretches, energy builds up, and suddenly the stuck truck flips right out of five feet of mud like a rocket."

Pero asked to see the images of the leopard on the screen. "Quick, blow that up, Heep." He did so. Heep panned back and forth, and suddenly there it was—barely seen through the branches of the tree—another truck's cab, the very top, and standing on top . . . *A white man*, Pero thought. *All this because*

one white guy far off in the distance thought they got his picture?
"Heep, what resolution is the scan we're seeing?"

Heep said, "About a fifteenth of the quality of the film, Pero. That's a ten-meg file. If I had a professional scanner with those Kodachrome slides? I could get one hundred and fifty megs. We might see who that is, Pero, we just might."

"Damn, so that's why they lifted Ube. He was on a camera safari, and there might be film. The noise you heard? The flipping of an overturned truck. And it explains why those two goons were in the lobby, to see if there was police activity with the film. We need to move fast now. Heep, call Gibson Nabana and get him to lock up that original film. Then use my phone and call Lewis." Heep started to protest. "No, Heep, I have to get other things done. So, call Lewis and tell him to arrange an embassy courier to collect the film from Gibson and get it to—hell, I don't know—whatever is nearest, maybe the Navy in Mombasa. Every fleet has top-notch spy equipment for photography. We will need to know what we're looking at. It may be what Lewis is looking for, too. And for God's sake, tell him we're giving him this help for whatever it is he has planned later. Use those words. But for now, we need to know what that film says for our safety."

Pero felt sure it was time to move, and move fast. There were two factors for him. One was the real time-lag concern for the hours it would take for the hijacked train to roll slowly from Dar to the mill. He had seen the train lumbering along, seemingly in no hurry. Freight by rail did not hurry anywhere in the world. In discussing this with Tone and Mbuno, the best guess was a ten- to twelve-hour trip from Dar. That meant they had to identify the next train, climb aboard, and take control. The next train, not the one after. If the train was on a daily schedule ... *It would mean it leaves Dar around five a.m., tomorrow morning. There's so little time ...*

The other worry was that he had no idea why one white guy's face could be so provocative. Simply not knowing, and seeing his opponents' reaction by resorting to kidnapping, coupled with the presence of Boko Haram, meant the whole damn business was a powder keg. Pero felt that speed was their only real hope for success now.

Meanwhile, he also had to make plans for protecting the arrival of the train in Kigoma, if they managed to hijack it in the first place. So, his next contact was with Virgi Singh, a friendly call on an open line, asking Virgi to have lunch with him that same day in Dar. Obliquely he added, "It would be great to see your brothers at the same time."

Virgi responded, "Would it be so? Great, you say? I see, I see. I do not think they will come to lunch with such short notice ..."

"It would be really great to see them, really great, too, if we could relive our fishing trip ... and I need to get special"—he emphasized the word *special*—"permits for a shoot as well."

"I see, I see. Well then perhaps if it is another great story time again. Why don't you come to my private office, and we'll go to lunch from there. Shall we say one o'clock?" Pero said thank you and hung up. He was pleased Virgi understood the fishing reference. Several years before, Virgi's fishing boat had been attacked by pirates. The Marlin trophy in his office was a fake, put there to commemorate the "fishing" trip that almost ended in tragedy after a deadly firefight with sea bandits.

Moments later, again on an open line, Pero called Sheila at Mara Airways, who confirmed the plane was back, waiting. He said he'd be there within the hour, to make a flight plan for Dar es Salaam—a wait and return flight. She said the plane would be ready.

If anyone was listening, he thought, *it was just a normal producer's life, going to Dar to secure permits.*

Niamba was in her room, making sure Ube was healthy enough to go. He had thrown up breakfast but assured Niamba it was because he had never had orange juice before.

In Heep's room, Mary had used Pero's phone to call Jimmy Threte in North Carolina, getting him moving as quickly as possible. Heep, meanwhile, was compiling a shopping list with Tom and Nancy for which supplies to buy: "So that makes it four video cameras, all digital; four tripods; twelve sets of batteries and chargers; and, above all, six reflectors. We have to assume we'll video outdoors because the lighting at Oasis is poor." Nancy added regular batteries to the list, plenty of them, in case the generator at Oasis was out of action. Heep continued, "Okay then, now we pack up. Tom, go ask Pero about transport."

Tom went next door, interrupting Pero's conversation with Bob, Mbuno, Tone, and the brothers. They had tourist maps and Tone's car map open on the table and were having a heated discussion. Tom asked Pero for transport to Loiyangalani for early afternoon. "By the time we've finished shopping and packing up, we could leave here around four. So let's say Wilson Airport at five, five-thirty."

Pero looked at his watch, "Okay, but I suggest you split up. Start getting equipment to Wilson and Mara Airways as soon as possible; they'll handle loading. I don't know what plane they have . . ." He hesitated, "No, wait, you take the four-fourteen; I'll have Sheila give me something smaller. I'm going to Dar for lunch. But whatever you do, you need to be airborne by five to land in last daylight at seven-thirty. Let Wolfie know."

As Tone and Mbuno continued discussing their plans, Pero reached for the satellite phone and called Sheila, asked for a change in the flight plan, with the Cessna 414 leaving to Loiyangalani when everyone was on board, but not later than five. "Also, please find me a plane to go to Dar, leaving within the hour. I need to get there by one." Sheila said it would have to be an older Piper Aztec, twin engines, plenty of range and speed. She would get customs working right away for clearance. Pero thanked her and rang off.

The last planning concern was how to protect the train as it entered and then left the mill compound. Mbuno had the answer—using the lake crossing again. Hearing this as he disconnected the call, Pero said that once was enough; the risk of swimming again was too great, especially as there may not be elephant around. Mbuno gave a little laugh. "I agree. I was thinking raft." Tone said he had an inflatable at his house in the garage. And so they pressed on with planning.

Finally, Mbuno seemed to approve the whole plan. "Keriako goes to Loiyangalani. Nancy, Ube, and Bob with Pero. Teddy with me." He looked at Tone. "You and Mr. Pritchett fly separately."

Tone agreed and then changed topic, saying to Pero, "That leaves you, Bob, Nancy, and Ube—and perhaps Mr. Singh—on the train? A lot of people to hide on a train, especially when you add all the girls and the four of us when we're leaving the area around the compound. Got any ideas?"

Pero did but wasn't ready to commit to anything yet. It all depended on if the train was scheduled to go there for a pickup or not. If it was, would he let the mill load the giant logs that were headed to Kigoma on the coast of Lake Tanganyika? If the train wasn't scheduled to go to the mill . . . Pero had too much to figure out and so little time to do it. He answered to the friends gathered in the room, "The earlier we can get in, the safer it will be. Speed is everything, I feel." Everyone seemed to agree. "That means we need to be ready when the train arrives late tomorrow afternoon. I'll figure that timing out, but I need more intel first from Dar. Gotta go, running late."

And of course, he thought, as he rushed around the room getting his passport and papers ready for the trip to Dar, *I hope having a woman who speaks Hausa will work with these terrified girls.*

When Tone asked Pero to confirm the expected arrival of the train, Pero's earliest estimate was the next day in the late afternoon, which again prompted Tone to do the arithmetic of the travel time. "Lord, we have no time left to dawdle." Tone looked at Mbuno, who nodded. Tone simply said to Pero, "We need to leave, and leave now. Mbuno, Teddy, and I. We'll rendezvous with Pritchett. Can I call him using your phone?"

Pero handed him the phone and turned to Mbuno. "How are you getting there? Why do you have to leave immediately?"

"We have a plan. It was the idea of Teddy. It is a good plan. We need to pick up many things. It is a long drive."

Tone concluded his quick call to Pritchett. He explained that they were going to split up. Mbuno would keep Tone's Land Rover and make the drive with Teddy. "All my safari permits are in the vehicle, and Mbuno is licensed as a safari driver. He'll say he's delivering it to Moyowosi Reserve if stopped. I am sure that's in order as we have permits from the last safari." Tone went on, quickly, as he went around Pero's room, picking up the notes and tourist maps they had been drawing on. "Pritchett and I are getting a friend, Robert, to fly us in his small private plane, a one-eighty-two." He meant a Cessna 182, a single-propeller bush plane. "Robert will drop us at Moyowosi early in the morning when it will be dim and misty, and we'll depart immediately." As they started leaving the room, he explained over his shoulder on the way to the elevator that they would jump off the plane as it turned around at the end of the field. The pilot would pull up to the hut, wait for a few moments to see if anyone challenged the empty plane, pretend to get a radio call to go elsewhere, and depart.

Mbuno added, "The Land Rover should still be where we left it in the forest."

Tone added, "Right. We load the raft, drive to the edge of the lake avoiding any logging trucks, and wait for Mbuno to make contact."

When the elevator doors opened, Mbuno ushered Tone and Teddy in. Turning to Pero, he said, "We will be there, Pero. We come another way."

Tone held the door. "Don't worry about us, Pero. We'll stake out a vantage point on the hillside on the other side of the mill. Easy to stay outside the fence and make our way around. Once you get the train in, load up, and then start to take the train out. We'll circle and hop aboard as you trundle past the mill entrance."

Pero asked Teddy and Mbuno, "And you two?" The Waliangulu and Okiek looked at each other knowingly.

Tone responded for them as he released the doors, "Better you do not ask Pero. They are deadly with poison arrows."

CHAPTER 25

Dar es Salaam, Tanzania

The Piper Aztec was indeed old. The pilot seemed unfamiliar with some of the controls, but Pero gave him a hand with the preflight checklist, and soon they were in the air, if a little late. The twin Continental engines roared in the high altitude, but all the instruments looked good to Pero.

Halfway to the border, the right engine quit. The pilot tried restarting it. "I left it a little lean, I think, saving fuel." The engine would not restart.

Pero realized that they were losing altitude. The pilot suggested they find somewhere below in the Tsavo National Park to set down. Pero asked a simple question, "Are you used to Continentals?" The pilot asked why. "The restart procedure you were using is for Lycoming, not Continental." Pero reached for the Aztec written instructions for engine restart. "Allow me?" The pilot, embarrassed, nodded. Pero followed the written instructions—throttle position, mixture, magnetos on, then blade pitch—and the engine caught the first time and ran steady. "Now, let's not save fuel. Make these two run a little rich and let's make it to Dar, okay?" The pilot was clearly ashamed. He agreed and apologized—rather handsomely, Pero thought. To put him at ease, Pero said, "That's okay. Happens to all of us." *Well, not really,* he thought. *Forced landing in a boulder-strewn national park is hardly normal.*

Pero settled back in the right-hand seat and appeared to doze off. It showed the pilot that Pero had confidence, and, more important, it gave Pero the headspace to continue planning. His main concern was still the Singhs. Why weren't they stopping the trafficking of drugs in their own country? That was not like Madar or Virgi, not to mention their brother, the Justice Minister, Amar. Pero knew that the Singhs were combative, feisty, brave, and, above all, patriots—all through pre-unification, during the communist period, and afterward in the current democratic government. Pero hoped lunch would provide answers and support.

Dar es Salaam was mainly a fishing and import-export port. It always had and still retained the smells and feeling of hugging the Indian Ocean. For millennia, Dar had welcomed sailors plying their trade all along the coast of Africa and across the vast Indian Ocean to the coast of India, trading in silk, spices, myrrh, gold, iron, foodstuffs, and fish. The harbor welcomed the deepwater fishery boats before sunrise, their exotic catch offloaded and sold on the docks and gone by nine. Then came the freighters—cranes dropping cargo into nets or pallets onto the slippery, fish-scaled docks—trucks pulling up, men arguing over prices, cash money being exchanged, trucks loaded, shouts and hailed greetings and farewells as the hustle and bustle continued. By noon, the docks were deserted, cleared out, some washed down. Mostly everyone escaped the midday heat for food and *kupumzika mchana.* (Afternoon nap.)

Of course, since unification with Zanzibar, the old Tanganyika capital of Dar es Salaam had also modernized. There was a massive new docking area off to the north of the old harbor suitable for floating tourist hotels, complete with shops and vendors of every description, colorful wares flapping in the ocean breeze. Even farther to the north of the new docking area was a peninsula where all the wealthiest lived and where the embassies demonstrated their importance by their superior sea view. True to its communist past, those countries without acceptable politics were relegated to inland acres with no view at all. The one-story US embassy off Bagamoyo Road, with extensive grounds mainly for defensible sight lines, was painted white against the heat, maintained razor wire fences, and looked out onto the rear servants' entrances of other buildings.

At the very heart of Dar near St. Joseph Cathedral on Kivukoni Road, facing the old harbor, was a one-block-long, glass-fronted Toyota dealership. It was the only Toyota dealership in a country dependent on the utilitarian and reliable nature of such vehicles. With import duty, sales tax, and other government add-on costs, the price of these vehicles was double the price for the same model in the US. The success of Toyota in Tanzania was due to one man, Virgi Singh. He made a deal with the government that said that until the truck or car was sold, it was technically not yet in the country. That allowed him to have stock and availability when his competitor car dealers, Nissan and Mitsubishi, had to prepay and finance all the taxes beforehand, which limited the number of vehicles they could afford to have in the country. Virgi Singh had a vast stock with every color and every modification ready to be sold. Toyota gave him a monopoly, and he made sure Toyota sold ten cars for every other marque combined. Virgi Singh was a powerful and well-connected man.

Pero's taxi dropped him off at the seaport on Kivukoni Road as he had asked. He waited for the taxi to leave and checked to make sure that no one else had followed them. The Julius K. Nyerere Road in from the airport was down to one lane, cars being forced to keep moving, and it would have been possible to tell, in the midday traffic, if there was anyone following. Satisfied, Pero crossed the road and went into the showroom. A startlingly beautiful woman greeted him, looked at a paper she had on a clipboard, and said in Oxford English, "Welcome, Mr. Baltazar, sir. Mr. Singh is expecting you. Please come this way." Pero followed, listening to the sharp click of her stiletto heels on the marble floor. At the elevator, she pressed the button, stood aside, and waved him in when the doors opened. "Have a pleasant lunch, Mr. Baltazar." Pero stepped in and the elevator rose to the top floor, only one floor up.

As the doors opened, the short, plump Madar Singh was waiting, revolver in hand, pointed at Pero's chest. Pero stepped forward and raised his hands. Madar frisked him swiftly. Then, putting the small pistol away, he pulled a box from his pocket, pressed a button, ran the box up and down Pero's right side, and repeated the procedure on the left. Satisfied, he smiled. "Welcome to Dar, Pero. I may call you Pero, may I not?" Pero nodded. He continued, "So glad to see you again. You gave me the slip last time, but I am forced to admit the outcome was most fortuitous, most fortuitous. For us all."

"May I ask why the gun and the little . . . what was that thing?"

"This?" He pulled the box from his pocket and showed it to Pero. "If you had, what do you call it, a wire on you, I would have known." He still had not offered his hand, and that made Pero nervous.

Pero asked, "What is the problem? Why the need to frisk me? And is Virgi here? If not, I'm leaving."

"Leaving? I am afraid not. Until we have some answers on what you were doing in Moyowosi . . ." He paused. "Such a vicious, short, little trip, don't you think?" Again, he paused. "Well, officially, you are supposed to be under arrest."

"For what?"

"Come now, don't let's play games, Pero. You and I know you are most resourceful and have connections in Washington. You see, people are dead, complaints have been made, a company has formally filed for an investigation." They were still standing next to the elevator. He looked at Pero intently. "Until I find out the truth, you are, shall we say, our guest. So, come, people are waiting." He turned and led the way, opened a door, walked down a corridor, and knocked twice on a paneled door.

The door opened and Commissioner Singh's brother, Virgi, extended his arms and gave Pero a hug. "We are safe here, Pero. Now we can talk freely." He nodded down the corridor Pero had walked. "Cameras recording everywhere. In case anyone ever asks why we allowed you in here, they can see my brother arrested you." Pero was confused. He knew Virgi's palace, as the Toyota dealership building was often referred to, was one hundred percent under Virgi's control.

As the thick paneled door latched shut, Pero spotted the third brother rising from an easy chair. He extended his hand. "Mr. Baltazar, it is a pleasure to meet you. I am Amar Singh, the only one here with official power to do anything." He saw Pero's eyebrows raise up. "Yes, this is all very strange. The truth is, there are problems. It is why we are being careful." He turned to Madar. "My little brother here likes you very much—trusts you with his life—so you can't be all bad . . ."

he laughed. Pero looked at Madar who was beaming and nodding. "What we need to know is what you know. And, I am afraid we need your help."

Pero had not expected giving anyone help; he had come to ask for it. He looked at Virgi. "Does the pact we made still stand?"

Amar asked, "What pact would that be?" Pero looked at Virgi, hoping he would explain.

"Brother, you remember the fishing incident?" His brothers nodded. "Well, we shot a few of the pirates, and I swore Pero to secrecy in the national interest. What he didn't know—but we found out, if you remember—was that it was part of a coup since attacks on you both were planned at the same time. I made a pact with a promise to help Pero if he ever needed assistance in return for his helping to stop the attack on me."

Amar said, "Yes, I see, that is reasonable." He turned to Pero. "And why do you want to know if the pact is still in place? Seems to me you had that help from Madar last time you were in Pangani..."

"No, I didn't. I ran with my crew from Pangani because Madar here was using us as bait to flush out al-Shabaab agents in Tanzania. I could not wait to also help him. I had to stop the attack in Nairobi, if you remember." Pero was getting angry; this was not like the Singhs.

"Ah, yes, seems I heard about that." Amar looked at Virgi and Madar. Turning back to Pero, he said, "And what do you want?"

Pero thought quickly. Three times since arriving he had felt the cold hand of danger in the room. The Singhs were wary of his presence when they should not be. He thought they were friends. Also, they had mentioned Moyowosi casually, yet they knew people had died. And then there was the revelation that the boat shoot-up was actually part of a coup. Just to use that word now, in his presence, told Pero that things were boiling over and that Zanzi-Agroforestry might be playing a larger hand. Last but not least, Pero reminded himself that he and Mbuno had instinctively theorized about a possible "coup" the previous day.

Pero raised his arms, saying, "Okay, I give up. You guys want to play games, go ahead. I'll go and leave you to it. But just know this"—he looked at Virgi—"I helped save you all those years ago and would do it again, unless you don't want my help. I know things, and I suspect you guys and this whole country are in trouble, but if you want to play games, forget it."

Amar sat back in his easy chair, motioned Virgi to sit next to him and told Madar to sit as well. That left Pero standing. Amar looked at Pero, and Pero could see he was making up his mind. "Okay, Mr. Baltazar, let's have lunch." He pointed to the free chair completing the circle around a coffee table laden with English high tea triangle sandwiches. Pero went over and sat. Amar said, "What you say makes sense."

Pero watched Virgi take a sandwich and start to eat. Madar took a glass of water and sipped. Both looked concerned. Pero thought, *Damn, they look like they are waiting for an execution.*

Amar continued, "Now, if we are going to share information properly, please, you start—ask us whatever it is you came to ask, but one item at a time, please." Amar pushed his fingertips together, almost as if in prayer, and awaited Pero's response.

Pero started with, "Do you know anyone who speaks Hausa?" Madar spat out his mouthful of water.

"Hausa? Hausa?" Madar was almost screaming. "What in Shiva's name does Hausa have to do with anything at Moyowosi?"

Amar took control. "Little brother, I suspect Mr. Baltazar was trying to shock us." He turned to Pero. "That is right, isn't it? Hausa is a ruse?"

Virgi saw Pero's face and knew it wasn't. He reached over and put his hand on Pero's knee. "I agree, Pero. If the word you just used is part of the problem we have here, then let us stop playing games. Tell us all, now, quickly." Pero was unsure, and Virgi suspected as much. Virgi said, "I can tell you this, a coup seems to be in the planning. Zanzi-Agroforestry is making very serious money selling tobacco to the Chinese. It gives them political power in the new Tanzania." He meant Tanzania no longer had a communist egalitarianism power structure. Money was beginning to rule the country. He went on, "And gold has come into the country. Bribery is everywhere, and word has reached us that rebels, maybe a small army, are being allowed by the minister from the region you were in. Moyowosi is in Tabora province. The Minister for Internal Affairs is the nephew of our country's founder, Julius Nyerere. His name is Stephan Nyerere. He has a powerful name with all the regional tribes. He is also Madar's boss." Pero looked at Madar, who nodded. "Now, your turn." Then Virgi added, "Please."

I have to trust that these are the same two men whom I trusted before . . . Pero thought. And so, he began to tell them the whole story, including the rescue of Ube and the presence of Boko Haram speaking Hausa, but not what he and Mbuno had seen in that first room. Virgi and Madar were shocked. Amar sat still, hands in the prayer position, eyes half shut, meditating.

It was Madar who spotted the missing part of the story. "You rescued your man. Your people are safe. Why are you here?" He looked intently at Pero and thought he spotted further concern. "You saw something, something that makes you come to us? What? Why?"

All three men watched Pero. Pero responded, "Mbuno and I saw something we cannot forget or allow. In the first room, three windows wide, there were twenty to thirty girls, half-dressed, young women, in what looked like school uniforms. We coupled that with the Boko Haram presence and added it up. The girls need rescuing."

This was shocking news to Amar. "In Tanzania? In Tabora province? How could this happen? It is an outrage!"

Virgi calmly asked, "How do you propose to do that? Those are armed men, Boko Haram—"

Pero interrupted, "Did you already know Boko Haram were in your country? And if so, why didn't you do anything about it?"

Madar responded, "Even I have to take orders, Pero. I was prevented from investigating when we arrested a Nigerian at the port in Kigoma, off-loading a crate we found to be full of guns, machine guns. He only spoke Hausa, and I suspected he was Boko Haram. I could not prove it."

"The guns, AK-47s?"

"Yes, like the one you saw, I presume. The man was most violent when we arrested him. He has since been released by the local police chief who is friends with the minister."

Pero had a question. "Was the guy working for Zanzi-Agroforestry? And, by the way, who owns Zanzi-Agroforestry?"

Amar looked at his brothers and, receiving their nods of approval, explained, "When Tanganyika became free of the German colonial overlords, certain families—ex-German families to be sure—vowed one day to take the country back. They relocated to Zanzibar at the time. Later on, when unification came about, they left Zanzibar quite angry, or very angry, I would say. We confiscated their houses and property. Some went back to Germany, East Germany, as you call it. Recently, some of those families have returned with considerable wealth and now sit on the board of Zanzi-Agroforestry."

Madar continued, "The man I arrested had no work papers. He did have a piece of paper with a phone number on it. I called the number. It was Zanzi-Agroforestry's number in Kigoma. So you see, we had no knowledge of the mill and Boko Haram there."

Virgi came back to his question. "Pero, how do you propose to rescue these girls?"

"I plan to hijack a train going to the mill. Go in, rescue the girls, and take them to safety. I have arranged transport with the CIA if we get them out. What transport exactly, I do not know yet. They are waiting for me to tell them what I need." Pero was being absolutely frank. Then he remembered Niamba's prediction about the Dar policeman who would accompany them. "And I guess you'll be coming along, too, Madar."

Madar's mouth opened, shut, and then he glared at Pero. Everyone was silent. "And why do you think I will be coming along?"

Beyond Niamba's prediction, it now made sense. Madar would be the only Singh who could be free, could represent the brothers, and, as he was a commissioner of police, would carry authority. "Let me put this another way," Pero said. "Besides rescuing the girls, which would make you a national hero, maybe an international hero, it could give you a power base, politically."

Ever the politician, Amar was nodding. "And you might find out where all the money is and where it is going to. The Russians may be sending the gold, but they are not giving it away. They are buying drugs. What and where, we do not know. If we can link—"

Virgi cut him off. "The link has to be there. We know it is cocaine because of the plants grown, but we cannot trace how it is being exported. We know it is not coming back through Dar."

Pero had an idea. "Look, you told Heep on the phone about the tobacco farms, and the CIA knows that the only transport leaving the mill is cut lumber to Dar . . ."

Madar said, 'We have searched those stacks—nothing."

Pero was guessing, too. "Okay then. That leaves the giant logs going to Kigoma. It must be hidden between the logs, or on the flatbed train cars under the logs. Maybe when we get there, we'll see how it is being done."

Madar agreed. "We have been prevented by the same police chief from examining the flatcars in Kigoma. But we know what happens to the logs; we watched them being unloaded in case something else was hidden there. Nothing. The crane picks them up, one at a time, loads them onto a barge on the lake. Then the flatcars travel back to the mill, get loaded with cut wood that is then offloaded in Dar and put on freighters to South Africa. The South African police have searched the freighter twice for us. Nothing."

Pero thought for a moment. "There was a customs story I remember. Every day a Mexican kid rode his bicycle with two watermelons in the front basket through into the US. Every day they saw him come through, waving him on. What harm could he do, selling watermelons? What he was smuggling was bicycles." He gave a little chuckle, as did the brothers. "So, where do the flatcars go?"

Madar answered, "The Siagwa-Bagir is a Chinese freight company. It's their freight system, and they shunt them in a holding train yard. Every day the train leaves the yard with six or eight flatcars attached and goes to the mill. It passes the returning train at Tabora. When the flatcars are in the depot? We have looked, carefully. Again nothing."

"So, it has to be the one thing you have not searched," Pero said. He waited. "The logs."

"How?"

"No idea, but if we have them loaded, we'll have time to find out on the way to Kigoma."

Amar turned to his younger brother. "Madar, you must inspect the logs on the way to Kigoma." Madar agreed.

Pero said, "Okay then, if we hijack the train tomorrow morning, you say there is one going to the mill from Dar early . . . well, we'll let them load the train, and then we'll find out where and how they are smuggling the cocaine resin."

Madar was suddenly inquisitive. "What makes you think it is resin?" Pero realized he hadn't told them what Ube was poisoned with. He explained, and Madar smacked his hands on his knees. "That's why! The dogs can't detect cocaine powder if there is no powder! They are exporting resin, maybe the cocaine curds mixed with kerosene. The dogs are trained to smell the sulfuric acids used to turn it into powder."

Amar said, "But that's ten times the quantity, ten times the volume. Why take the risk?"

Pero thought he had the answer. "Two years ago, we did a shoot in Colombia with small cocoa farmers. The acid boiling and drying processes are different. Small holdings can boil it after adding acid to break the cocoa leaves down into the paste or resin that they mix with kerosene to stabilize for transport, but to dry it into powder takes sophisticated chemical labs, away from prying eyes. I think they're extracting the paste or resin here, shipping that out, and it is being processed elsewhere."

Amar added, "But the gold comes here and funds criminal activity. And if Minister Nyerere has his way with even more privatized tobacco farming cooperatives, they could refine the cocaine here in hidden factories, increasing profits, giving him more money from the Russians. And the only way he can do that is to overthrow the law. Bastards."

Pero agreed, "A coup." The three brothers sadly also agreed. Pero knew then for sure that they were the same reliable, trustworthy, patriotic Singh brothers he had come to respect. He also knew that although they were determined to stop the corruption and a possible coup, they were frightened.

"Fellows," Pero began, "we'll all have to pull together to make this work. I have a team in place . . ." and he explained who was helping and the plans they had started. He asked Madar if he still had his Interpol satellite phone. Madar pulled it from his pocket. "Good, then we have secure communication. We have a plan, of sorts, and surprise is on our side."

It was Madar who concluded their meeting, saying, "It seems I am taking a train trip."

Leaving the Toyota dealership, Pero called Sheila, told her to get the Piper Aztec back to Wilson Airport, and then Pero settled back in the Singh's chauffeur-driven limo to the Julius Nyerere International Airport, where he took the afternoon jet commuter to Nairobi's Jomo Kenyatta International Airport. He had called ahead, and the Interconti had sent a driver. He was back at the hotel in time to say goodbye to Susanna, Heep, Mary, Keriako, and Tom who assured Pero they were ready and would be standing by with Wolfie before nightfall.

Susanna's last words to Pero were, "I love you, *mein dummer* . . ." Then she threw up in the gutter next to the car taking them to Wilson Airport. Mary told Pero she'd be fine. Pero kissed Susanna's cheeks and watched them go.

Back in his room, Pero called and reached Tone, who was already on the road. Pero wanted to confirm the small plane arrangements Tone had made. Tone was circumspect. "Sorry, Pero, you have to trust me on this old boy. It's a friend, you see; I don't want names mentioned."

Pero wanted to know if they had everything they needed. Tone pressed the cellphone loudspeaker button and the sounds of the Land Rover straining diesel came across the airwaves. Earlier, Pero had handed Tone his satellite phone, saying, "I'll use Madar Singh's." Pero wanted to make sure Tone had it with him. "In case we get separated, use the satellite phone. Okay?"

Mbuno and Tone assured him they had it and were ready. They also vouched for Teddy, who looked keen and eager. Pero wanted to be sure they understood the plan. "When the train starts leaving, no matter what, get on the train. You have to get on the train or you will be stranded and we won't know where you are. Agreed?"

Mbuno answered for them all, "Pero, my brother, you rescue the *wasichana*. We will protect and then we leave."

An hour later, Pero, Ube, Nancy, and Bob were driven back to the airport by the Interconti driver. Pero decided to keep their rooms to create the illusion that they were coming back.

The regular commercial Kenya Airways flight to Dar landed at nine-thirty, and Virgi picked them up in his Toyota extended cab truck. "I have arranged for you to stay at my house tonight, most private. My staff thinks I am away, and I have given them the day off. Then Madar will pick you up tomorrow morning at four to go to the freight yard. You must try and sleep."

When they got to the house, there were no servants. Pero thanked Virgi adding, "Where are you sleeping?"

"There will not be much sleeping tonight. Amar is planning what you call a counter-offensive, ready if you are successful." Pero suspected Virgi was going to add "or not" but then thought better of it. He continued, "What you have found out, deep inside our country, is intolerable, and that treason will be used to secure the loyalty of many in Parliament. We will be busy this night." Virgi prepared to leave, but not before handing Pero the front door keys. "Be sure to lock when you depart. Leave the keys in my brother Madar's car, if you wouldn't mind."

"Wait a moment . . . did you have any luck with the extra caboose or guard's van for the train? We have to put these girls somewhere."

"My staff is making other arrangements. It will be"—he paused, looking for the right word—"suitable, if not comfortable."

Pero was content at that and shook his hand. "Want to wish us luck?"

"It is not luck we all need, it is strength. These are serious times. Our country is at risk." And with that he drove away. Pero went back inside and made sure everyone found somewhere comfortable to rest. Pero slept on the sofa in the front hall, wanting to be near the door.

CHAPTER 26

Dar es Salaam, Four a.m.

The banging on the door dragged Pero from a fitful sleep. He opened the door to near pitch black. Two potted palms framed the open doorway. Between them stood the squat, rounded figure of Commissioner Madar. He was looking furtively right and left. He softly asked if they were ready.

Pero heard a noise behind him and turned to see Nancy, awake and ready. Then Bob appeared, flipping on the hall light, hopping while trying to tighten a sandal's strap. Turning further, Pero spotted Ube standing, ready, silent. Pero wondered how long he had been standing there.

Pero made introductions, and Madar said softly, still looking around, "Let us get going. I will explain developments on the way." He raised his hand as he walked toward the police SUV parked outside the property gates. In his hand was his satellite phone.

Madar drove the SUV quickly, lights flashing, but no siren. He said they were not headed for the main railway station. "All Tanzania Railway freight transport has to be assembled in the main station yard for departure. There it is checked and rechecked to prevent smuggling and theft. It is also a matter of timing for safety, to avoid collisions. I watched the locomotive already hooking up flatcars. So the planned departure is to be still at or near five. I do not think we can board the train at the station. If anyone is watching, it would be there. Already there are workers from all over Tanzania at the depot at this hour. When the train leaves Central Station, it will next be halted at Kiumbe Road. It is a crossing by the back road to Nyerere Airport. I have made sure there will be a truck blocking the crossing. We need to get on board there while it is still dark." Pero thought it was a clever plan and said so. Madar's determined expression, dimly seen and illuminated only by the instrument lights, reinforced Pero's feeling that the commissioner was not so sure. Madar added, "Yes, yes, let us hope the train driver is awake and brakes in time."

Madar had already reached the edge of town near the Julius Nyerere main highway. There were no cars at that early hour, so he turned off the police lights. With the windows open, the slightly stale and fetid air of the city gave way to the scent of the natural beauty of Tanzania. Green and lush, trees and plants alike filled the morning mist with their aroma that would soon fade away under the midday sun. Pero had only brought his Swiss Army knife, a halogen pencil flashlight, and a pair of binoculars with him. Bob had brought his medical kit. Nancy had a hunting knife she had smuggled the night before through airport customs by hiding it under her shirt. And Ube? Ube seemed unarmed but carried a small leather pouch that dangled from his waist belt. When Pero asked him what it was, he would only reply that Mbuno had given it to him and that Mbuno had asked Niamba to bring it from home.

Pero looked at the determined Madar and asked, "Okay there, Commissioner?"

"No, not really. I am breaking the law. If this goes badly, I may be out of a job, and Tanzania may be lost."

Ube, sitting behind Madar, put his hand on Madar's shoulder and said, "It is good. You do good. It cannot be wrong." Madar nodded.

Pero asked, "Any idea how many are on board the train in the driver's cab?"

Madar nodded. "We have been busy while you slept. Tanzania Railways Limited is now partly private, and Virgi's Toyota dealership shares some of the same board members. He called some colleagues after you left yesterday, and others he woke up late last night. We have made some arrangements without arousing suspicion. It seems there is a cargo of dried fish from Zanzibar recently arrived in port that has to go to an important client in Kigoma. It is a real client and a real shipment that happened to miss yesterday afternoon's train, which my brother made sure of. So, a boxcar has been added to the eight flatcars that the mill ordered for today's shipment. Virgi made sure it was a normal business arrangement."

Pero looked at Madar approvingly. "Well done. But will the boxcar be detached before the train enters the mill?"

"No, it is not possible. Some workers at the depot mistakenly hooked up the boxcar next to the locomotive. It seems that the side track that the mill is on, a spur line as you call it, requires the train to stop on the main line. Then the points—what Americans call *switches*—are thrown by the driver by hand, and he backs the train into the siding, all the way into the mill. The mill does the loading and securing of cargo as part of their contract. The locomotive moves back and forward as required to position each flatcar where the crane can deposit the logs. It takes them four or more hours to load the logs apparently. The train cannot rejoin the main line until at least ten at night when the track is clear. Last time the train driver said the men were lazy and took six hours to load the logs. Also, there is a signal, you know—red, yellow, green at the siding points—and the train cannot rejoin the main line if the light is not green. We have ensured there will not be a red light."

"Incredible. How'd you manage all this? And how'd you talk to the driver?"

"The train driver, the engineer as you call him, for today's freight had beers with my assistant who was disguised as an official of the company. He had said he hates going to the mill because they never let him leave the engine cab, don't even offer him a beer or chai. He even said they won't let him down to urinate so he has to carry extra plastic bottles."

Pero was more and more confident. "That means we don't have to hijack the train, yet. We'll let everything proceed as normal and, I presume, hide in the boxcar with the dried fish. Right?"

"That is my plan, yes. You have a better one?" Madar sounded a little testy.

"Nope. You did brilliantly. Thank you, Madar. Really great job." But Pero had to ask, "And I suppose the only popgun we have is your twenty-two?"

"Ah, thought you would never ask. Brave or foolish of you. Feel under your seat, there is a drawer . . . and you, Bob, in the back, feel behind the seat for a shotgun I keep there. There is also a box of shells." Pero felt the drawer, pulled it out, and extracted a Luger. Next to it was a box of nine-millimeter shells. Pero looked at Madar questioningly. "Left over from the war, the Great War. Found it when I was twelve. Quite good German engineering. Can you use it?"

In response, Pero took out and loaded the clip. Before he put it back in the grip, he cycled and dry fired the pistol.

Satisfied with the action, he inserted the clip. "Nice gun. For you?"

In response, Madar shook his head and opened his coat. He showed Pero he was wearing a shoulder holster with what looked like a cannon under his left armpit. "Python, powerful, American three-fifty-seven magnum." Pero nodded.

Sounds from the back seat told them that Bob was cycling the pump-action shotgun. Bob simply said, "Ready." For Pero, the armament did not give him comfort; it only made him more aware of the dangers they were facing. Then he remembered the faces of the girls and tightened his resolve. *Courage certainly does come in waves,* he thought.

Off to their left, paralleling the highway, Pero could see the glint of partial moonlight on steel rails. The road signs for the airport began to get more frequent, but at the last kilometer before the main passenger turn-off, Madar turned left and started down a paved but deserted road. Up ahead Pero could see there were lights.

Madar said, "Good, he is there. Now we go here . . ." and he yanked the wheel, skidding off the road to the left, bumping across open ground and dodging dumped rusty car carcasses and other trash. Pero saw an abandoned and leaning hut just ahead, its gaping roof caught in the headlights. Madar stopped the SUV to the right of the hut and said, "Now we're on foot."

Everyone got out. Madar made sure he put his brother's house keys in the glove compartment. Then he went around and manually locked every door, whispering, "Don't want the damn thing to beep." Gathering their gear, they marched single file, with Madar in the lead lugging a two-gallon water cooler toward the train tracks, a hundred yards to the east of the road they had been on. As they took up their positions, lying down next to the two-foot-high rail embankment, Pero could see that there was a large white delivery truck positioned across the tracks, and that the truck's driver was swinging a bright light in their direction, back and forth, back and forth, causing Pero to muse, *The train driver would have to be blind not to see that ... or asleep.*

There was no need for silence anymore, yet the men retreated into their own reverie. Suddenly, Bob asked, almost to himself, "Anyone ever jump a train, like a hobo? God, it's dangerous. You have to make sure you get a good grip with your hands and then find good footing."

Pero said, "Bob, the train should be stopped. We'll just get on and into the boxcar."

"Yeah, I know that's the plan, man, but if he don't stop, I'm getting on anyway. Better to be prepared."

Nancy offered, "I've done this before. He's right. Hands first, feet last. Maybe knees next. Get a firm grip; that's critical."

As it turned out, Bob was indeed right. At that moment, they saw the triangle of three lights on the oncoming locomotive to their left. To their right, another truck pulled up next to their decoy truck and was helping, shouting, and then pushing the stranded vehicle off the crossing. Madar's man did the best he could to make that job impossible. Even from where they were, in the reflected headlights, they could see the two drivers start fighting. But Madar's driver wasn't waving the warning light anymore, and the train wasn't applying brakes yet. *Damn, he is asleep ...* Then the train's horn sounded quickly, followed by the sudden screech of emergency brakes. The ear-ripping squeal nearly deafened the five prone hijackers as the locomotive rolled on, albeit more slowly, past them. Pero had to shout to be heard, "Now, let's get running, we have to get on!"

Even though Bob was carrying the water container, he was the first aboard the boxcar. While holding the metal rail next to the sliding door, he pulled the latch pin and kicked the door all the way open. He reached back and caught Nancy by her free hand, as she held the shotgun in the other, and swung her inside. Then Ube jumped on and dropped to his belly and extended his arms out the door to try and help Pero and Madar. Pero was urging Madar Singh along. The roly-poly man, as Mary had described him, was having trouble, his small feet slipping on the train gravel beneath him. But the train was slowing, and he caught up with the help of Pero who was pulling his hand, tugging him along. Ube let Madar pass and instead reached for Pero's jacket's shoulder material, grabbing a handful. When Madar got to Bob, he reached up and firmly grabbed the handrail. Bob grabbed his jacket collar and landed him like a fish on the deck of the boxcar. Pero leaped up as Ube flipped him up and over the boxcar sill, dropping him next to Madar.

Bob slid the door closed just as the train came to a halt. The men waited, wondering if they had been spotted. They could clearly hear yelling. They were close to the truck drivers. The argument abated, and then the train started up again. Smiling, Madar said, "My assistant will probably want a bonus for this."

Pero looked around. It was predawn dark. Truck lights were barely filtering through the sides of the boxcar, but he did not dare turn on his flashlight until they were clear of the outskirts of Dar. As the train sped up and they crossed roadways, the flashing red crossing-barrier lights shone through the old boxcar side planks, giving them enough light to stack crates of the dried fish and get comfortable. The old, pitted, planks of boxcar wood allowed sounds to seep in, and when Pero pressed his face against the wood sides, peering through cracks, he could see the crossings roll by. About forty minutes in, they passed through a station, brightly lit. Madar said, "Ruvu. Now we climb to Kilosa and then down to Dodoma."

In no time at all, Pero could see no more lights or houses, as the train started the steep and slow climb over the Mitumba Mountains. Pero lit his flashlight and checked to see that everybody was settled. Like a travelogue, Madar continued, "The Kaguru people live here. They are loyal." It seemed to Pero that Madar was conducting a census of who could be trusted if there was indeed a coup. Pero thought that even in modern-day East Africa, so much was still dependent on tribal loyalties.

Madar continued, "When we reach the top, it is a plateau for twenty kilometers, all Kaguru land."

Ube seemed to like the Kaguru people. "They are good people. They are a woman tribe." Bob asked what he meant. "The women are the bosses; they own the cattle."

The train rolled on and then seemed to speed up as they stopped climbing. "The plateau," Madar explained. When they reached Morogoro, Pero realized it was a major town, well-lit in the predawn. The train came to a complete stop at the station, and Madar and Pero whispered their fear that someone would open the freight doors—"to steal a little," was how Madar put it. Luckily, no one approached. All breathed sighs of relief when the train started up again. Madar passed the water cooler around, suggesting they keep hydrated. "It is going to get hot in here soon."

Pero asked for Madar's phone, extended the antenna through a crack in the wall slats, dialed, and Wolfie answered. Pero gave him an update and asked that Wolfie reach Tone and tell him they were in the boxcar. Ten minutes later, Pero turned the phone back on and called Wolfie to confirm. Wolfie gave him the good news. "Tone and Pritchett have linked up;

we have Pritchett's cell phone number. They are waiting for first light, but before sunrise, to fly. Mbuno and Teddy have already driven through Tabora—they called Pritchett on Tone's mobile, which Mbuno had kept. They are going south, and they will be approaching the mill from the south side, over a stone hill, they say. Tone agrees to join up with them there. He's going to go west on the lake, away from the mill, through marshes on the south side, and climb over the rocks to link up with Mbuno." Pero was delighted with the news and, on sharing it with his team in the boxcar, spirits rose.

The run to Dodoma was fast, mostly on the downgrade, and pretty. For three hours, light filtered in as the sun rose in the east. The track wasn't straight. Several times, some of the team fell off their crates as the train rattled and rocked its way across Tanzania, sometimes heading north, sometimes south, slowly making its way toward Tabora in the west.

Dodoma station again called a halt to the train's progress, but Pero could see they were past the platforms. "Probably waiting for a green to proceed." The curiosity caused Pero to shift his view from the side of the boxcar to the gaps in the slats at the front. What he saw there frightened him. There were two men on the platform at the rear of the locomotive. They were smoking and talking. One man had a bottle with clear liquid. The way they drank told Pero it was likely water. In a whisper, he explained this to his crew.

"There is no need to whisper, Pero. There is too much noise from the diesel engine." Madar was right, but still Pero felt nervous in case their voices carried and alerted the men.

"Who are they?" asked Bob.

Madar pressed his eye to the slat gap and had a closer look. "They are wearing TRC uniforms; they work for the railway. Here, take more water."

"Oh, deadheaders." Bob seemed relieved and then drank.

"What is this deadhead?" Madar asked.

"It's an expression for someone from a transport company, you know, like pilots or flight attendants, who are traveling to work or traveling home. They are likely to be dead tired and are not pleasure travelers." Bob seemed happy to have a normal conversation. The train journey was already monotonous and long, the calm before battle. Bob recognized the anticipation, the boredom factor he had felt in Iraq years before. He changed the topic back to avoid too much pre-battle nerves. "So those two are simply taking a ride to go to work somewhere or return home, right?"

Madar seemed to think so. On through the station of Manyoni, hour after hour, the two railroad employees stood or sat there on the locomotive platform, smoking, talking, or dozing off. It was only as they approached Tabora station that they seemed to become animated again, and as the train slowed, entering the Tabora siding to allow downgrade trains to pass, both men alighted onto the gravel, skipping along next to the still moving train. Pero watched through the side slats of the boxcar intently to make sure no one opened the door. The train came to a dead halt. The heat became instantly oppressive without the flow of air. Pero kept watch. For over an hour the train waited, ticking metal sounds punctuating the silence. Then the engine revved up again, and they heard a passing train on the other side. Pero climbed over boxes to peer out the left side, only to watch a locomotive and—he counted them as they passed—six flatcars loaded with lumber roll by. He whispered, "The cut lumber train from the mill."

Their train started rolling. They knew they had only two hours left before they reached the mill.

The approaching event started Pero's mind working on the complexity of the mill operation. He felt that the more he understood what they were doing, the more likely he would be able to improvise when they got there. Before he started talking, he checked to see if there were any more deadheaders. *Good. None.*

"Anyone besides me ever been to a sawmill, a lumber yard like this one?" he asked. Bob said he had, much smaller. The others shook their heads. Pero felt an inexplicable need to explain, perhaps even clarify his own knowledge. "Here's what happens—" Madar interrupted to ask what purpose his explanation had for their rescue. "Humor me," said Pero. "I have these hunches. Something is missing in our planning, and maybe we can talk it out."

"Very well, sorry."

"Okay. The logs are cut down miles away. They use the massive Volvo trucks to transport the cut logs to the plant, using the barge and winch across the lake. When the trucks arrive, they offload the logs, stack them, and, in daylight presumably because we didn't see the mill operating at night, they begin to saw the logs into planks. Some of the logs they do not slice up or cut up with the saw. Some are chosen, maybe because of species, to be uncut and loaded and exported to a client far away. Where?" Pero thought out loud. "Yeah, where?"

Madar had already found that out. "It is on the rail cargo manifest. From Kigoma they travel across the lake to Kalemi in Zaire, then by rail down through Zambia to Zimbabwe to Mozambique, where they are loaded onto a freighter at Beira."

"Do you know where the freighter takes them? What is the end destination?"

"I do not know." He picked up and waved his Interpol phone. "But I can find out. The shipping company, I do know. It is still Siagwa-Bagir."

Pero asked, "May I borrow that for a moment?" Madar passed it over. Pero extended the antenna and pointed it through a gap in the car's wooden side. He dialed the numbers he had memorized for emergencies. "Baltazar requesting patch to Lewis, urgent."

"Standby."

Moments later: "Where are you? Never mind. What phone is that?"

"It is Commissioner Singh's Interpol phone—remember him? And the speaker is on. I have a question that needs answering. Siagwa-Bagir, big cargo company, ships logs out of Tanzania, long train route, ending up in Beira onto a freighter, we presume."

Lewis cut in, "What is that background noise?"

"It is a train—stop asking. I need the destination of the freighter and logs, paramount importance. Also copy this, possible coup being mounted in Tanzania by nephew founder, one Stephan Nyerere using Russian gold being shipped in, possible connection, hiring mercenaries Boko Haram, all located at the mill site. With Madar Singh now, exploring realities." Pero thought that the word exploring would set Lewis's teeth on edge. "Will be at the mill shortly. Will keep you informed. Meanwhile, this phone will be with Singh. Urgent you get Siagwa-Bagir information ASAP."

"It won't take that long; it's on their website. Beira departures show freighter leaving ten days from now with what is manifested as raw lumber as a contracted load, bound for—now that's interesting—North Korea. It has been there, in port, loading whole trees, according to their port license, for three weeks. What's in this log business?"

Pero had the aha moment he had been waiting for. It had been tickling his memory for some while, and Lewis's comment of "what's in this log business" brought it to the fore. Pero smiled as he explained, "That's where the resin is, in the logs. Lewis, remember that German logging company in Bolivia that was hollowing out the Amazon logs and using the massive logs as smuggling containers for cocaine? That must be what they are doing here, too. Only they are smuggling cocaine resin for refinement later. Large quantities, too. I saw hundreds of bales of the leaves in a storeroom, waiting for processing, I guess."

Madar interrupted, "Our labs estimated that the number of cocaine plants that they have grown could produce over twelve tons of cocaine. But unrefined? Ten times that weight."

Lewis heard Madar and responded, "I was saying, the cargo manifest for that freighter leaving Beira says max cargo weight is one hundred thousand dry-weight tons. Assume half that is the ship's weight, that leaves a cargo-carrying capacity of fifty thousand tons. Hang on a moment." They heard Lewis asking someone to find out what a log weighed. "Any idea how big the logs are?"

Madar responded, "They are trees with the bark. Most are eucalyptus or Mutunguru, we have discovered. Bottom diameter about two meters, top about one and a half meters, twenty meters long each. The wood is very dense, heavy."

Lewis was relaying this to someone. "Okay, that's about sixty to seventy-five tons each. That means the ship can hold maybe six hundred and fifty to eight hundred trees. And if you are right about them being hollowed out, the weight of the cocaine resin would be less than the weight of the raw wood, so the load factor for the freighter is no problem."

Pero had one more question. "Lewis, find out who is paying for the freighter. That's your lion pride. Baltazar out." Pero thought, *As usual, Mbuno was right.*

The train seemed to be laboring up an incline, approaching the junction for the mill. Pero peered through the front slats. "When we stop, everyone must keep really quiet. The train driver will have to switch the points, passing this boxcar on foot twice. And once we're into the siding, he needs to reset the points, but he'll be ahead of us. And then he'll climb back into the cab and back the train down into the mill siding. Remember, we back into the mill. And that means the loco will be pushing and the driver will be watching this boxcar as he guides the flatcars on our other side into the mill. No movement—everyone on the floor behind boxes in case someone at the mill decides to check this car out. And remember, every time he's going to move the train as they load logs, he will have to be looking this way if we are going backward—we must remember that." The team seemed to understand and agree. "Okay then, I estimate a least four hours loading." He held up four fingers. "It'll be dark by the time they finish—that's good cover. Well, as good as we'll get."

Madar agreed but was still worried. "But the moon will not be up until midnight. Will we be able to see?" He meant inside the mill compound.

"Each occupied building has only a single bulb illumination, front and back. It was enough last time." Pero felt they needed a morale boost. "We'll be fine. There were no guards, no one really walking around. If it's late, they should all be asleep, except maybe the cooks that we saw arguing. We'll manage."

Ube added, his voice strong and determined, "*Ndiyo*, and if not, we will help them sleep." Ube was nearest the door, off to the left, and crouched down behind three fish crates. He waved at Pero.

Pero motioned Madar to sit next to him, both pistols drawn, facing the door from the opposite side of the boxcar.

Pero waved back at Ube and then waved over to Bob and Nancy who were all the way forward and barricaded behind crates stacked tall enough to hide a standing man. Bob gestured with his shotgun to make sure Pero knew he was ready. With that, Nancy and the men settled down behind boxes and crates, most reeking of fish, to wait.

They didn't have to wait long.

CHAPTER 27

Wanaotaka Kuna Ndovu—
Wishing There Were Elephants

The screeching of brakes was followed by the train coming to a complete halt on level ground. The diesel engine throbbed on idle as the cars rocked forward and back, the kinetic energy of the springs dissipating in the buffers. Soon after, they heard the crunch of gravel as the train driver walked back the length of the train to switch the points, allowing the train access to the mill siding train tracks. Five minutes later, they heard the crunch of gravel on the other side of the boxcar as the driver returned to the locomotive. About five minutes later, the diesel was powered up and the clanging of the cars being pushed reverberated through the floor of the boxcar, making all of the team acutely aware that their moment of truth was approaching.

The siding was a sharp, ninety-degree curve toward the south, followed a few miles later by another sharp bend to the west. The train slowed, sounding its horn three times. Clearly the gates to the compound were open because the train never stopped. It just kept slowing. Eventually there was a shout from somewhere, and the brakes were applied, bringing the train to a complete stop, the locomotive diesel left at idle. Another motor was heard, a straining diesel whose exhaust noise seemed to change direction. Pero thought it must be a crane, picking up and swinging a log. When he heard the crash of a log hitting the floor of a flatcar some distance behind them, it confirmed his assessment. *Sounds like they dropped it,* he thought, *and it is not the next flatcar, so they are loading from the back. Good, maybe . . .*

Abruptly, dispelling his thoughts, footsteps were heard outside, men talking. Pero put his lips to Madar's ear and whispered, "Translate?"

Madar listened. The muffled sound made it difficult. "He wants the driver to come out." Moments later they heard the driver being called, then men walking next to the boxcar, arguing. "They want to know why the boxcar. Wait . . . he is showing them something . . . ah, it is the manifest. They do not agree, they say it does not match their orders. Another man is coming . . ." They heard someone climb and put a foot on the lower step of the boxcar, just under the door. So quietly that Pero had to strain, he heard Madar continue translating, "He is told to wait. The new man asked for the papers . . . He says it is approved, that the fish is for a Kigoma friend . . . The man at the door wants to check. No, the man says, you want to steal. Lock the door." They heard the latch pin being slipped into place. They were locked in!

Pero whispered to Madar, "I guess we'll have to shoot our way out."

Madar shook his head. "Wait . . . they are still arguing. Someone else now." Pero heard the new, deeper voice. "Bad Swahili . . . telling one man to go back to the mill." Both Pero and Madar heard the cocking of a gun. Madar translated, "The new man said *ku tafi*. That is not Swahili." They both listened. Pero thought he heard footsteps going away.

Thankfully, night had fallen. Through the cracks in the sides of the boxcar, the glaring yellow intensity of the sodium lights that illuminated the mill allowed shadows to play across the boxcar crates as people and machinery moved outside. Pero wanted to sneak a peek but did not dare in case someone outside was looking in. He and Madar stayed still and silent. Between the bottom of the uppermost crate in front of him and the top of the next crate below it, there was a slit that allowed him to watch the doorway. He waited, intently.

Ten minutes later, he saw movement, a yellow glow obscured by a human form. A man was standing there. Another voice approached, said something, and the man outside the door laughed, saying, "*Kifi*." Pero looked at Madar, who shrugged in the near darkness. The new voice said something neither man could understand, but they heard the word *kifi* a few times. Then the door latch was pulled and a man gave a command, "*Kai kadai*." Madar nodded, and whispered, "Nigerian language, means 'only one,' I think." The door opened quickly. The man stepped in, lifted the nearest crate, and jumped out of the boxcar. The other person slid the door shut. The two were laughing, their voices quickly receding with their stolen treasure. Outside was silent except for the idling engine of the locomotive and the straining of what Pero felt was the crane diesel working as it loaded logs.

The noise made a pattern. Low roar, shouts from men, loud roar as the crane took the strain, change of direction of the roar, then low roar, a crash as the log hit the flatcar, more shouting, then a change of direction as the crane swung back to get the next log. Each log took less than two minutes. Pero did the mental calculation and thought each flatcar could only hold twenty logs. Eight flatcars made one hundred and sixty logs. *Each weighing, say, sixty-five tons—that's a total weight of ten thousand tons.*

Suddenly, after another crash of a log, there was shouting, and the locomotive went backward. Not far, just far enough, Pero assumed, for the next flatcar to be loaded. Madar had perhaps been making the same calculations. Madar was shaking his head as he whispered, "Only ten logs, half a load?" Pero had no explanation and simply shrugged.

With the door closed, the four men and one woman could do nothing but wait. As each flatcar was loaded, this time, Pero kept count. Madar was right—only ten logs were loaded onto each flatcar. Pero assumed the reason was overall weight and the pulling capacity of the locomotive, yet he knew that the route from the mill to Kigoma was mostly downhill.

There was nothing to do but wait. *Until we have to blast our way out.*

When the seventh flatcar was about to be loaded, everything suddenly went silent. Orders were being given. Madar heard the Swahili more clearly as the crane diesel had been shut down. "The man is not a habitual Swahili speaker; he's a *mzungu.*" (White man, a European.) "His Swahili is bad, but he is saying that this is the last load until the special logs. The mill men are being told to finish their shift, just this flatcar, and then clock out; their dinner will be ready. Tomorrow the mill starts operation at six when the claxon sounds. The special logs will be loaded by his people, *watu wangu.* That is the term he has used, his people." Madar sat back a little. "This man commands two workforces." The diesel crane engine started up, and the shouting began again in earnest, followed by the crash of a log, and the procedure repeated five times until the diesel crane was shut down. Voices became distant until all was silent.

Inside the humid boxcar, no one dared move. The team waited, unsure what was happening next.

Soon Ube recognized the sound of the truck, as did Pero and Bob. Pero explained to Madar and, carefully in a louder whisper, to Nancy, "It's the logging truck—Volvo, a giant." They heard it approach the train and then the crane diesel started up once more. There were no commands, no shouted orders—but the sequence was the same. However, instead of a crash of a log, the log was nestled into place, causing only the coupling with the boxcar to clank as the weight of the log was transferred to the flatcar. The crane swung away and was turned off. The truck drove away. No noise was heard for ten minutes. Then the truck came back, and the procedure was repeated exactly as before. This happened a total of five times. When the truck drove away and the diesel crane was shut down after the fifth log, the only sound the team heard was a man talking. Then they heard two sets of footsteps on one side of the boxcar and another set of footsteps on the other side. The single set of footsteps continued past the boxcar to the locomotive. They heard the driver being called.

The two footsteps stopped again by the door, and even Pero heard the word *kifi* clearly. The men were laughing. One started to slide the door open. Ube grabbed him as he put half his body in the car and spun him away behind the crates, Ube's hand over the man's mouth. Pero just had time to think, *The guy's not fighting back.*

The second man was facing away from the car, probably keeping watch as his colleague stole another crate of fish. But he had heard the faint commotion and put his head over the edge of the boxcar floor to peer inside. There was nothing to see. Where had the man gone? He called out, "*Ina ku ke?*" No response. Then Ube said, "*Secours . . .*" French for "help," in a weak voice.

The second man climbed in through the partially opened door, lifting his AK-47 to a ready position. Ube moved so swiftly that Pero saw him as a blur. Again he put his hand over the man's mouth, and the man went limp. Ube dropped him to the floor and quickly shut the door. He put his finger to his lips and lay down on the floor. Pero and Madar resumed their hideout.

The train diesel began to rev up. The man who had gone to talk with the driver walked back, crossed over the coupling of the loco to the boxcar, and called out for the men. He called again. Not hearing a reply, Pero heard, quite distinctly, his German as he muttered to no one in particular, "*Beschissene Schwarze.*" (Shitty blacks.) The team heard him walking off. Pero moved quickly to check on Ube, to see if he needed help with the two men. Ube rose and patted Pero on the upper arm to tell him there was nothing to do. Pero turned, knowing it was only a matter of time before the men were found missing. The man who had sworn in German would want to know where they were—and soon.

"Madar, we need to keep the train here, parked, not moving. It is hijacking time." Madar nodded. They slid open the door a crack, peeked out, and then Madar slid it open enough, jumped down, and ran toward the locomotive driver's cab.

Pero asked Ube, "Dead?" He pointed to the man on the floor.

Ube showed Pero his hands, which were dusted with a white powder. "Maybe, or will not wake for many hours." Ube then slid open the door, checked, and dropped down. He moved back under the boxcar into the shadows. Pero imagined that the powder was from Mbuno and Niamba's small leather pouch, no doubt something deadly from their Liangulu hunting days. Whatever it was, he was glad Ube had silenced the two men, one of whom Pero recognized from the other night, the man with the AK-47—Boko Haram.

Pero motioned to Bob and Nancy to follow as Pero alighted from the boxcar, pistol ready. Bob landed next to him with the AK-47 ready, followed by Nancy, who had the shotgun in one hand and her hunting knife in the other. Pero felt something tugging at his ankle. He looked down and saw Ube, who was smiling. Behind him were Mbuno and Teddy. Teddy was holding a large satchel.

Pero pointed at the huts. The mill sodium lights had been extinguished, so they needed to rely on moonlight, just rising in the east, to identify the different structures. They could see no one in the compound, but he knew, just knew, the German would come back soon. "Let's move, and fast. Madar will hold the train. That German will want to find those two men," he said, pointing back into the boxcar.

As Pero took in his view of the compound, he realized he was turned around from the last time he had been there. He looked at Mbuno, who pointed to two huts in succession. "Kitchen, other building." Pero nodded and started to run, the others quickly following. Pero thought, *I wish there were elephants to trample them all to death.*

They reached the kitchen and dining hut first. It was full, men talking, some yelling, laughing, plates rattling. Mbuno looked at Pero and whispered, "Get girls."

Pero ran on to the next hut and peered into the windows, one by one, carefully. He felt Bob next to him but saw Ube with Nancy by the front corner, awaiting Pero's instruction. He peered inside and there they were. Same room, same huddled mass. He nodded to Ube and Bob, and he ran to assist.

Entry into the building was simple. The guard in the hall, not so easy. Nancy threw her hunting knife, which struck the guard's collarbone and fell to the floor. Startled, the man fired a shot that also hit the floor and muttered, "*Farin arya.*" (White bitch.) The noise of the shot was deafening in the narrow space. Ube walked up and grabbed the man's throat, silencing him, while Nancy picked up her knife and gave it to Ube, who stabbed the man through the heart. Pero opened the girls' door. Terrified, they were already moving away, even more frightened by the gunshot.

Ube stepped in and said, "*Tueal maei, walssalamat, wanahn 'iinqadh.*" Pero thought, *That's not Hausa.* What Ube had said in Arabic was, "Come with me, safety, we rescue." But Pero had learned one word in Hausa from Nancy, and he used it, "*Aboki!*" (Friend!) He said it again and again, pointing, one at a time, to Bob, Ube, Nancy, and himself. Nancy kept saying, softly, "*Muna abokai.*" (We are friends.) One of the girls started crying. Bob picked her up and said, "Let's go!" Nancy urged them on, explaining in Hausa that they were safe and that they had to hurry, to get out of this horrible place.

The group obediently followed Bob and Nancy, who, like Bob, also carried a girl in her arms. Nancy's and Bob's instinct to carry and protect was the opposite of the girls' treatment at the hands of Boko Haram, so they instantly followed. Ube retook the lead, leaving Pero to guard the corridor in case anyone stuck their head out. Pero was dreading leaving the hut. He was sure they would meet armed resistance since the gunshot had been loud. As he ushered the last girl outside, he still heard no fighting.

There, in the middle of the compound, was Mbuno, saying, "You must be faster . . ."

The girls sprinted after Bob and Nancy. They reached the boxcar just as the first shots rang out. It was one man yelling, firing. Pero turned, dropped to one knee, and raised the Luger.

He saw the white man who was yelling and waving his hands over his head. His firing was not at them; he seemed to be shooting in the air. Pero didn't much care for the man anyway, so he took aim and dropped him. He was not sure where the bullet hit but was glad an obvious boss had gone down. Without a leader, the remaining men might not follow. *A guy can hope for a little luck, no?* And he sprinted for the train.

Pero saw Madar climbing back into the locomotive cab carrying a bag he had gotten from somewhere. Then Madar was looking out the cab window, waiting for a command.

The twenty-six girls took a while to get on the train. They were malnourished and filthy. Some were embarrassed to be roughly lifted up and into the boxcar, but Bob, Nancy, Ube, and Pero persisted. Mbuno and Teddy kept watch—Mbuno's bow was unslung, and an arrow was notched. Pero knew that any hit from the tip would be deadly.

Once all the girls were aboard, Pero urged them all to get further inside and waved at Madar to leave. As the train moved off, Pero slid the door partially closed and turned to Mbuno. "I don't understand, the dining hall was packed with Boko Haram soldiers. They never fought back!"

Mbuno smiled. "Teddy is Okiek. Okiek know bees."

Pero was stunned for a moment. "You mean? You don't mean that was what was in the satchel!" Mbuno nodded. Pero called over to Teddy. "Bravo, Teddy, and all Okiek beekeepers!" Teddy beamed with pleasure.

Bob was puzzled. "What did you do, throw a beehive in there?"

Teddy answered, vigorously nodding, starting to laugh, "From my koret! Then Mzee lock door." An Okiek's koret is his honey farm with as many as fifty hives of African bees who do not like being disturbed. They do not like it at all.

Pero thought, *Flying elephants, thank God*, then brought matters back to the urgent present by saying, "We still need to locate Tone and Pritchett." Then he realized he didn't have the satellite phone; it was up with Madar. The train was making good time now, maybe five or six miles an hour just entering the first ninety-degree turn to the north. *Where are they?* Pero looked out the open door and felt a crack next to his head, making him recoil quickly. "Shooters!"

Bob pushed all the girls who were in front down to the ground, while Nancy motioned them to tell their sisters to do the same. Like a wave, the mass of women descended to the floor between crates. Several crates fell over, and their flimsy tops came open, spilling dried fish. The girls looked pleadingly. Nancy offered them a piece, encouraging them in Hausa to eat, and they all grabbed pieces. Bob crawled to the doorway, opened it a crack, and sighted along the AK-47. He simply said, "Ready." Pero knew Bob was trained for this. Medic or not, a Marine is always trained to protect. Moments later, Bob said, "Shots." But Pero heard nothing. Bob continued, "More shots, muzzle flash, not here." He was silent for another moment. "Men on tracks, running alongside."

Pero felt the train slowing. The train advanced slowly on the two men—one was limping, being helped by the other. Bob opened the door all the way and asked for help. Pero moved over and leaned out. Leaning down they scooped up Tone first, who had been limping, and then Pritchett. Both had hunting rifles slung across their backs. Pritchett said, "There's a truck following on the tracks, making headway, I am afraid. Couldn't stop it. Good shots when they get the angle."

Bob looked at Tone's leg and asked Nancy for his medical bag. Nancy brought it over, and Bob started administering medical attention.

Mbuno patted Tone's arm, adding, "First aid, very good."

Tone looked up and said, "Bloody embarrassing, getting slow in my old age. He nicked me before I could—"

Pritchett completed his sentence, "Shoot him dead, single shot, two hundred yards. Marvelous shot, Tone, marvelous. Pity you dropped that satellite phone in the marsh!" Pritchett was laughing, in an adrenaline high, then he spotted the girls and laughed harder. "Damn good show! Rescue central! Hello, ladies!"

Tone was silent. His teeth were clenched as Bob treated the wound, saying, "Not too bad; he'll live."

Pero was concerned about the truck following on the railroad ties. "We need to take a look at what's following. How fast are they going?"

"A bloody sight faster than this train, mate. They'll catch us any moment now."

Pero thought fast. The train was picking up speed again, maybe doing twenty miles per hour already. He peered out the door and could see lights approaching the last flatcar. "Bob, I need a hand. Boost me up, I have to get onto the roof. Nancy, keep the girls from panicking. Tone, can I borrow your rifle?" Tone handed it to Pero who wore it, rifle strap across his chest, the rifle at his back. Bob made a cradle of his hands, and Pero was thrust up, just grabbing the top rail running down the length of the boxcar roof. He hung there for a second or two, trying to get a foothold on the slider mechanism of the door. Once his toes caught grip, he pushed up and somehow, in the moonlight, wriggled onto the galvanized metal roof.

He took off the rifle, lay prone, and fired two quick shots at the truck, which swerved a little and dropped back, then started forward again. Pero held the top of the strap by the barrel and lowered the butt to the door entrance. He shouted over the noise of the diesel train and steel wheels screeching on the rusty rails of the seldom-used siding, "We have to deal with them before the next corner. I need Ube up here. I'll lift." He felt the weight on the strap and instead hauled Mbuno up.

Mbuno smiled, "Brother, we do this together."

Pero asked, "Can you shoot at them while I disconnect the flatcars?" He handed Mbuno the rifle.

"*Ndiyo*, I shoot; you be careful." Mbuno assumed a shooting position on his belly.

Pero crawled forward and spotted the vertical ladder every freight car has leading down to the coupling and the gap between cars. In the old days, the brakeman could walk along the train top, down the ladder, and apply manual brakes. The need for a walkway persisted with trains, even container trains. Pero lowered himself, taking a firm grip as the carriage swayed, almost as if it were alive and trying to buck him off. As the loco reached the next bend that would lead to the points, it slowed. Pero thought, *Of course, we need to slow to a stop to reset the points. But we'll be sitting ducks.*

Pero jumped the gap to the first flatcar. He landed on a clear portion of the flatbed as the logs were not long enough to reach the ends. He stood just as Mbuno started firing. There was a little curve to the left, and he heard Bob open up with the AK-47. Pero could not see the truck, yet. As he climbed the logs to crawl to the other end of the first flatcar, he noticed that the flatcar had box-construction sides. With the logs fastened and chains holding the logs tight, he could walk along the side as he would on a yacht at sea, holding onto each chain, and make it to the other end faster. He squirmed down the side of the logs, gripping the nearest chain, and felt his feet make contact with the steel side. He stood and began to make his way along. Fortunately, Pero had chosen the right side of the train. As the corner started, it followed the tracks to the left, which meant he would have been exposed to the truck's gunfire if he had been on the other side. Quickly making his way along the safer right side, he reached the coupling between the two flatcars. He could not see anything in the darkness between the cars.

Reaching for his flashlight, Pero felt unbalanced and gripped the end chain fiercely. The train lurched, and the chain pinched his fingers. He removed his hand quickly to save his fingers, felt he was falling, and dropped the flashlight to regain hold with his other hand. *Now what?* he thought.

Mbuno was firing again. Then silence.

Pero knew how the cars were attached. He had to keep the first flatcar with the special logs and let the others go do some harm.

Unlike American train design, which had two claws that interlocked and could be popped open, the Germans had built the Tanzanian rail cars using the classic European turnbuckle system. A hook at the end of each car had a turnbuckle attached. You looped the end of the turnbuckle over each hook and tightened the turnbuckle to pull the buffers together so the trains could not accidentally become detached. Pero's problem was that the turnbuckle had a stop thread—it could not be completely undone. What he had to do, he realized, was loosen the turnbuckle all the way and wait for the cars to be pushed together, then lift the loosened turnbuckle off the hook. Next time the train accelerated, they would be detached.

He was halfway through the process, holding the loosened end, waiting for the brakes to push the cars closer together, when a voice said, "*Nein*, halt!" Pero looked up and recognized, partially anyway, the face of the man he had met at Moyowosi airfield. The man's face was covered with red welts from bee stings. Pero was hidden in deep shadow, and the man could not see him well. If he had, he might have simply shot Pero, realizing his connection to the events over the past few days. As it was, he hesitated. It was all the hesitation Mbuno needed. Crawling over the logs, he had seen the man approaching Pero. However, Mbuno was out of bullets, so instead he threw and hit the man with the scope off his rifle. Unbalanced with the train's swaying, the man reached for the nearest chain, lost his footing, and slid into the gap between the cars. Desperately reaching out with both hands to grip the nearest buffer, the pistol fell and clattered away beneath the steel. Holding on, his face showed pure terror. He knew the danger he was in. Being crushed by train wheels was a gruesome death. Pero reached out. "*Schnell, gib mir deine hand.*" (Quick, give me your hand.)

The man swung between the cars wildly, the train picking up speed around the corner, rocking back and forth. He reached out with a free hand, and Pero grabbed it and pulled. He was halfway out of the gap and got a foot on the buffer, but then he let go with the other hand, reached inside his jacket, and produced a pistol. Before he could aim it at Pero, Mbuno cried out a warning. But Pero had been watching the other hand, hoping the man would try and help pull himself up. Seeing him reaching, and then as the gun came out, Pero merely let go. The man panicked, reached for a handhold, dropped the gun, and his fingers missed as he fell beneath the train. The sound was sickening, like a melon being dropped on concrete.

At that same moment, the train traveled down a slight decline, brakes were applied, and the cars came crashing together. Pero reached down, thankfully remembered to disconnect the brake lines and connect them to each car's dead-end brackets, and then quickly disconnected and lifted the link before dropping it. As the train resumed speed, he watched the gap widen. The properly disconnected brake lines would prevent the brakes from being automatically applied. The electric lines parted, spewing sparks as the flatcars separated.

From on top of the logs, Mbuno could see clearly. He called down, "The truck is stopped." He told Pero to come up and see. Pero put his feet into the gaps between the logs and climbed, looking over his left shoulder as the train continued around the quarter circle to rejoin the main line. The released flatcars represented hundreds of tons of inertia, and the line was slightly downhill to the truck. At first the flatcars slowed down, then reversed backwards. Had the truck turned off, it could have been saved. Instead, the truck was impacted and then pushed, turning partially sideways and then toppling over. On the detached freewheeling flatcars, Pero and Mbuno could see other figures on top, guns glinting in the moonlight. They weren't firing, just observing their transport being destroyed and the danger of the logs coming loose and crushing them. Even with the flatcars going faster than ten miles per hour, one man jumped clear, and the others followed.

As the loco, with Madar at the helm, finished navigating the corner and dieseled away the last mile to the main line, Pero could just see the men walking back to the truck. The truck was still spewing sparks as the weighty flatcars pushed it relentlessly. *There goes a perfectly good Unimog.*

CHAPTER 28

Futa Reli Kabla—Clear Rail Ahead

Pero was waiting for the train to stop at the points before returning below. Seeing the man fall was too much of a warning. He told Mbuno to wait until they stopped. Mbuno said he thought so, too, adding, "I do not like falling."

As the train came to a stop, Pero and Mbuno got off and fast-walked up to the locomotive. Madar stuck his head out the window, looking at Pero six feet below. "Ready? The down-track light is still green, although the man here is worried it might go red soon. I know it won't. Still, we're running late. Can you switch the point lever?"

Mbuno said he would handle it and trotted off. Pero asked if Madar needed any help with the engineer. Pero saw Madar stick his head back in and another face appear in its place, barely visible in the moonlight. "I am a good citizen. I am happy to help," the engineer said, with a somewhat concerned look on his face.

Madar reappeared, and he, too, appeared worried. "The engineer thinks that they have missed the schedule and that the line might go red for him past Uvinza. He says it happens when they take too long to load the logs."

"What does that mean for us?" Pero saw Madar's head disappear.

When he came back, he said, "A six-hour delay in a siding at Uvinza."

Pero thought. "That's too damn long. How much time can he make up, now that we're lighter?" The head disappeared again.

"He says he'll do his best, but some of the track is not so good, and he's afraid we'll jump the rails if he goes too fast." Pero agreed it was the best they could do and, seeing Mbuno trotting back and waving them on, told Madar to get rolling. Pero jumped onto the locomotive ladder and pulled Mbuno up after him. Madar opened the small door to the cab, and the two men came inside as the locomotive gained speed over the points, going slowly, pulling the log cars behind, clear of the points.

"*Lazima mabadiliko ya pointi.*"

Madar translated, "He wants the points changed back."

"*Siwezi kwenda mpaka pointi ni nyuma. Ni si salama.*"

Madar said, "He cannot go unless the points are back. It is not safe, he says. He is right, the next train carries thousands of passengers. Mbuno?"

"*Ndiyo.*" Mbuno opened the door and hopped off the ladder. The train came to a halt shortly after, and Pero looked out the window as Mbuno ran to regain the ladder rung. Then Pero saw the lights at the mill. All the sodium lights were on, and he could see lights along the tracks behind them as well. Mbuno, hanging onto the ladder as the train began to make headway, turned his head and followed Pero's line of sight. "We must hurry." He climbed in and shut the door. Madar had heard Pero and told the train driver. They watched, in the nighttime vision, the red-lit interior of the car as the driver pushed the throttle fully forward. Without the extra weight of the lost flatcars, the diesel accelerated rapidly.

Pero looked down out the side and could not see anything other than the dim reflection of the loco headlights. Moonlight or not, there was no other definition in the blackness. What he wanted to know, but had not been able to see on their way to the mill, was whether there was a service road next to the rails. "Madar, ask him if there is a road next to the tracks here."

When asked the engineer nodded and replied, "*Ndiyo. Macho yake. Baadaye hakuna.*" (Yes. Here, yes. Later, no.)

Pero tried out his broken Swahili. "*Wakati hakuna? Ni kiasi gani baadaye?*" (When is no? How much later?)

"*Baada ya Usinge. Kisha inarudi baada ya Nguruka.*" (After Usinge. Then it comes back after Nguruka.)

Pero did a quick mental calculation based on the maps they had studied. "Okay, that means for the next ten or more miles, there is a road next to us they can use. Then no road, and then there's another road alongside after Nguruka." Madar looked pleased. "Don't be so happy, Commissioner. I saw lights back there; they may have gotten past the flatcars and may be coming on strong. And here's another problem. Nguruka is at the bottom of Moyowosi Reserve, and we know they are logging there. If I were them, I'd barricade the rails. We have too much evidence here against them."

Madar gripped Pero's arm, his fingers digging in. "What evidence?" Madar's eyes darted to a case standing against the back wall of the cab.

"We're towing a boxcar full of kidnapped Boko Haram girls . . ."

Madar seemed disappointed, "Yes, that is evidence, but not against Zanzi-Agroforestry and Stephan Nyerere..."

Pero continued, "And we have the cocaine-paste-filled logs as cargo." Mbuno nodded and moved to the left-hand window to watch for trouble.

"How do you know? Are you sure they are the ones?" Madar gestured toward the rear of the train.

"The last logs were loaded carefully and without the local employees. The Boko Haram soldiers carefully loaded all six logs. That cannot be a coincidence." Then, as an afterthought, he said, "Oh, and the guy we killed when he dropped beneath the train? He was white as me, and he spoke German." Madar was soaking it all in. "Now," Pero asked, "May I borrow your phone."

"No, I need it first." And with that Madar extended the antenna, pointed it out the right-side window behind the driver, and dialed. He spoke quickly and in a language Pero and Mbuno did not understand but assumed to be Urdu, the language of the Singh ancestors. When he disconnected, he handed the phone to Pero. "Virgi and Amar are ready and most grateful. Loyal officers of the People's Defense Force will be airborne within minutes. We have had them on standby. They will surround and capture the mill. Amar wants us to proceed to Kigoma port depot where the Tanzanian Naval Command will declare martial law from eight tomorrow morning. They will secure the cargo."

Pero had an uneasy feeling. "You do not mention the girls."

"They are not in Tanzania; they never were in Tanzania."

Mbuno heard and spun quickly from the window. He said forcefully, "*Wasichana ni hapa. Wao si kupotea.*" (The girls are here. They will not be lost.)

Madar was shocked that Mbuno did not understand what he meant. "*Hapana, hapana*, Mbuno. *Mimi maana sisi lazima si kuruhusu vyombo vya habari kusikia wao ni hapa. Wanapaswa kuondoka kwa usalama, lakini ni lazima kuondoka.*" (No, no, Mbuno. I meant we must not allow the press to hear they are here. They must leave safely, but they must leave.)

Mbuno was silent, then he looked at Pero and said, "He is right. It is bad the girls are here. They make Tanzania bad."

Pero put his hand on Mbuno's shoulder and said, "That's why I planned a safe place, my brother. The girls need to go to the Oasis at Loiyangalani, away from any prying eyes. Until they are ready." Then he looked at Madar. "But you know the truth will come out, don't you?"

Madar nodded, "Yes, but later, when we have made sure this attempted coup is stopped."

Then the impact of the girls' plight really hit Pero. "Madar, you knew, didn't you? The girls were not here by accident or as a prize of Boko Haram terrorists. Someone planned that they would be discovered, maybe already dead or in a mass grave, in Tanzania . . ."

Madar looked ashamed. "Yes, then Stephan Nyerere could claim the security of the country was corrupt and that only he, the grandson of our founder, could restore order. This is the real threat to our nation. The gold and drugs are a police matter, my concern. They give Stephan Nyerere money power, yes, but not the means to become a dictator."

"It's a Reichstag event, is that what you are saying?" Pero said. Mbuno asked what he meant, and Pero quickly explained, "In Germany, Hitler, to come to power, needed a terrorist event to show the government was weak. So his agents burned the capital building to the ground, claiming it was caused by the terrorists of the day. Hitler soon took power as the law-and-order leader." Madar was nodding his agreement. Pero was dismayed. "And if we had failed? If we had gotten into a firefight at the mill?"

"I did not think they would. They would not want that to happen on Zanzi-Agroforestry property since the Minister is a director."

"But now?"

"Yes, now we are a target, giving them what they need. We are escorting fugitive girls—maybe we are working with Boko Haram. It would be unfortunate to get caught now."

Oh great, out of the frying pan and into the fire, Pero thought.

CHAPTER 29

Kimbia, Kimbia Haraka—
Run, and Run Hard

Pero remembered Lewis advising him to get in and out and run like hell. Now he knew what Lewis had been intimating. He put his hand out to Madar and said, "Give me the phone."

At the same moment, Mbuno, who had been watching out the side window, brought his head back in and said, "There is truck, large truck, catching us on the road, Pero. Ten minutes unless we go faster."

Madar talked with the driver, who was shaking his head. The throttle was already fully open, and the speedometer showed eighty kilometers, fifty miles per hour.

Pero opened the antenna and dialed Lewis. "Baltazar for Lewis, most urgent."

"Standby." The wait seemed interminable. "Lewis here. Where are you? I hear that noise again—still on the train?"

"Yes, now here's the rundown, copy?" Lewis told him to go ahead. Pero relayed all that had happened to make sure there was a record of precisely what they had done in case it was needed later to prove that Tanzania did not harbor Boko Haram nor kidnap girls.

Lewis did not sound that impressed and said, in a cold and unfeeling way, "You sound like a lawyer at a deposition. Just give me your assessment of the situation now."

"We have a truck gaining on us, on a parallel service road. That road ends in about three miles. That may be enough time."

"Copy," was all Lewis said.

Pero quickly added, "Okay, but there's another road later on that connects with Moyowosi Reserve and crosses the train tracks, and we know they have logging operations in Moyowosi. They may have already radioed ahead for help or a barricade."

"And by help, you mean they plan an armed attack? Why?"

Then Pero realized that not even Lewis would be so careless with the lives of the girls. Angrily, he almost screamed into the phone, "You are mistaken to think they would not attack the girls. We are not on Zanzi-Agroforestry land now. If the girls die here—especially at the hand of a CIA agent and the commissioner of police—Tanzania will be lost. Do you understand?"

Lewis' calm voice came through clearly. "Oh yes, we always did." He yelled back at Pero, "That's why I told you to stay away. Now you are there, putting an entire country and the United States in danger."

Mbuno, hearing only part of the conversation, got Pero's attention and said, calmly, "It is the girls."

Sighing, Pero responded to Lewis, "Mbuno is right—we needed to save the girls. Can you help or not?"

Lewis was still angry, but the edge had left his voice. "We always planned to rescue them, you idiot, but you have ruined our plan!"

Pero gave in. "Okay Lewis, but please, we do not have time for this political crap. Can you help us now or not?"

"Yes, yes, of course." Lewis had calmed down. "You asked for airlift to standby. The best I could do for that big of a load—and yes, we figured out what it was you wanted to lift— is a Sea Knight off of the Eisenhower currently off the coast of Kenya. It is en route to you already, second air-to-air refueling being completed. Expected ETA for Kigoma vicinity within one hour. And, before you ask, a C-130 tanker is loitering for further refueling."

Pero was impressed. He had not expected that much support. The Sea Knight was a heavy-lift, twin rotor, helicopter. The C-130 was also called the Hercules, four turboprops and . . . Pero had an idea. "Lewis, is the C-130 armed?"

"Standby."

Pero looked at Madar and explained what was coming to help. Madar asked, "On whose authority did they get overflight permission?" Pero shook his head. Madar pleaded, "It is vital we know who!"

Pero asked, "Lewis, Commissioner Singh wants to know who gave the Navy overflight permission?" Pero motioned to Madar to put his head next to Pero's to hear the answer.

Lewis responded, "Permission was asked through US Central African Command in Germany to Tanzanian delegation. They reached . . . let me see, I have that here somewhere . . . the Minister of the Interior."

"Quick, Mr. Lewis, what time was that permission requested?" Madar's desperation could be heard by Lewis clearly.

"Midnight Zulu, why?"

Madar grabbed the phone. "It is a trap. Tell the helicopter to divert, go away. The Minister of the Interior is Stephan Nyerere, and he's the one planning the coup."

Pero took the phone back. "For God's sake, Lewis, call them immediately . . ." But Pero could hear nothing. He waited, then heard, "Standby."

Mbuno said in Swahili that the truck was no longer gaining ground and that it seemed to be bouncing on a very rough road. The train driver confirmed that the road was ending because it had been washed away several times in the last year.

The phone beeped. "Lewis here. Got through. Emergency divert undertaken. C-130 pilot reports possible SAM fired, no target. Countermeasures deployed." SAM was a surface-to-air missile.

Pero, feeling desperate, needed to take control; he felt it in his bones. "Lewis, am I still in charge?" He heard a somewhat reluctant, "Affirmative." "Good, then here is what I need. If there is an ambush coming for us, it will happen at Moyowosi Reserve north-south road where it crosses the train tracks. Copy?"

Again he heard, "Affirmative."

"I need C-130 to loiter that area and be prepared to destroy anything, repeat, anything other than this train anywhere near that junction. Confirm?"

"Confirm destruction requested. Estimate time of arrival junction?"

Pero asked Madar, who talked to the engineer. Madar responded, "Twenty-five minutes if he can keep up this speed, but it may be longer."

Pero related that to Lewis and added, "By destroy, I mean lethal, big show, kill every last one. Copy?" Madar, listening in, was nodding.

"Confirmed destroy everything. May I ask why?" And Pero heard Lewis issuing instructions while he waited for Pero's response.

"Lewis, we have here, on this train, a lethal combination for all of East Africa. US meddling with internal affairs, a corrupt government seen to be harboring Boko Haram, and terrorist-kidnapped girls from one country held in another, which will infect all Organization of African Unity relations, so the OAU ..." And Pero stopped. He thought. "Question: Who paid for the freighter in Beira?"

"Back on that? We found out it was a company owned by Mikael Petrov."

"Petrov ties to the Kremlin?"

Then it was Lewis's turn to be silent. When he came back on, his voice sounded more worried than usual. "Petrov is the main financial backer to the current president, you-know-who. Do you mean to tell me you think all this is part of a plot by the Russian government to destabilize African unity?"

"Think about it, Lewis. The Chinese are buying up everything—logs, tobacco, all the mineral rights, food production. But the Chinese refuse to lend military or defense support, being mainly merchants. That leaves the OAU underfunded for defense, which is why the US created the Central African Command, like NATO. But Russia and the ex-communist allies are left without any reason to link up at all—there are no spoils left. What better way to destabilize the whole region and have some countries reestablish ties with Russia than to cause international strife and possible war? Do you think Nigeria and most of the world's press will believe Tanzania wasn't harboring Boko Haram and the kidnapped girls? Forget the Arab Spring; this is like lighting the fuse on the African Split."

Madar took a step back and stared at Pero. Then he bowed, and Pero could barely see, in the glow of the nightlights' red glare, tears rolling down Madar's cheeks. Mbuno understood as well and shouted so that Lewis could hear, "This must not be allowed."

Lewis came back on. "Okay, we're linked here with State and an old friend of yours, Pontnoire. He says you are right." Pontnoire had been the ambassador in Berlin the previous year and had helped thwart the uranium smuggling operation. Lewis continued, "We're also linked up here with General Tews at Central African Command . . . good guess by the way, Baltazar. General, are you there?" Pero heard an "affirmative." Madar pressed his ear closer. "General," Lewis continued, "your assessment?"

"Sea Knight now loitering near border with Kenya, passing over Lake Victoria, out of SAM range. C-130 at altitude, beyond SAM reach, awaiting instructions."

A new voice chimed in, "This is Pontnoire. General, can you lend more military assistance to the region the train is in, top priority, effective immediately?"

"Affirmative, awaiting command and control instructions."

Lewis cut in, "We're getting that, General. White House is informed; president will be issuing orders ASAP. But we need something in the air, in case."

The general's soft Texas twang came in clearly, "No shit. Two F18s scrambled seconds after SAM attempt. They will arrive on scene in minutes to protect the Sea Knight and the C-130. Inbound, from within Kenya airspace, are four Harriers undergoing a joint-training exercise near Malindi that have been diverted to Lake Victoria, flight permission granted by Burundi. On station within minutes." Burundi was only a couple of hundred miles to the northeast of the train. "I need permission for hot weapons, but not to protect assets."

Lewis thanked him and said they would await the White House Situation Room's assessment and orders.

However, Pero was not convinced. "General, this is Pero Baltazar in Tanzania. Am I not an asset?"

"Affirmative, you are," came the reply from African Central Command in Germany.

"Okay then, I would like this asset protected, please. Come and get us!"

"It ain't that simple son . . . hold on." The line went silent. When the general came back on, he called for a roll call and then stated, "Permission for hot weapons received, diverting F18s to overflight protection inbound Harrier squadron, ETA ten to twenty-five minutes."

Lewis's voice sounded elated. "That was quick . . ."

Mbuno, leaning out the window, started yelling, "*Hatari! Hatari!*"

The driver peered into the gloom and reached for the brakes while pulling the throttle control back. Pero felt the shift. Lewis called out, "What's happening?"

Just before he disconnected, Pero said, "It may be too late. We're in trouble here."

Mbuno turned to Pero. "Big Volvo, I think."

Pero peered ahead. Maybe a mile away he could see big lights, right in line with the tracks that were now straight as an arrow. He said to Madar, "We need all the power we can get. We need to smash our way through." And with that he handed Madar the phone, opened the cab door, stepped out, and ran along the locomotive's side, grabbing the railing to keep from falling. When he reached the gap between them and the box-car, he leaped across, grabbed the ladder, and climbed on top. Inching his way as fast as he could to the middle, he lowered himself to find the foothold on the door's slider mechanism and then kicked the door with the other foot. The door opened. He extended his arms, lowering his torso, and then felt arms holding his legs and then his middle before he let go. He managed to swing inside as many hands grabbed him and pulled.

Pero could see they had restacked all the crates of fish against the side walls. Pero thought, *Bullet protection, good thinking.* But the two dead men that Ube had silenced were still on board. "Tone, Bob, Nancy, dump those two and then get everyone down, flat on the ground. We're going to crash." Pritchett dragged one man, then the next, and dumped them out the door. Bob, meanwhile, pushed, as gently as possible, the girl nearest to him down to the ground. Ube, Nancy, Teddy, and Tone did the same with the others. Nancy was yelling instructions in Hausa, telling them it would be all right. When all the girls were down, the men covered as many of the girls with their own bodies as possible, Nancy still chattering away in Hausa to keep them calm. The open door allowed Pritchett to peer ahead, and, seeing vehicle lights ahead, he grabbed his rifle and squeezed off shot after shot. Pritchett saw that one of the lights went out.

They were within ten yards of the obstacle when bullets started hitting the boxcar. Pritchett stood and kept firing, saying, "Got one . . . and you, ya bastard . . ." The rest was lost in the din that followed.

The crash, when it came, was louder than anything Pero had ever experienced. Thirty tons, however massive the Volvo truck was, was no match for almost a hundred tons of locomotive. That and its cargo of thirty tons of logs crashed through and swept away the Volvo truck like it was a toy. The train shook, the boxcar contents flew about the interior, and some girls were hurt by the boxes of fish that fell off the stacks piled against the walls. One hit Pero square in the back, causing a sharp pain.

There was a new strange sound coming from behind the boxcar.

"Is everyone all right?" One by one, voices of his team confirmed they were still alive and helping the girls.

When the bullets stopped and they were clear of the roadblock, Pero rose and leaned out of the open door. Up front he could see the locomotive had sustained massive damage—metal was twisted, and it looked like the top of the cab was torn partially back. The train powered on, but Pero could see no movement from the driver's compartment. A clanking sound behind him made him turn around. One of the logs was partially hanging off the side of the flatcar, held in place only by a remaining chain, the other four chains dragged along the side, whipping and lashing the side of the flatcar.

The log was cracked open, and globs of what looked like wallpaper paste were blobbing out, splattering on the gravel along the train tracks.

Pero looked at Bob, who had gotten out the flashlight and was checking on the girls with Nancy's help. "Bob, I need to get back up front. Give me a lift?" Bob laced his fingers and hoisted Pero back up. Pero, exhausted, nearly missed the handhold. He was thinking everyone up front must be injured and needing his help. He leaped off the boxcar front ladder onto the loco and made his way along the side. His trousers ripped on jagged metal. The door would not open to the cab. There were no lights, and the front window was gone, blasted away by the impact. He called out "Mbuno!" through the hole where the window had been.

"I am here. Mr. Madar is hurt. It is very bad."

"The driver?"

"He is dead. I drive."

"Okay, hold on." Pero went to the back of the loco and yelled back to the boxcar. "Can you hear me?" Pritchett's head appeared. "We need first aid here. Can Bob come over?"

Pritchett's head disappeared. Bob stuck his head out. "On my way!"

Pero watched first a figure, presumably Bob, make his way up and over and onto the roof. He was followed by a second, and when the face turned forward to crawl across the roof, Pero saw it was Ube. Both made their way to the ladder, climbed down, and jumped onto the loco. Pero said, "Bob, we cannot get in this side; see if you can on the other side." The two of them inched their way along the right side of the locomotive. Pero went back along the left side and considered climbing in through the mangled window opening. Then he heard, "We're in—this door works." Pero could not make out the conversation, but Mbuno was telling Bob about Madar. Pero went around and joined them.

A smashed body is both horrifying and messy. The driver had been ducking down behind his console. A chunk of metal, torn off the Volvo, had impaled him through the upper chest, the yellow truck fragment passing clean through and sticking into the cab deck. Pero and Ube, working together, took hold of the upper part of the metal skewer, said sorry to the driver's soul, and moved it back and forth, easing it from the decking. Eventually, the metal shard and the driver fell sideways to the floor. The two men tugged the bloody mass clear of the driver's station.

Madar was on the other side of the cab, sitting up while being administered to by Bob who held his pencil flashlight in his mouth, leaving his hands free. Mbuno had been jammed into the corner of the right-hand side of the cab, standing next to the impaled driver, keeping the throttle wide open. None of the instruments seemed operational, although it was hard to tell because there was no light in the cab or from the console. Ube crossed behind Pero and went to assist Bob.

Weakly, Madar said to Pero, "That case, it has documents. Get it to my brother." Bob told him to save his breath while he tried to assess the damage.

That the locomotive was functioning at all amazed Pero. No one was operating the deadman switch. Pero knelt and felt for the foot pedal. It was depressed, being held in place with a metal clamp. Many drivers did that—hour after hour of pressing on the spring-loaded pedal was exhausting. It meant, however, that accidents could easily happen. In this instance, the illegal clamp had saved them when the train had not stopped within range of their guns once the driver died. *No, he didn't die.* Pero corrected his thinking. *They killed him.*

When Bob eventually stood after attending to Madar, he told Pero, "I've sedated him. He's badly wounded, looks internal. There's massive bruising across his chest, and he's coughing a little blood. Could be a pierced lung. I can't tell more. We need—"

"Yeah, I know, as soon as we can. Search his pockets. I need the phone." Pero went over to Mbuno and said, "I think we need to slow down a little, brother. This train may be too damaged to keep up with this speed."

Mbuno pulled the throttle back halfway. The diesel engine seemed to slow but the deck still pulsed beneath their feet. "I do not know how to stop, brother. Do you?" Pero shook his head. "Then we will just have to go so slow until we can turn it off . . ." He pointed at the master control switch that had the words *On* and *Off* printed in luminescent paint.

It was the only control they could discern in the darkness. Pero looked ahead, the oncoming wind blowing mist and the smell of the forest into the cab. He realized there were no longer any functioning headlights. The train and tracks ahead were dark.

They were also invisible to anyone out there, friend or foe.

CHAPTER 30

Yupo Pale Kusaidia?—
Is There Anyone There to Help?

B ob interrupted Pero's thoughts and handed him the phone, saying, "Sorry." Pero looked at the small metal antenna, ripped clean off, and sighed. They were on their own.

No! We're not! Pero opened the cab door and went to the back left of the loco. He called back again to Pritchett, who responded. Pero asked as loudly as he could, "Do you or Tone have your cell phone?"

The boxcar had started making a terrible hissing noise. Pero looked down and saw that the air brake tube was whipping around, unconnected. He lay flat on the loco back deck and caught the hose on the third attempt. It was no use. The hose was severed. The only brakes they had ... Again, Pero corrected himself. *No! That's not right ... when the tubing is cut, it applies the brakes!* Pero leaned over and tried to visually check the wheels and braking mechanism. All he could see under the box car was glowing red-hot sparks showering the tracks.

Pero yelled back to Pritchett, "Look, brakes are on in the boxcar, full on. They will fail and take a wheel assembly with them. We need to slow down. The satellite phone is broken. On your phone, call Tone's office, get Sheila, and tell her to radio the Oasis. Tell Wolfgang to have Mary call Lewis." He paused. "You getting all this?"

Pritchett yelled back, "Tone and I are listening—go on."

"Mary needs to tell Lewis emergency support and rescue Sea Knight now. Can you repeat all that?"

Pritchett did and added, "No mobile signal here, but when we get past this range of hills coming up, we'll be coasting down to Uvinza, about an hour before we reach Ujiji, two maybe to Kigoma. The line of sight for mobiles might be okay soon."

Pero was grateful for Pritchett's calm and knowledge of the area. "Thanks. We're going to have to slow, so it may be an hour, but keep trying, okay?" Pritchett said they would and waved. Pero walked, carefully, back to the cab and asked Bob, "How's Madar doing?"

Bob rocked his head back and forth. "So-so. Actually, he seems better, but I have seen that before; it might only be the effect of his natural endorphins masking the pain. Any idea when we'll get help?" Pero explained what he had asked Tone and Pritchett to do. Bob added a suggestion, "Couldn't you have them also call his brother?"

Pero patted Bob's arm and thought, *Stupid, I should have thought of that.* He rushed back to the rear of the loco and passed the message to Pritchett. Pritchett responded, "No signal yet, but Tone also thought of that. We'll get through, don't you worry."

Coming back again into the cab, there was just enough of an early daylight glow to begin to make out the cab interior.

Mbuno said, "Pero, you are bleeding." His hunter's eyes had seen what neither Ube, Bob, nor Pero had seen.

Pero, looking around his body, asked, "Where?"

Bob spun Pero around and saw the red patch below Pero's scapula on the left side. He lifted Pero's jacket and saw his shirt was soaked. Bob put his flashlight in his mouth again, aiming the beam at Pero's back. He pulled the shirt up and said, "Bad one. Plenty of blood." He probed around the wound. "Puncture. Doesn't look like a bullet, too messy an entry." He reached into his bag and pulled out long tweezers. "This is going to hurt. Lean forward over the dash there." Pero did as he was told. Bob probed gently into the wound. "Aha, hold still." Pero felt something moving in his body as Bob grabbed and then tugged it out. Bob held it out for Pero to see under the flashlight beam. It was a piece of wire. Pero recognized it from the boxcar cargo, the wire used to secure the fish crates shut.

Bob moved back to looking at the wound, now oozing fresh blood. "Should be okay—it's not too deep—but you'll need medical attention." He puffed some powder at the wound and then applied a gauze patch and several strips of medical tape. "Try not to do any more acrobatics." Bob smiled. "That's a professional opinion. Five dollars, please."

"I'll do my best." Pero looked at Ube, Bob, and Mbuno. "Anyone else injured and doesn't know it?"

Bob played the flashlight on each one of them. "All clear."

The train rumbled on, Mbuno at the controls. Pero watching the line ahead, suspecting there might be another ambush. Mile after mile—it was nerve-wracking, what seemed like time inching along.

To change the thoughts in his head, Pero asked Mbuno, "What was the powder you gave Ube to use?" Just as he said that, bullets rang out from behind. Pero went through the cab door quickly and peered down the length of the train. He could see nothing, but then suddenly the train started a right curve, and he could see lights following. Whatever it was, it was firing and catching up. He went back to talk with Mbuno.

"I do not think we should go faster, but something is catching up with us, and they are shooting. They are too far behind to actually aim, yet."

"Headlights?"

"Yes, why?"

"They are not a train." Pero realized Mbuno was right. Then he had an idea. Could he release the last log flatcar and achieve the same result twice? Mbuno clearly was thinking the same thing. "You like trains, Pero—you drive." He put Pero's hand on the throttle, opened the door, and left.

Mbuno was smaller than Pero, but, whitening hair or not, he was stronger and more physically fit. He leaped to the boxcar, climbed the ladder, ran across the roof and down the ladder. There was room for him to lay flat and undo the coupling, but then he got an idea. There was still moonlight, and that, coupled with the faint glow of the coming sun, enabled him to see the one log now sticking out at an angle, far out, as well as the single chain left holding all the logs in place. Peering under the flatcar, he could see and smell that the wheel assemblies were glowing red-hot, almost orange.

Mbuno climbed onto the flatcar, went to the remaining chain ratchet fastener, and released the safety pin. The chain, under tremendous strain, whipped apart. The one log pivoted, quickly rolled off and bounced onto the train tracks. A bullet whizzed past his ear. Mbuno watched the remaining logs now jostling, moving. But they looked well set in place, three on the bottom, two on top now. Mbuno paid no heed to the bullets being sent his way. He had been shot at before, but when he had a job to do, nothing could deter him.

Mbuno calmly but quickly unlatched all four of the loose three-inch-wide chains and tugged them, one at a time, back to the end of the flatcar, ducking down out of the path of the bullets. He pulled and pushed the hundreds of pounds of chain across the gap onto the boxcar, resting them across the boxcar buffers. There was nowhere for him to lie down on the boxcar, so he laid down on the flatcar end and undid the turnbuckle. When it was fully out, he went to the side of the flatcar. A bullet passed, sounding like an angry bee. He waved to the engine driver's cab. Ube was watching and waved back.

Pero pulled the throttle to slowest to put pressure on the buffers. Mbuno lifted the link and leaped to the ladder on the boxcar. The train started to accelerate, leaving the flatcar behind, brakes fully on. It came to a halt within a hundred and fifty yards. The train continued onwards.

It was as Mbuno expected. The vehicle he recognized as the Mercedes SUV drove off the railroad ties, around the flatcar, and then back up onto the railroad ties. Now Mbuno was exposed, and they were gaining quickly.

While the SUV had been taking evasive action, Mbuno had simply dropped one chain after another across the rails. He heard them clanking away as steel hit steel, one side of the buffer, and then the other. Each one was a hundred pounds, like a steel snake.

Mbuno knew about driving on railroad tracks. You do not need to look for potholes or obstacles because railroad ties and rails are uniform, predictable.

When the tire of the SUV hit the first chain, it exploded, instantly flat. The rim of the wheel scraped along the rail, sending a shower of sparks. The driver was fighting to control the car when the other side slid into the second chain that wrapped itself into the wheel well and ripped the left front wheel assembly clean off. The SUV's energy was pitched forward, and, for a moment, it looked like it would skid. But the bumper caught a railroad tie, and it pitched the SUV into the air.

At that moment, the SUV burst into a ball of flame.

Mbuno hadn't seen the missile and didn't understand what had happened, but nonetheless he was quite pleased with his handiwork. He climbed back up the boxcar ladder and leaned over the open doorway, asking, "Everyone is all right?"

Tone, waving his cell phone, was laughing, "Mbuno, you silly idiot, look over there!" Tone's arm pointed off to the side of the train. Mbuno had never seen anything like it. An almost dragon-like metal airplane—at least he thought it was an airplane—was looking right at him. Lights flicked on, blinding him, and the plane seemed to be dancing sideways.

Ube had seen the Harrier Jump Jet, too, and pointed it out to Pero. Pero flicked the loco switch to *Off* and, slowly, the train came to a halt. Pero got down from the locomotive and waved to the pilots who were shining their landing lights at the train. He ran to the open boxcar and peeked his head over the transom. "Everyone okay here?"

Tone answered, "Frightened—a few bumps and bruises—but all fine otherwise."

Nancy said, "The girls want to know if it is over. They want to go home."

Then a tremendous noise was heard, and blinding lights illuminated the whole train. Pero waved as the Sea Knight settled moments later off to the side of the train tracks, its loudspeaker hailing, "Baltazar, report! Baltazar, report!"

Pero ran over, arms up, waving, "Baltazar, I'm Baltazar. We have a badly injured man in the cab, internal injuries, some of us have small wounds and another shot in the leg. Do you have a medic?" And he added, surprised at his own desperation, "But Christ, first get these girls out of here!"

The airlift took under twenty minutes to load; Pero nervously eyed the forest on the one side of the tracks and the cleared land on the other. He felt vulnerable, sitting in a trap.

Nancy helped guide the girls aboard, encouraging them all the while, telling them repeatedly that they were going to safety and would soon be home. The Navy crew had come armed with candy. Pero smiled at that simple gesture. Communication with the Harriers and the F18s zooming overhead was constant; Pero could hear them chattering through the helicopter flight-deck speaker from the pilot's open side window. Pero made sure they got Madar aboard with an IV plugged in. He handed the medic the case that Madar had brought into the train cab. "Make sure this always goes with him, okay?" The medic said he would.

When Tone was settled comfortably, with Bob and Pritchett fussing over him, Pero moved up to the flight deck and talked with the pilot. "New orders, we are flying to Lake Rudolf—all of us except for the commissioner who needs a hospital. Can you drop him off and then continue on?" The pilot said those were not his orders. Pero insisted. "Call in for new orders; let's get General Tews on the line."

The pilot's head swiveled, amazed at Pero's suggestion. "I can't call the general!"

Pero calmly said, "Try, and try now, please."

The pilot called the C-130 and asked for a link to General Tews. The C-130 responded that it was authorized, and the general came on. The pilot flicked on the cabin speaker. "Tews here. That you, Baltazar?"

"Yes, General. Our thanks. But we still have a problem. We need to get the girls out of here, away from Tanzania. What I suggest is that you allow me to transport them to the Oasis Lodge at Loiyangalani on Lake Rudolf for a week. Reverend Threte is already there, or about to be, with specialists in hostage debriefing and rehab. Make a damn good story in the *Stars & Stripes*. Then, we can fudge the dates and have you fly them back to their families in Nigeria . . . not bad for Central African Command."

The general's Southern twang came through loud and clear. "Pontnoire gave me a little lecture, son, on your abilities. Said you were a devious S.O.B.; happy you are on our side. Suggested I agree to anything you propose. Your Lewis ain't so sure—he's worried what you'll get up to next . . . but heck, son, so far you've done okay. That chopper pilot listening?" The pilot said he was. "Orders: Do what the man says. Out."

The pilot's expression was one of amazement. He got on the radio and told the C-130 and the Harriers to follow him. "Where to then?"

"Dar es Salaam; we've got a patient to deliver to his brothers. Then on to Lake Rudolf."

With an "affirmative," the pilot checked that his crew were all on board, buttoned up, pulled the commutator throttle up, and the Sea Knight lifted off.

Once airborne, Pero went back into the hold and checked that everyone was doing well. The girls looked both terrified and hopeful. Bob, Nancy, and the onboard Navy medic were seeing to wounds, bruises, and other minor medical problems. The flight staff was handing out blankets and more candy. Madar was unconscious but looked to be breathing regularly. The IV was half empty. Pero went over to Tone and Pritchett, who were sitting together and watching the people around them. Pero said simply, "Thank you."

Tone looked at Pritchett, and both had to raise their voices to respond. Pero could see the two men were feeling safe, winding down after an experience that must have been as terrifying for them as it had been for him. But Pero had not counted on the British sense of humor to defuse tension when Tone replied, "What for? Did us good to be in the thick of things again. To win again. Wonder if we can ever tell anyone, though."

"Speaking of telling anyone, may I borrow your phone?"

Tone passed over his cellphone. Pritchett, who Pero had come to understand was a bit of a prankster, commented, laughing at Tone, "Oh, sure, the cheap cell phone you save, but you lose this fellow's expensive satellite phone tripping in the marsh!"

Tone backhanded his friend's chest. "Oh, do shut up, you idiot." Both men smiled, still enjoying the feeling of success. "Try and remember I'm badly wounded here; you should have some sympathy. Go, fetch me a pillow and a cup of tea."

Pero left them to their banter. He asked the petty flight officer if he could use a cell phone in flight. The man nodded. Pero dialed Virgi and reported in. "It's a bit noisy here, but packages retrieved, all safe as far as we know, so far. Need to drop off a slightly broken package to you for family care. Can you suggest where?"

The chop-chop-chop of the helicopter blades carried across the airwaves. Virgi responded, "Ah, Mr. Pero, I have had a most useful conversation with your Mr. Lewis. Excellent planning. Most excellent. The bad"—he paused—"*postmaster* has been apprehended, so there should be no more illegal shipments or discussion of laws being broken. And a family of German rats from Zanzibar are enjoying a trap. A most sincere thank you. And a cable just came in from Lewis that says Avanti aircraft splashed crossing the Mediterranean Sea and to tell you ASAP. That make sense?" Pero knew then that Lewis had ordered the destruction of the Avanti carrying, as Mbuno had called them, the lions to Albania.

Virgi waited a few moments, expecting no response. Pero could hear someone also talking to him. Then he said, "Amar says you are most welcome to come for lunch when you can."

Pero felt that was a generous gesture, and promised it was one he planned to agree to in the coming weeks. "What about the personal family package I need to deliver? It has gotten quite a bit damaged, but we hope it can be repaired."

"Ah, that is most sad, but we have a most wonderful building here, same name as the one in Nairobi, named after a generous spiritual leader..." Pero knew instantly he meant the Aga Khan Hospital. "Can you deliver the package there? We will have you met. It is most secure."

Pero said that would be fine and to expect arrival within two to three hours, before hanging up. He went and explained to the pilot, who only commented, "That's a bit obvious in broad daylight... can I suggest we set down, transfer him to a small medical chopper, and then bug out to Loiyangalani?" Pero checked with the onboard medic, who said the patient was improving and was stable. As for Tone, the wound was superficial, and he was already telling the medic to leave him alone. "Had worse than this from an infected thorn last year. I'm staying with you. I want to go home when you're ready." Nevertheless, the medic gave Bob antibiotics with instructions. Bob promised him that Tone would take them. Tone gave a "harrumph" and pretended to be going to sleep.

The transfer for Madar should work out fine. Pero went forward and told the pilot to set it up and gave him Virgi Singh's number. He left him to it. *It's time I stop trying to run everything.*

CHAPTER 31

Mwisho wa Safari—
End of the Safari

The transfer of Commissioner Madar Singh at the Tanzanian Air Force base on the outer rim of the Julius Nyerere International Airport took twenty minutes. The base commandant wanted to detain the US Navy helicopter, accusing the Americans of subversive activity. As the Singh brothers had been alerted of the transfer site, they had arranged for Defense Forces, who showed up just in time and impounded the airbase, just in case. As soon as the commandant had weapons pointed at him, not to mention four Harrier Jump Jets patrolling his base perimeter, he changed his mind quickly. He claimed he had no idea what was going on. The hospital's medivac chopper took off immediately, headed for the Aga Khan Hospital.

The Defense Forces major, busy arresting the commandant, was also intent on listening to his radio. Finally, he came over to the Sea Knight, leaned into the helicopter doorway, and asked to speak to Baltazar. He shouted to be heard over the turbines above, "Message from Minister Singh: the logging camp of Zanzi-Agroforestry was captured after a deadly firefight. Our forces had some losses, but we have managed to capture twenty-one Boko Haram and the drug chemists working at the mill. The logging site in Moyowosi has also been captured, but no one was found to have remained. We are searching the area. The total count of dead and wounded on the train route you took is eighteen, six of whom are in medical custody, including one of the Schmidt family, recently returned to Tanzania from Germany. The last part of the message I do not understand, but I have written it down." He pulled a folded paper from a breast pocket. "Postmaster now deceased, must not be mentioned for good of country."

Pero understood. The relative of the great and revered father of their country could not—should not—be allowed to tarnish the population's faith in their nationhood. *Stephan Nyerere will*, he had no doubt, *have probably officially committed suicide*. Pero wondered what was going to happen to the Schmidt family. He had one more message for Amar, which he hoped the major could pass on. "Major, can you relay a message for me? We will honor our silence on the postmaster, but ask him to look into the Treuhand Bank's financing of Zanzi-Agroforestry. Treuhand is a bank riddled with ex-Soviet spies and sympathizers." Then he handed the major the case that Madar had brought into the cab. "Madar nearly died protecting this; you might want to take it to Minister Singh. I had a look. This is the financial record of money paid through Zanzi-Agroforestry to Boko Haram and others." The major said he would pass all that information along immediately, saluted, and cleared the Sea Knight for departure.

As they crossed the border into Kenya, the pilot advised that two of the four Harriers and the F-18s loitering above were leaving them. The C-130 was still on station above, ready for refueling. The day was past noon already, and Pero could see shadows below as they passed over Tsavo West where that Piper pilot had contemplated setting down with only one engine. *When was that?* Pero wondered. *Yesterday? No, two days ago.* He shook his head to clear the mental cobwebs.

Four hours and one exciting aerial refueling later, the Sea Knight drifted over the Oasis Lodge, its twin turbines and rotors shaking the roofs and alerting everyone there to their presence. The Harriers did a low fly-by and then zoomed up doing barrel rolls in celebration. Pero had already asked Central African Command to contact and ask Lewis to notify Wolfie. As the helicopter landed between the Lodge and the docks, a billowing cloud of dust settled as the Sea Knight doors opened. Nancy stood in the open doorway, turned, and joyously called out to all the girls sitting in the canvas seats, "*Mu ne a nan. Abinci, da ruwa, da tsabta gadaje, likitoci da a cikin 'yan kwanaki ka je gida!*" (We are here. Food, water, clean beds, doctors—and, in a few days, you go home!) Some of the girls started clapping, some crying. The girl Bob had carried from the hut clung to him every time he walked past. Now he undid her arms from around his leg and offered his hand. He walked her off the helicopter and toward the Oasis.

Strolling down the slight hill from the Oasis was a Nigerian giant with bulging muscles that Pero recognized as Kweno Usman, and a bull of a man, Reverend Jimmy Threte. Bob recognized Mary's uncle, the famous pastor, immediately. Next to them were two women, both in traditional Nigerian *buba* and *iro* dress complete with headscarf. They started keening, and at once Bob's young girl detached her grip on his hand and ran to them. As the girls poured from the Sea Knight, following the sound of the two women keening, a crowd formed with Jimmy Threte at the center. In his sonorous voice, he proclaimed, "The Lord has delivered them safe; what a joyous event. Blessed is the Lord!"

After the girls deplaned, Nancy, Bob, Mbuno, and Ube left to join the happy reunion. Tone and Pritchett carefully unloaded and were greeted by Wolfie, who helped Tone hobble toward the Oasis. Pero could hear Wolfie exclaim, "I want all the details, you owe me that . . ."

Pero was going to be the last to leave the helicopter, taking time to thank the crew and pilots. He also asked if he could speak to the remaining Harrier pilots and the C-130 crew. The pilot patched him through. "Fellows, from the bottom of my heart I thank you. You stopped an atrocity with your action and bravery. And, more important, you stopped my good intentions from turning into a God-almighty, international disaster. If you guys talk to General Tews, please thank him for me as well." The cockpit speaker emitted a round of welcomes and Pero was about to leave when the pilot grabbed his sleeve.

"Mister Baltazar, I really don't know who you are, and I know I'm not supposed to ask, but let me assure you all of us are mighty proud to have rescued those girls. In aviation we have a saying: Any landing you can walk away from is a good landing, good enough. Seems to me that you touched down just fine." There was nothing else left to say, so Pero patted his shoulder, turned, and exited the aircraft.

His foot hit the peaceful soil he loved so dearly in Loiyangalani, and, to complete the contentment, he saw Susanna waiting for him. She was holding Mary and Heep's hands. Behind her, Mbuno and Niamba stood waiting, smiling. Pero could see that all their faces were streaked with tears and dust, brown trails they had no intention of wiping away. Happy tears are always that way.

He walked up to Susanna and simply said, "Enough. That is enough." He looked into his wife's eyes and added, "You almost lost me. I know what it is like to lose someone. No more. No more."

Susanna was made of sterner stuff. She took her husband's face in her hands and told him, "*Mein dummer Mann*, I could lose you if you did nothing. I could lose you if you do something. But never will I stop loving you. You are who you are." And she kissed him.

Pero was thoroughly confused. The impact of what they had risked and achieved, the full geopolitical implications that he hadn't understood until it was almost too late—all of it was making him feel guilty for the risks he had taken. He found it oppressive to his very soul. Mbuno's perspective was simple: Rescue the girls. Pero didn't have the luxury of that simplicity. The threat was not just to themselves, but to the very stability of Africa and, by extension, world affairs. Pero knew thousands could have perished—could have been faced with war and instability—if his do-gooder action had fallen into the trap that had been set. Those thousands of lives would have been on his conscience; they would have been his fault for agreeing to the instinctive decision to rescue the girls. *Damn the Kremlin*, he thought angrily.

And yet, the girls. *They were safe. And the Tanzanian coup failed. Wasn't that worth the risk? Wasn't it?* Pero feared he might never be able to weigh out the answer. It seemed an unsolvable puzzle with his guilt at the middle.

Mbuno and Niamba shook their heads, waved to Pero, and slowly ambled back up the hill holding hands. Watching intently, Pero felt the two Liangulu formed the perfect image of the hunter safely home from safari, reunited with his loving wife.

Susanna, Mary, and Heep were studying Pero's face, seeing a familiar pensive look. They knew Pero well. They knew that his reaction was not one of anticlimax or self-doubt. They knew his mental capability; in Heep's case, he knew his partner would be evaluating the overall risk and judging his past actions accordingly. Heep had seen it repeatedly on location shoots. Pero always took responsibility. He always put himself at risk emotionally and philosophically because, as Heep knew, Pero was a micromanager. Micromanagers rule themselves with an iron hand.

Pero allowed his friends to walk him, deep in thought, back toward the lodge. Suddenly, Pero felt exhausted. He told them so, and Mary said soothingly, "Yes, Pero, just as Mbuno has already gone with Niamba to eat and sleep. We're taking you . . ." she let the end of the sentence hang.

Pero had no idea where they were going, which hut they were lodged in. He imagined the rooms were all packed, couples doubling up. *That's okay, I just need sleep.*

Pero felt a nudge, then he was falling into the refreshing cold water of the pool. He looked up when he surfaced. "What the hell?" And Mary, Heep, and Susanna, all still dressed, jumped in next to him.

Susanna paddled over and, in her Geman accent, said, "You think too much."

Heep and Mary were laughing as they chimed in together, mimicking Susanna's accent, "*Jawohl,* you zink too much."

Pero laughed, the tension ebbing. He felt, at last, that it was good to feel safe and be with the people he loved. Besides, he suddenly realized, he was hungry. "Hey, I'm hungry! Is there any toast?" And he burst out laughing at the childishness and the emulation of Mbuno in that question. *Maybe it'll be all right . . .*

As could be expected, the next few days were chaotic at Wolfie's resort at Loiyangalani. Kenyan authorities, with the assistance of Central African Command, kept all aircraft and transport away from the lakeside retreat except for doctors and experts that Jimmy Threte had commanded to appear. The Nigerian ambassador in Kenya was brought in by a small Kenyan Air Force plane. He met with the girls, the doctors, and Heep's video team. He held Nancy's hand the whole time he was interviewing the girls, patting it, and saying what a wonderful American she was. An uncomfortable Nancy kept looking about, wondering what his motivations were. In the end, Mary tipped off Jimmy Threte, and Kweno Useman walked the ambassador back to a Land Rover to take him back to the airstrip and then Nairobi. Threte and his bodyguard, Kweno, could be quite forceful and protective that way.

The Nigerian girls were reclothed in Kenyan kangas, which were almost like their national iro skirts, but without a blouse. So, Mary and Nancy went through all the women's clothing that the tourists, who were staying in the other wing, had donated from their luggage. Even Mary, Nancy, and Susanna came up with blouses and T-shirts to serve as buba.

Meals for the girls were initially in their huts, delivered via room service, but within a day Wolfie had gotten rid of any other guests, and the dining hall became a place of giggles, tasting of long-withheld treats, and incessant talk.

"*Ach*, it is too noisy now, I eat in my room," said Wolfie as he marched out of the dining room at lunch. Pero knew Wolfie didn't mind the girls being happy and talkative; he just minded not being able to have dining room behavior as he expected it to be. It was almost as if he felt they were taking over his place. Which they were, until they would leave, and then Wolfie would equally hate the goodbyes.

Tone and Pritchett left on the third day, sworn to secrecy, and flew back to Wilson Airport and to their families. Before they left, Wolfie patched them and the whole crew through on the RT to Virgi Singh. First Virgi reported that the locomotive driver was given a formal burial and that his family would be getting a pension for life. Pero and Mbuno were especially pleased with this news. Virgi then went on to tell them that not only was Madar recovering well, but that he had made his full report, and both of the ex–white hunters were being awarded honorary Tanzanian citizenship. Tone asked, "What about the rest of the team?" Virgi told them the Tanzanian government had something special planned for them, as well, perhaps a parade. Pritchett, ever the joker, pretended to be offended. "What, I don't get to be the grand marshal of my very own parade?" Tone smacked his arm, smiling.

Bob and the Okiek brothers, Teddy and Keriako, spent most of every day fishing for small tilapia from the dock. Bob said that he had "thinking to do, and fishing helps." The brothers were happy simply to be fishing with a man they looked up to. Besides, they were pestering him to invite them to this "pencil vania" he talked about. Bob considered them fast friends— they had been through a baptism of fire together.

Every day, Heep and his team, rejoined by Nancy, videotaped interviews and statements. Jimmy Threte's experts, all of whom spoke Hausa, worked to reassure the girls, to assuage them of any guilt for anything they had done or said and anything that had happened to them. As Jimmy Threte put it privately to Pero and Bob one evening over Tusker beers, "You see, kidnapped kids feel they deserve to be treated badly. Our job is to make them realize that they were doing good, the Lord's good, that they did nothing wrong, ever. The girls were not being tested by God. They don't have to feel guilty. God loves them; God provided you to rescue them. They are survivors, not victims." Pero thought it was partly psycho-babble and partly sound reasoning. *Anyway,* he thought, *I know nothing about that area, so as long as the authorities and survivor experts he's brought in are happy with Jimmy Threte, then so will I be.*

Pero recognized that it had become a Jimmy Threte show. No one seemed to care if he, Susanna, Mary, Mbuno, Niamba, Ube, or Bob were even there. Not even Lewis was in contact. It was as if the raid to rescue the girls had never happened, and Pero was being ostracized by the CIA for having risked so much. Pero knew that their luck had held, but he also recognized that it had been luck and Mbuno's skills that had prevented them from falling into a trap—a trap Pero had not anticipated. As a producer with overall responsibility he felt he had clearly failed.

Pero was not depressed, but he was a realist and spent his days staying close to Susanna and Mbuno, knowing they understood both his feeling of elation at having succeeded, as well as his dismay at having miscalculated. As Susanna assured him, "*Ach,* give it time. You won, that is the truth, nothing else counts anymore. See the girls? It was worth it, *nein?*" Pero hoped that, in time, he, too, would feel like Susanna and Mbuno—that rescuing the young women may have been worth the greater potential risk.

The fourth morning after they got back, Pero could not find Ube, Mbuno, or Niamba. He asked around, but no one had seen them coming or going. Around noon, a Land Rover drove back up to camp, and Pero went to see who was in it. Mbuno stepped out of the driver's seat, smiling. In the passenger seat, Niamba fiddled with and failed to open the latch handle, so Pero opened the door for her. She alighted, patted Pero's arm, and slowly started making her way back to the Oasis Lodge.

From the back of the Land Rover, Ube emerged, and asked Pero to give him a hand. Pero rounded the corner of the car, peered inside, and asked, "Spearfishing in the croc-infested reeds?"

Ube nodded. There on the floor in the back of the Land Rover was a Nile perch, about fifty pounds, with a broken spear stuck in its side. Pero looked inquisitively at Ube, who explained, "I never caught one, *bwana*. *Baba* said we could try." Mbuno, Ube, and Pero jointly lifted the fish and started up the hill to the Oasis, following Niamba, who was proudly leading the way. Ube, looking at his mother's back as she walked ahead, lamented, "But Mama said she only came to watch."

Confused, Pero jokingly asked, "And I suppose Wolfie is going to charge full price for the fish that we'll eat at dinner?"

Mbuno shook his head, "Oh no, brother, it is not for us. Niamba has told Ube it is her fish now. Niamba loves fish. We may get nothing."

Ube pretended to sulk, saying, "Big Fish! Small Mama."

Niamba turned and addressed her son, her voice exaggerating a stern tone, "*Ni samaki wangu. Napenda samaki.*" (It is my fish. I like fish.) Then, giggling, "Ha, *Kwa hiyo sasa huwezi kuwa na kitu chochote.*" (Ha, so now you cannot have any.) She marched off, clearly amused.

Mbuno paused in his steps, causing the other two men to stop walking. He smiled at Pero. "Brother, sometimes, it is better that way. You plan a safari to catch fish, and then, if you are lucky, you get to catch fish . . . maybe even a big one, like this. Bigger than you expected." He hefted the fish a little. "*Ndiyo*, yes, like this maybe. More than you expected."

Mbuno paused further, squinting in the noonday sun, eyes fixed on Pero's. "Ah, but brother, sometimes someone else gets to eat the fish, and maybe not even thank you." He paused, then added with emphasis, "It does not matter." Sharpening his gaze he added, "Remember, brother, there is always the honor of the safari, fish or no fish. Honor cannot be taken away here." He waited, with effect, to add, "Or in Tanzania." Then he smiled. Knowing, as only a brother could, that his message had hit home, he changed the subject, chuckling, "Now, our only problem is we may have to beg Niamba for a share of this fish."

Starting back up the hill, lugging the huge fish, a silent, resigned, and yet-now-happier Pero knew, as always, that Mbuno was right.

About safaris, fishing, and, above all, living.

End